Trade Agreement

by

jj Keller

I0687579

This is a work of fiction. Names, characters, places, and incidents are either the product of the author's imagination or are used fictitiously, and any resemblance to actual persons living or dead, business establishments, events, or locales, is entirely coincidental.

Trade Agreement

Cover Art by *Kim Mendoza*

The Wild Rose Press
PO Box 708
Adams Basin, NY 14410-0706
Visit us at www.thewildrosepress.com

Publishing History
First Crimson Rose Edition, 2009
Print ISBN: 1-60154-491-X

Published in the United States of America

"Why, Jake?" Her voice cracked. Her hands didn't know where to land and fluttered in front of her. She didn't care if she came across as weak.

His rejection hurt.

Tears clouded her vision.

She backed away and held a hand to the lowest button of her blouse. Then she got angry. What gave him the right to dominate all her time? He discouraged her from dating other men by monopolizing all her time and discarded her himself? Not one single indication from him led her to believe he didn't care for her.

He rubbed his chin and dragged his hand, the very hand a moment ago made her skin tingle, through his blond streaked hair. He didn't appear to want to answer.

Fine.

"You should go. I guess we want different things from this relationship." She grabbed his discarded T-shirt and threw it, his woodsy scent filtered through the air.

"Gee, you don't understand…"

"Then explain it to me." Her voice rose with a fury equal to the wind blowing outside. "I don't need a commitment from you. What do you want? It's evident what I want." Damn. Her voice continued to be raspy. She blinked back the tears. She would not cry. *Be strong.*

Her chest hurt with closed-in sobs.

No, her pain came from unrequited love. She loved Jake, and her self-esteem couldn't handle the rejection. The tears pooled on the edge of her eyes. She sniffed, pulling the water back into the abyss of her lonely heart.

CAPA finalist, 2007.

Multi-published with Cobblestone-Press:
The Watcher, Believe, Melody's Song, &
The Ghost Inside

Dedication

This book is dedicated to my husband,
who makes me laugh.

Chapter 1

Atlantic Ocean

Shivers cascaded over Georgina's body, the November cold penetrating her thin dress. She braced herself against the bumpy jolts as the speed boat hit rough water. The night was moonless, deep black ink surrounded them. The closer they got to the freighter, the faster her heart beat, a quick cadence to match the waves hitting the side of the vessel.

Georgina drew in a shaking breath and tried to lessen her grip on the rail of the boat as they pulled beside the ladder. Her fingers ached with the chill of tension. She glanced at the freighter. It was oh-so-tempting to simply fall into the water, but she'd freeze to death or get eaten by sharks. No, the only logical means of escape was catching a ride on the gray metal whale floating in the dark night, on a black ocean, surrounded by a mysterious fog.

She glanced at Kandi, her ex-husband's current femme-de-jour, dressed in a sleek strapless azure dress and spiked heels, then to Tristan himself. She'd loved him once, but now even looking at him made her colder. His fingers wrapped around the rail of the freighter's ladder. He grabbed her hand and tugged her from the seat.

No.

Her spine tingled with dread. Tristan couldn't be trusted. She knew better.

"I've changed my mind," Georgina said. "You can let me off at the next port."

Tristan gripped her hand tighter and pulled her

toward the ladder. "Can't."

"Why not?" Georgina jerked Tristan's arm, ready to throw him overboard. Did demons sink? Her stomach tumbled. Getting on that freighter would be a mistake.

Kandi slid beside Tristan and snarled, "Just get on the ship, Georgina, or I'll throw your spoiled ass overboard and you can swim back to Virginia."

Shocked at Kandi's language and the threat, Georgina glared.

"It's too late. There's no going back...not for Gemma either," her ex-husband spewed.

Damn him for using her best friend as a pawn. Georgina's heart rate went tachycardia. She blew slow breaths trying to slow the pace. She released his forearm, sat down on the padded boat seat, and crossed her arms.

"Georgina, climb the ladder." Tristan's jaws snapped together.

Kandi sighed and tapped her foot on the metal rail of the rocking boat.

Had Tristan really kidnapped Gemma? He had to be bluffing, but Georgina's heart rattled against her chest. What if Gemma wasn't safe? She'd already lost one baby, she couldn't lose another. "I decline."

Tristan gripped her arm and jerked her upright. She reached up with her other hand and dug her nails into the tender skin of his palm.

"She'll go," Kandi said.

Georgina sneered at the two, pivoted, and clutched the nearest brass rung.

The three-inch heels clipped the metal, and she slipped on the third rail of the ladder. Determined, she tightened her hold and stepped to the next rung. Homeward bound. A precarious scramble on steps or fear of the unknown wouldn't prevent her from returning to her little house and Jake. Thoughts of the sleepy little town of Nero intruded. She'd often complained about the boredom and photographing nothing but dog and garden shows. Well, she'd trade her current situation for some of that routine any day.

Jake, her lover. Her heart clutched a little in her chest. Was he searching for her? She maneuvered up one more rung. In the back of her mind, she hoped Jake would come to her rescue.

A wintery breeze blew up her dress and she shuddered. She was beyond chilled in the clingy little dress. She clutched a metal bar and pushed the hem down. Her foot slipped, and her spiked heel dug into Tristan's fingers. She applied as much pressure as possible.

Tristan roared. He slapped her rear with such force she pressed flush against ladder. "Keep going, Georgina. Move it."

Bastard. She stepped to the next bar, releasing his hand.

Finally, she reached the top. Two goons, heavyweight bookends with matching blank expressions, hauled her over the rail. Tristan crawled on deck and helped Kandi onto the platform.

"Come." One of the goons, with a melodic Russian accent, motioned with his head.

It didn't sound like a request.

The men led them down a staircase, through a corridor, and into a square, frigid room. A stainless steel table and two metal chairs were the only furnishings. One seat was occupied by a man she assumed to be Aleksandr Stypopas, the captain of this fine vessel.

Like the gentleman he was, Tristan sat down on the other chair. A bottle labeled IKON Russian vodka sat in the middle of them like a referee. Kandi stood behind Tristan, her hand resting easily on his shoulder. Georgina stood to the side, as close to the door as possible.

While the men talked, in Russian or Ukrainian, Georgina deliberated how to convince Aleksandr to return her to the States. He was as dark and mysterious in appearance as the freighter. His shaggy black beard seemed blacker as a result of the elegant gray shirt and pants covering his thin body.

Would this nightmare ever end? It had to be a dream, because Aleksandr was wearing Armani for God's sake, at midnight, on a freighter, in the middle of the Atlantic Ocean. He didn't look like a man who did favors out of the goodness of his heart. Would he want money? She didn't have anything to offer. Or did she? She shuddered at the thought. A raised voice captured her attention. What had she missed?

There was a palpable sense of menace in the air. Had they walked into a trap? Would they all be killed?

Aleksandr's voice was oily and his smile insincere. "Kaplan, we've been comrades for almost a year. Why the mistrust?"

"Do we really trust one another, my friend?" Tristan took a sip of vodka.

From Georgina's viewpoint, Tristan's hand appeared to be trembling. Damn. There were some underlying messages being sent back and forth that caused her alarm radar to go off. She glanced at Aleksandr. He was smiling. Like a crocodile.

Okay, Tristan, it's time to leave—now! You'll have to drop me off at the next port.

"Are you calling me a thief?" Aleksandr's deep, heavily accented voice filled the tiny room like a sonic boom. He bolted to his feet and his chair clanged to the floor. The angry red glow on his face, either from the heated argument or from the drink, accentuated his gray appearance. His lips virtually disappeared into the mass of black facial hair as he sneered.

4

Tristan's face remained calm. "Of course. Aren't we all? We take items and sell them for a profit. The buyers are not important, nor the nationality, nor the cause, nor how illegal the goods. We steal them for the thrill of making a deal. For money." His blond cropped hair, light crystal-blue eyes, and winsome smile widened, giving him the appearance of the boy next door.

Georgina stared at his devilish dimples while trying to get a grasp on the situation. She'd fallen in love with his dimples, before she'd fallen in love with the man. Now she looked past the façade and wondered how she'd been so foolish.

"I've never cheated anyone in my life, and I resent the implication, Kaplan." Aleksandr nodded his head to one of his henchmen at the door.

Georgina's fight or flight urge was strong. She tensed and glanced at the exit, calculating whether she could get to it before the goons caught her. What she would do after reaching the entrance, she didn't know. But she desperately wanted to go through that door.

"Please accept my apology. I meant no offense." Tristan calmly lifted his half-empty glass of liquid fire and held it out to Aleksandr, for a customary salute.

Aleksandr stared at Tristan, a long, intense, soul-searching glare. "Ah, none taken. However, I do insist the whore be given to me as a fair trade agreement."

Aleksandr slid his black-eyed gaze down Georgina's body and came back to stare into her eyes. His thoughts about her were as clear as the vodka between them: brown hair, heart shaped face, an ordinary body, and not worth his time. The brunt of his perusal landed on Kandi. Georgina's heart rate slowed from its marathon speed. Aleksandr lifted his chair and lowered to the seat.

Kandi gasped, edged closer to Tristan, and reached toward her diamond and jade bejeweled bodice. She tossed her long auburn locks out of the way and pulled the limited blue silk material of the strapless dress higher, trying to cover her endowments as much as possible. Her nipples protruded further as a result of her efforts. She folded her shaking hands at her waist.

"Consider it done," Tristan said, the words ice-cold.

"Tristan!" Kandi screeched, her voice, shrill and full of shock. Her pale pink lips quivered, and her bare shoulders twitched back and forth. Tristan had offered her as a door prize.

Could this be happening? The scene was a Saturday B-movie event. People in real-life did not trade off their friends or family to get a shipment of...of...of whatever obviously illegal thing they were exchanging. The goods had to be contraband to make Tristan sweat. Georgina knew him well enough after six years of living together to recognize the signs of his anxiety. Regardless of how calm he appeared, he wasn't in control of the situation.

Aleksandr's eyes glittered with dangerous ecstasy. He turned his cold, calculating stare onto Tristan and leaned back in his chair. His jacket gaped, revealing an old fashioned .44 revolver in a gray holster strapped to the side of his chest. Her father had one just like it in his gun cabinet. The racketeer's don't-mess-with-me attitude made him the perfect bad guy for any mafia movie.

Georgina tried to ignore the chills running through her body. She pushed a dry wind-blown strand of hair behind her ear. In an effort to appear to be in command of her emotions, she clasped her hands in front of her and waited.

Kandi's brown gaze turned toward Tristan. She reached over and grabbed his arm, spilling vodka

6

onto the table top. He peeled her fingers loose one by one.

"You can't do this!" Georgina didn't care how much she angered either man. Part of the reason she had filed for a divorce concerned Kandi and all of the Kandis before her. But she was still a human and Aleksandr, regardless of his designer suit, was scum.

"Shut up, Georgina," Tristan barked.

Aleksandr's glance took in the clear pool of vodka, and a scowl formed on his hairy face. Apparently he valued his alcohol.

"How barbaric. Stop this right now, Tristan," Georgina reasoned, hoping he'd understand this was illogical and perverse.

The oppressive atmosphere grew weighty and thick. Sympathy coursed through Georgina. The black Russian wouldn't give Kandi the spa treatment on this tub as she'd had on Tristan's yacht. Tristan had to do something. Why didn't he act?

"It's done. Take her away," Tristan spoke softly, as if the words were for his ears alone. He lifted his hand to his mouth and sucked the alcohol off. The goons started toward the door.

Georgina glanced at Tristan and witnessed the truth in his eyes. Kandi wasn't the whore being handed over as a door prize.

"No!" Georgina's voice vibrated off the walls. She wrapped her arms across her waist and backed into the corner. She was the one being traded for a load of whatever.

The burly guards rushed forward, Georgina's vision became blurred.

"You're soiled goods." Tristan turned back to the vodka, lifted his glass, and slowly sipped the beverage.

The two henchmen's pungent breath gushed around Georgina's face.

In those few seconds, Georgina's future changed into a kaleidoscope of unreality. She prayed Jake Callahan was alive. Her hero would find her. He had before.

Aleksandr's men picked Georgina up under her bent arms to carry her away. Tristan set her up. Instead of having a sweet ride home, she was part of his trade agreement. Soiled goods? Beg!

"Tristan, you love me. What about our time together in Mexico? Remember when you said you'd never stop loving me; you'd never let me go?" Her voice loud and clear, she struggled for some saving grace.

Kandi grimaced and glanced at Tristan, but said nothing.

Aleksandr alternated his beady eyes between the Tristan and Georgina.

Did she mean nothing to Tristan? He loved her. He fought the separation a year ago and resented the divorce papers recently delivered to him. Why would he give her to the Russian?

The value of the goods must be great and Tristan's circumstances dire. What existed in the hold of this ship that was so valuable?

Georgina tried to elbow the two men, but she wasn't a pugilist. She couldn't get her legs up high enough to kick out.

"Let me go!" She shrieked, her voice resembling a screaming banshee.

They carried her down a narrow corridor of the ships underbelly, permeated by the smell of fish. The men were almost identical, with short blond hair, ice blue eyes, and no necks. Their massive shoulders were twice as wide as her body. How could she fight them? What would they do to her? Where were they taking her?

"You can't hold me against my will." She butted her head against the man on the right. An ache radiated through her neck as the muscles pulled tight. Her chest hurt from intense fear constricting her lungs.

"Damn you robots, let go of me. I'll kick your asses."

They spoke in Russian. The guy on her right must have said something humorous, because the clone on the left laughed out loud. The smell of onions and garlic coming out of their mouths penetrated the air. She couldn't breathe. Her thoughts struggled with how to deal with her situation. She stopped and let them carry her. Instead, she'd fight with words. Maybe calm controlled reason would work.

"Let me go." She tried to keep her voice low, powerful, and dangerous, regardless of how much her stomach tightened and her hands shook.

Two corridors and one staircase later they threw her into a small rectangular room. She landed on her feet and glanced around the cabin. One tiny porthole had been punched into the side of the metal vessel. She visually measured the hole, the only access to the outside universe, a world where stars and hope existed. Her head might fit through the tiny cut out, but certainly not her shoulders nor her generous rear. The bed, a mere bunk, took up one entire side with cables holding it to the ship's side. It was hardly large enough for one person, let alone a woman and a large hairy man.

Good. Positive thoughts are good at this stage.

One blanket, one sheet, and one pillow. No bathroom, no sink, no desk or chair. A bed and coverings, period. She turned and pounded on the door with her fists.

"Let me go." Fear made her heart pulse hard in her chest. Thirst matted her lips together, and her hoarse voice sounded weak to her own ears.

Georgina twisted the knob on the door. The

handle moved. Strange. She inched it open enough to peek through the crack. One of the clones stood outside. At the sound of the creak of the rusted metal, he turned to glare. She tried to swallow the dread lodged in her throat.

Fighting didn't work and reasoning had done nothing to promote her release, so she tried calm trust-building logic.

"Um, I hope," she began demurely and then stopped herself. She reflected back to her childhood, straightened her shoulders, and imitated her mother's most haughty voice. "I demand you give me a glass of water, a notebook, and pen."

A guard nodded. His partner took off at a lope down the hall. Georgina smiled and shut the door. She sat on the bunk, to wait. If she was going to be a concubine, or a white slave, or fish food, she wanted to leave a message to her family. And to Jake, if he was alive, and she intuitively knew he lived. There had to be someone with an ounce of decency on this ship full of criminals to mail the letters. Certainly a challenge, but she only needed to find one person.

Georgina was a smart chess player and considered this an important game of strategy, so she didn't waste energy on anger or remorse. Her next move would be determined according to her opponent's play. She had to find a way to reach Tristan before he left, to convince him to change his mind. If not, she needed to find out Aleksandr's game and a means to beat him at his own scheme.

A knock resounded on the door. The guard entered and extended a notebook and two pens. A Russian insignia was on the side of the ballpoints, probably an advertisement for vodka. Georgina took the items and to her surprise, he handed her a bottle of water. Fresh spring water. Her glance met his, and she smiled a true smile.

If he had a neck it would have become beet red

as the glow flowed from beneath his collar up to his cheeks. He smiled in return and backed out. His partner said something in Russian, laughed, and the door clicked shut. She crawled onto the bunk and used the pillow as a back rest. She pulled her legs to her chest, covered her lower body with the moss-green blanket, and opened to the first page of the hard cover book.

The notebook surprised her. The silk cover had a dark taupe background with cherry blossoms woven within. It was a quality diary, and might have been a gift for a sweetheart or family member of one of the crew. Oddly enough, she appreciated No Neck Number One getting the journal for her.

Taking the pen in hand, she wrote in small perfect print: Georgina Grey Barrister ~~Kaplan~~. She felt a sense of relief by having a plan of action and proceeded to put on paper how she came to be in this odd and frightening circumstance.

Chapter 2

Nero, Virginia
Six months earlier

"Oh, Gemma, isn't it beautiful?" Georgina whirled around the small, dingy room seeing freedom. The cracks in the walls and the ashes in the fireplace didn't trouble her, but the expression of horror on her friend's face did.

"The building doesn't live up to what we grew up with, but on such short notice, it's the best Robert could find. It's a tract house." Gemma said the words as if she were talking about a tar paper shack in the deep woods.

"Tract? I don't know what that means, but I love it. Your home's close, right?" Georgina watched Gemma frown as her beautiful brown eyes glanced down at the dirty carpet and then to the door hanging askew. Gemma's husband was a commissioned officer and could thus live in relative luxury. This house was in an area where enlisted officers dwelled while awaiting base housing or a promotion.

"Yes. So, what do you honestly think?"

She thought it was Gemma Sheraton who contrasted with the squalid surroundings. Her elegant Italian features, innate grace, and designer clothing created a bright spot in the otherwise dreary room. "Although the house doesn't have plush luxury and doesn't meet your standards, for now it will suit me just fine. More importantly, Tristan wouldn't think to look for me here. At least, that's what I'm telling myself."

Georgina's gaze scanned the room, decorating as she went. The late afternoon light shone on the dirty brown walls. If she painted them creamy beige, the space would appear larger.

"Gee, why don't you just come to live with us?" Gemma moved closer to the front door.

Georgina just shook her head. "Your house would be the first place he'd look. I think we'll have a wonderful time fixing the tract. I can't wait." She hugged her childhood friend, then grabbed her sleek arm and pulled her up the creaky stairs. Two bedrooms and one bath were on the second level. The largest bedroom had a fabulous wide window, overlooking the recently clipped back yard. The view was wonderful, but the wallpaper would have to go. She rested her hand on the pink wallpaper with pelicans marching across a moss ridden swamp. Nasty.

The two quarters were separated by a simple bathroom, which was the prettiest room in the house. The beautiful lavatory with an old fashion claw footed tub gave the area a quaint appearance. Someone had installed a shower pole, which ran from the floor to the head of the unit. A moldy curtain surrounded it. If the cracked and rusted stained porcelain were resurfaced, the bath would look adorable.

"Egad, Gee. The wallpaper's falling off and the tub must be over one hundred years old. At least the bathroom doesn't look like mold has invaded. I'll have plumbers come out tomorrow and replace everything." Gemma shoved a strand of dark brown, thick, hair behind her ear.

"They can replace the sink and loo, because I don't believe I could possibly get those clean, but leave the bathtub. I love the tub. Refinished it'll be beautiful. I think lavender and green decor will work to brighten this room. Very Feng Shui. What do you think?" Georgina smiled. For the first time in a long while, she had a sense of purpose. She would survive. Her plan was to get lost in the mainstream and eventually become a productive member of the work force. And above all else, remain hidden from her husband. Soon to be ex-husband.

"Loo. How funny. I haven't heard that word used in years." Gemma laughed softly.

Memories of when they escaped finishing school and traveled through Germany and the United Kingdom flashed through Georgina's mind. Then, they hadn't known what loo meant, but found out quick enough.

Georgina knew Gemma's thoughts centered around their adventures...rather misadventures, too. They had pestered the American Embassy in Switzerland so many times a poster of their faces with a diagonal line through it must have been tacked up in the break room.

They had met at boarding school. Their last names brought them together as roommates. Georgina G. Barrister and Gemma G. Balinnie. Their shared initials were a sign. From the moment they met, they were known as the GBs, inseparable and eager to experience life.

"I'll get a plumber. Robert's friends can come over tonight, and we'll pull out the carpet and try to remove the wallpaper." Gemma heaved a sigh. "Let's go look at the kitchen."

Georgina struggled to keep the laughter inside. Gemma acted as though a life sentence had been declared, and she wasn't looking forward to the time.

Gemma led the way through the smaller bedroom. One of the burnished copper walls sported a small rectangle shaped window topped with a torn and tattered paper shade. She sighed and Georgina stifled a giggle.

Downstairs, Gemma stopped in the doorway of the kitchen.

"Oh, my. We must replace everything in here. It's horrible." She held her nose with two fingers.

"On this we agree. I'll take care of it." Georgina too, plugged her nose and took short shallow breaths. "If you'll take me to a car dealership, I'll pick up something to drive. Then I can go shopping for supplies."

"Maybe we should wait and have Robert go with us. It'd be better to have a man with you when you buy a car. Especially around here. The women in my book club say the men at dealerships are chauvinistic." Gemma had joined a book club, and along with the variety of literature, she got tips on various ways to handle difficult situations. A car purchase must fall into the top-ten list.

"Are you kidding me? The GBs need a man?" Georgina tossed her friend a look of scorn and noticed the green cast on Gemma's face. "You're pale. What's wrong? Are you ill?"

Georgina slid the patio doors open and let the fresh, early summer air into the mold-ridden, cabbage-scented room. She took hold of her friend's arm and led her outside. Gemma sat down on an upturned pail, took great gulps of air, and scrubbed her long straight locks into a ponytail with shaking hands.

Georgina took another bucket, emptied out the putrid brown water, upended the container, and plopped down. "Tell me what's wrong."

Gemma raised her fathomless dark eyes. Georgina searched into the depths to realize the news was good, not bad as she had anticipated.

"I'm pregnant," Gemma whispered.

Georgina held her hand to her chest, thankful it was good news and not bad. "I'm so happy for you. You're going to have a little Bobby or Georgina." She laughed at the look on Gemma's face, which came and went as fast as a flash of lighting. "Okay, we'll rethink Georgina. How far along are you?"

"Second trimester. Robert and I haven't told anyone. I couldn't bear all the sympathy if I lost this one as well." Gemma's hand shook as she reached out.

A memory of Gemma sitting on a rocking chair in a nursery painted with blue airplanes and all the sympathy baskets surrounding her made Georgina want to weep. She choked back tears, took the offered hand and held on tight.

"You'll be godmother, Gee, won't you?"

"I will." She smiled. "But I'll be Auntie Gee, because Godmother Gee sounds awfully old, don't you think? I can't wait." She jumped off the bucket and pulled Gemma to her feet. "Come on, you go home and get some rest. I'll have Robert go out with me this evening to get a car. We can start renovating tomorrow."

Georgina took Gemma's arm, locked the house, and led her to her red Aston-Martin. She opened the door, tucked her into the passenger seat, and climbed in behind the wheel to play chauffer. "Tell me where to go. Do you think we could get some really strong guys with a truck to take away the appliances in the kitchen?"

"Yes, but Georgina…"

Gemma generally called her Gee. Uh, oh, serious talk alert. She held the wheel in a death grip. Please don't let it be the disasters-come-in-three speech.

"If you're hiding from Tristan, how will you pay for the house and your expenses?" Gemma paused and then continued. "I've access to my trust fund. I'll give you money to get started. But to blend into the community you'll need a job."

Warmth spread throughout Georgina. How generous her friend was. "I love you, and I appreciate your offer, but I'll be fine. I've got a high-class education and experience. If I can't get a job right away, I'll dip into my own trust fund. Tristan doesn't have any connection with the money, and my attorney, Mr. Sinefield, won't tell him about the account or where I'm living."

"Seriously? What experience do you have?" Gemma shot her a can't-wait-to-hear-this look.

"While Tristan traveled this past year—"

"You mean, while he sailed the seas and sent a man to attack you?" Gemma's mouth formed into a tight straight line.

"Yes." And Tristan killed someone, but Georgina didn't have the courage to voice it aloud. "I took classes at a local college. I'm certified as a photojournalist. And under my pen name, George Grey, I've written three articles for the Boston Inquirer and sold a couple of photographs."

"Oh my gosh, and you never told me? You always were interested in photography. I'm so glad you're able to do something with your artistic talent. I'll ask Robert if there are any contractor openings at the base for a photojournalist."

"Thanks," Georgina replied, "You look better. Has the nausea passed?"

"Yes. I'm starving. Let's go eat." She laughed.

Georgina reached over and ran her hand over Gemma's arm. She would be fine. Gemma would carry this baby to term, and Georgina would be there to support her.

****

The days passed by in a happy blur of redecorating. Georgina used her trust fund to pay expenses and prayed for a job interview. When a job offer came along, she called Gemma.

"Guess what. Andy Hall from the Navy recruitment office called and offered me a one-time job. I'm covering a recruitment fair in Newport. If I do well, he'll recommend me to the Nero News." Her excitement bubbled over, and she laughed with giddiness.

"I'm so happy for you. When is the fair?" Gemma asked.

"In two days. I'm going to meet him tomorrow. We'll go over his requirements, and I'll lay out my ideas." Georgina took in a deep breath. "Let's go celebrate. My treat. Too late for lunch, let's go for dessert. Is there a café somewhere close that specializes in baked goods?"

"I'll pick you up in ten minutes, and we'll go to Nourish Bakery."

"You're talkin' now, girlfriend. First, you can eyeball my new next door neighbor. He moved in a week ago."

"What happened to the Smiths? I liked Jeanette."

"Beats me, the Smiths disappeared overnight. Strange." Georgina hummed the theme to the Twilight Zone.

"Interesting. So is your new neighbor dating material? It's been three months since you filed for divorce and over a year since you left the jerk. You should consider dating," Gemma declared. Georgina could envision the mental wheels turning in her mind.

"Is this your method of telling me three's a crowd? Is Bob tired of me?"

"Robert isn't tired of you. We think you should, you know, get to know other people. Guys. Andy Hall, as a matter of fact, asked about you." Gemma's breathing sounded labored as if she were walking and talking, and the two exercises together were overwhelming.

"Ah. So, Bob arranged the job. I suspected he had something to do with the interview. I'd applied at every news, magazine, and publication in Nero.

My portfolio looks exquisite. No awards, but I've testimonials from professors and professionals in the business and despite all that, not one call. Out of the blue, this opportunity comes up." And thank goodness it had. Unable to withdraw funds from her trust until the fifteenth of the month, twenty days away, she was clipping coupons. Georgina and Bob had rescued her, once again.

"Hey, they just talked and you came up. Robert showed him your work and Andy thought your pieces were brilliant. Andy's smart, he listened. Anyway, I'm in the car. I'll be there in ten and I have some exciting news to tell you." Gemma rushed the words.

"What news? Is everything okay?"

"Yes, I just want to tell you in person. I need to concentrate on driving. I'll be there in a few."

Georgina hung up the phone and walked to the patio doors. She knew Gemma, so what had she left out of the story? "Eye of the Tiger" played on the radio, creating energy in the kitchen, exuberance in her. She leaned against the frame and watched the amazing specimen next door. Textbook perfect.

He worked in the weed patch masquerading as a yard. His shirtless, muscle-defined chest gleamed with sweat. He stood up and stretched, arms straight out and legs spread, resembling DaVinci's illustration of Vitruvian Man. Oh my. Her vaginal juices started flowing from just watching him. She didn't know about what was under the jeans, but she wasn't opposed to finding out.

A small spade and a set of clippers weighted down his jeans, and she wished they'd slide down a little further. His light brown hair wasn't the military short clip she typically saw around Nero. Rather, it lightly brushed his neck and rolled over the tops of his ears. She clenched her fists at her sides, preventing the urge to run over and touch his—hair.

He picked up a baseball cap with a large red C embroidered above the bill and settled it on his head. Swiping the sweat off his face with his discarded blue T-shirt, he bent over exhibiting his tight, hard rear.

Two years had passed since Georgina had been intimate with a man. Now she had an Adonis next door creating all types of temptations in her mind. She sighed. Tristan had been her one and only. The memories of kissing, touching, and experiencing a climax made her yearn for a man's touch. Gemma was right. This celibacy needed to end.

Soft footsteps tapped on the tile floor of the kitchen. She smelled Gemma's Channel perfume. Georgina wiped the neighbor-induced drool from her lips.

"What a stud. Did you introduce yourself yet?"

"You know, you should work on the quiet approach if you want to sneak up on someone. Since you're into your seventh month, you're not a light walker." Georgina smiled at her friend, taking in the expression on her face, and a quick scan of her body to make sure everything remained in place.

"Guess not if you heard me while you were mentally seducing him. Come on. Let's go meet the neighborhood hunk." Gemma laughed. Walk down any street in Nero, a military town, and you could spot uniformed men with hard bodies and precise movements.

"I can't," Georgina stated. To see his eyes, to hear his voice would encourage her to continue the sadistic trip into lustdom. She'd been watching him for a week and had made this weird metaphysical connection to him. Hell, she could accurately predict what body movement would follow each action. If he scratched his right ear, his hand would lower to rub his neck, and then to scratch his left forearm.

"Yes, you can." Gemma leaned over, pulled open the door, and shoved her out into the bright sun.

Georgina stumbled onto the patio, bumped into the tag-sale wicker set, and knocked the acrylic top off the coffee table. It banged onto the cement with a loud twang, and she fell. Gravel and cement ground into her knee. She gasped. "Ouch."

"Oops, a little too hard. Sorry." Gemma awkwardly bent from her side and held out a hand.

Georgina glanced up to see the hunk scale the fence with ease. He rushed forward and lifted her to her feet.

His touch.

God, his touch caused tingles to lodge low in her belly. Even her breasts ached. She tried to act nonchalant by flipping her hair. The movement stirred up the airflow and filtered her musky jasmine scent through the air, making her think of the sexy commercial advertising the spray. Man and woman locked in a tight embrace. She shook her head to get the thought out. Gemma backed away wearing a too-innocent expression.

"Are you okay?" His voice was as deep, sensual, and as heavenly as his body. With trepidation, she shifted her glance to meet his eyes. They were gray-blue, the color of storm clouds. She could not break the connection. Damn, her heart hooked onto the feeling of familiarity as he continued to hold her hand.

"I need to use the restroom. I'll be back." Gemma rushed into the house. At the snap of the door, the spell ended.

"Thank you. I'm clumsy." A photojournalist should be able to use some of the thousands of vocabulary words in her head, yet Georgina couldn't create a sentence. She couldn't pull her gaze from his.

"I'm Jake. Jake Callahan." He continued to hold

her hand, so a shake seemed unnecessary. Sweat glistened on his brow. A firm jaw was the perfect infrastructure for his flawless flushed lips. They stretched into a smile as she stared.

"I'm Gee. Georgina Grey. My friends call me Gee." *What is wrong with me? Construct a sentence; impress him with my wit. Otherwise, I'm simply the bug-eyed, graceless, woman next door.*

He released her hand and picked up the acrylic tabletop. She cringed as she bent to help.

"Let me see your knee." Jake lowered her into the bench, crouched at her feet, and lifted her right calf in his hands. He propped her leg across his lap and pushed the hem of her dress to her thigh. She fought back a shiver at his touch. His broad chest with a light sprinkling of hair was directly in front of her. Her breath hitched. Get control!

"Your dress is torn," he said.

Georgina opened her lips to respond, but could only stare into his intense eyes. Warmth smoldered within.

He broke the contact and looked at her injury. His rough fingers on her knee multiplied the tingling in her lower region.

"There's a small abrasion. You'll probably have a heck of a bruise."

"Are you a doctor?" She glanced at her right knee to see a nice round, red, spot forming underneath the white roughed skin.

"No. I have two nephews and a niece. So I see a lot of this, especially the knees and elbows. I recommend ice." Jake lowered her leg, but his fingers lingered on her ankle. His fingerprints burnt imprints onto her skin, making her an unbridled woman. "Can I get some for you?"

"Oh. Ice? I usually like my ice floating in tea. I think you'll find some in the fridge." Georgina resituated on the wicker bench sinking into the palmetto-leaved fabric cushion. Her knee was already starting to stiffen up.

Jake slipped on his shirt and stood still. His beautiful eyes focused on her. Maybe she had spider webs on her hair or face. She reached up to check. She didn't feel any foreign matter.

"Ah, what's wrong?"

"Well, princess, within one minute of meeting, you're giving me orders." Jake hooked his thumbs in the belt loops of his jeans. His voice had gone from pleasant hero to complaining I'm-watching-the-game male.

Gemma always had the best timing and came through the patio door.

Georgina leaned over to blow on the now burning abrasion. Between puffs, she introduced them. "Gemma Sheraton, Jake Callahan, vice versa."

"Nice to meet you, Jake. Georgina, are you okay?" Gemma edged over toward Georgina and took a seat next to her on the bench, her blue dress contrasted with the light green palmetto leaves.

"Georgina?" A light brown eyebrow raised in challenge. "I thought you said your friends call you Gee?"

My goodness, what was this, the third degree? She knew it had been a mistake to meet him. Her heart continued to pound, and her knee throbbed in tune.

"Who said she's my friend?" Georgina quipped. Friends didn't force the people they love to meet hunky guys and then make a fool out of themselves.

Jake looked puzzled. His glance bounced from one woman to the other. Georgina restrained a laugh.

"We're closer than friends," Gemma said, narrowing her eyes at Georgina as if to tell her to behave. "We're sisters of the heart."

Ignoring Jake, Georgina turned to Gemma,

desperate for the news her friend had yet to share. "So, is it a boy or a girl?"

"According to the ultrasound, he's one hundred percent boy."

"Oh, a boy!" Georgina put her leg down, leaned over, and drew Gemma to her. "My first godson." She sat back on the settee, and Gemma put her feet on the small round wicker table. "Is Robert pleased?"

Jake went into the house. Georgina continued to carry on the conversation, but she kept glancing at the door, waiting for him to return. Was he real? Handsome, buff, kind, and intelligent, so, what was wrong with him? He opened the door and came out with a tray of iced tea and a cold pack.

"Find everything okay?" Georgina could have sworn a flash of shame crossed his face. What could he possibly be guilty of? Had he been snooping? Listening to their conversation?

"Oh, thank you, Jake. How nice." Gemma smiled, her dark eyes glittered with secrets.

Georgina could tell she was plotting something and with Jake standing there, she couldn't tell Gemma to forget it.

Jake held a tray like a professional waiter and handed Gemma a glass of ice tea. The scent of citrus from the lemons permeated the air. When he held a glass out to Georgina, her fingers grazed his, and electricity flowed as fast and powerful as lightning through her nerve endings. Did he feel it as well? His face remained impassive, so she assumed he didn't. Little flecks of white paint from the wicker scattered over the cement as he lowered his hunky bulk into the dainty chair across from the bench.

He placed the tray on the ground, leaned over, and gently lifted Georgina's injured leg to rest on the table top. He took a cloth from the tray, placed it on her knee, and then arranged the cold pack on her injury.

"Ouch, that hurts." She grimaced and shot him a fierce frown. He just smiled in return, making her lose her way in the ever-expanding lustdom maze. She sipped her tea and tried not to look at him. She could not keep staring, because she was a sex-starved woman, and he was a sweet handsome luxury wrapped in faded denim. And oh, how she wanted to indulge.

"Jake, Georgina mentioned you work in the yard a lot. What else do you do?"

Georgina reached over and pinched her. Now he would know she spent time watching him.

He smiled at Gemma. "I'm a freelance photographer."

"What a coincidence, so is Gee." Gemma patted Georgina's knee and then took an exaggerated look at her watch.

"Wow, look at the time. I need to take off. I haven't decided what Isabella should make for dinner." She rose, leaned close, and kissed Georgina on the cheek.

"Thanks, Gemma. Tomorrow? After?"

"Okay. Wear the bright blue."

"Will do," Georgina said. She could tell by the confused expression on Jake's face he didn't understand. Just as well. Friend-speak had been invented first and foremost for that purpose.

She heard the slam of a car door and the motor rev as Gemma drove away. Jake looked at her, and her heart beat as fast as a hummingbird's wings.

"Thank you, for helping me." She lowered her head as the blood rushed to her face. Six years was a long time to wait to flirt with a man. She had forgotten how. Did she embarrass herself? What were the rules? Since he was the next door neighbor, she couldn't jump him. Or could she?

"My pleasure."

Embarrassed by her thoughts, she met his eyes

and then pushed the ends of her hair behind her ears. What was the probability of someone with a similar interest, moving into the house right next door to her? Why was she suddenly suspicious?

She narrowed her eyes. "Do you prefer Anne Geddes or Alfred Eisenstaedt?"

"Huge difference. Eisenstaedt was the father of photojournalism and captured spontaneous shots. Geddes, an equally interesting photographer, poses babies in cabbage patches." He grinned. "Don't make me choose."

Oh, he was clever. "I think my favorite of Eisenstaedt's work is VJ Day, 1945," she declared.

"Is that the one with the sailor kissing a nurse on the street? Times Square?" He tipped his hat back on his head.

"Yes, that's the one. I think he was a genius and incredibly lucky to be able to capture moments in time that have lasted for over sixty years. People still clamor to see his work. The sign of a true artist, don't you think?" She tried to think of other famous photographers she could test him with.

"He had humility and humanity." He lifted his hand, rubbed his cheek and resettled his baseball cap on his head. She drew her gaze away from his beautiful gray-blue eyes to notice his crooked nose, which appeared to have been broken and never reset.

"I'm debating on what artwork to decorate with. Which would you purchase for your home, a Christopher Burkett or Dorothea Lange?" She bent her knee as the skin painfully tightened, and placed her hands underneath to brace it.

"Probably Burkett. I like trees, especially his Panther Mountain Maple taken in Virginia. I have a print of Old Aspen Trunk."

She lifted her eyebrows. Really? "I didn't know that had been released?"

"I was in a show in Colorado. He was there and gave me a copy."

"I'd like to see the print."

"Sure. I'll have it in a few days. Right now I'm having it framed." He smiled and didn't flinch. His eyes remained fixed on her. He told the truth. She had a great deal of experience with a liar. Tristan was the best.

"What do you think of the Brit, can't recall his name. Late, maybe nineteen hundreds. He was brilliant, probably created the first freeze frames. Did a lot with human movement, collotype. My favorite was about a man walking and turning around. He had a satchel in one hand and a cane in the other." She tapped her chin with her index finger, as if contemplating his name.

"Could you be referring to Eadweard Muybridge?"

"Yes. Unusual name don't you think?"

"Yes. Are you done testing me, princess, or did you want to ask about Elliot Erwitt and his dog photography?" He leaned forward, placing his elbows on his knees, and cupped his chin. He didn't smile, but a flash of humor held residence in his eyes and a grin threatened to appear on his perfectly shaped lips.

"I think I'm done. Although Garry Winogrand will be in Tampa in a few months. Do you know this photographer?" She tilted her head and waited.

"Fascinated with beautiful women?" The flash of humor zinged across his eyes.

Georgina couldn't suppress the laugh. "You're good. I threw old and new photographers at you. You pegged each one."

"I'm good at a lot of things, princess, and I do like beautiful women." Jake gave her that stare again. The intense, hot look that made her stomach tingle and her skin heat up. She held his gaze. After her body raged with lust-filled warmth, she moved her glance to his perfect soft mouth, and then his large rough, green-stained hands. He picked up his tea and sat back in the chair.

"Do you want me to carry you into the house?" His voice was soft, husky, like leaves rubbing together.

She shivered. Damn lustdom.

Hell yes, she'd like him to carry her inside, up the stairs and...She kept her face lowered and willed him to go away, before she did or said something she'd regret.

"No, that's okay, I'll manage."

He reached over, placed two fingers on her chin and raised her head. "Your turquoise eyes fascinate me. I wanted to see them once again before I leave."

Her glance traveled up his muscular legs, outlined in the soft, worn, blue jeans, to his chest, halted briefly, and continued up to meet his clear intelligent gaze. He had a five o'clock shadow, with blondish-brown sprouts of hair, and a sincere expression. No smile. No grin.

She croaked out, "Thank you." She took the ice bag in her hand, stood, and limped toward the house. *Thank you? What a moronic thing to say. Quick, say something bright, funny.*

Too late, she turned around to see Jake Callahan scale the three-foot picket fence and go into his house, leaving the door open. She looked down and saw his garden spade lying on the porch. She picked it up and hobbled over to the fence.

"I screwed up, gave away my name. Yeah, I'll be here." His voice, loud and tense, carried well. Hmm, interesting. She hovered, but there was no more conversation. Did he suspect she was listening? She lifted the spade over the fence and let it go. The shovel fell with a clang, and she wasn't sure, but she thought she heard Jake's door click shut.

Chapter 3

Aleksandr's Freighter

Georgina berated herself for foolishly trusting Tristan. Despite him being a consummate liar, she'd been surprised by this latest deception. She thought he only wanted to trap her in their love-less marriage. She'd gone along with it to keep Gemma safe, but Tristan could have lied to her—probably had. He'd given her to the Russian. She'd never trust him. Ever again. She hoped Gemma was safe. Georgina had made a promise to help with the delivery. Little Bobby's due date was close now. Unfortunately, Georgina wasn't.

The squeak of the rusty door brought her back to the present. She stopped writing and scrutinized her captor as he stood in the doorway. Aleksandr's keen eyes focused on her. The urge to squirm and to throw things at him was almost uncontrollable. She forced herself to remain calm and in control, pushed back on the firm bunk, and pulled the ugly green blanket to her chest.

Her heart beat as fast and rough as the lights flickering off the waves. Would there be a chance of getting home soon? Especially with the Russian trafficker staring at her as if she were the main course for tonight's dinner. She wanted to cry, but refused to let this monster see her vulnerability. Her eyelids half-lowered to hide the hurt and angry emotions roiling inside. She would win.

Aleksandr spoke English. His voice was heavily accented, but understandable. "You requested paper and pen, da?"

"Yes. Thank you. I like to write." Georgina prayed there would be time to scribble a few words, but she still didn't know what was going to happen. What game existed in Aleksandr Styopas' world?

"I want you to be comfortable while you're on Fortune's Jewel." Aleksandr stepped closer to the bunk. His shiny black shoes peeked out from under his perfectly pressed pants.

So I'm not scheduled to be fish food.

"How long will I be on this jewel of a ship?" She drew her legs up to her chest. Clicking open the pen, she exposed the point and slowly slipped the journal under her pillow.

"We travel to St. Petersburg. Two to three weeks, depending on the weather." He sat down on the bed, forcing her to bump against the wall.

"Will there be any stops along the way?" The swells of her breasts were exposed. She tried to pull the covers close to her chin, but his weight on the blanket prevented any movement. In her upright position she'd have a better chance of stabbing him, but she needed to get her legs free.

"One stop, Norway. You do not get off." He ran his index finger down her face, onto her neck, halted briefly on the crest of her left breast. He pushed the bodice of the dress below her left nipple. The areola, responding to the stimulus, puckered.

Georgina flinched. Her hand came up with the pen in hand, knocking his fingers away. She brought the pen down as the door flew open and No Neck Number Two rushed in.

"It has happened," he said in broken English.

Aleksandr rolled off the bunk and shot out the door. Georgina halted mid-air and drew a deep breath. Without thinking, she pulled up her bodice, threw off the cover, and followed. Even the guards were absent. She ran back to her bed and grabbed her shoes. The bronze high heels were cumbersome and would slow her down, but the floor was metal, cold, and rough. The bolts alone would tear her bare soles to shreds.

She slipped on the heels, checked the corridors, and took off running. The exit was five feet away, at least, or did she remember it wrong? She halted, closed her eyes, and tried to bear in mind which way her guards turned en route to her cell. Rapid footsteps echoed through the hall, she ducked into the nearest room.

The cramped space had three bunk beds with individual chests at the end of each and six hammocks. Two of the three silver metal trunks were open. She grabbed a blue chambray shirt and pulled it over her dress, tucked her hair into a woolen cap, and searched for pants. Did the men on this vessel only own one pair of pants each? The sound of scampering footsteps stopped. Time was out. Of course, once she got to the top deck, where would she go? Maybe Tristan's yacht was close by. Hell, she'd swim if she had to, to get back to the devil. At least he was a Satan she recognized.

She eased the door open and looked both ways. All clear. She kept to the side, trotted up the staircase, and crept onto the top deck. The wind furiously blew, broadcasting a hint of wood smoke. The harsh pungent scent of fuel oil burned her nose. No guard or deck hands were visible. She edged around the wall, surrounding the staircase, and gasped.

Instantly she realized why she had been left unguarded. Red and yellow flames rose high into the star-speckled sky. Gray, white, and black plumes of smoke drifted toward the frigate vessel. Bits of burning wood and ship parts floated on top of the calm Atlantic Ocean, creating prismatic shadows on the glassy water.

Tristan's yacht had been destroyed.

Tears ran down her face. Whether from the smoke or out of sadness, she wasn't sure. Sobs stuck in her throat, shutting off air. She grabbed her chest and leaned against the rail, fighting intense pain. A hand touched her shoulder, she didn't turn to look. Instinctively she knew. Her fate had been sealed.

Aleksandr whispered into her ear. "He is dead. Of this I make sure. I will take you back to your room now. You should not be here." Numbness overrode fear. Fear overrode sadness and left her body an empty emotionless shell.

****

Georgina hid in her room for the next two days. Tears flowed until dehydration prevented another drop from squeezing out. When she did leave to use the facilities, she returned to find cold soup, dried fruit, and bottled water. Much to her surprise, a table, chair, and lamp appeared as well. Her cell slowly closed in on her.

Her mind flashed back to the good times of her marriage to Tristan. He was the heir to one of the largest software empires, centered in Boston, Massachusetts. While his money hadn't interested her, his young Robert Redford appearance and prep school charm had. Her heart had been tripping double time when he escorted her to her coming-out ball. That day she had decided to become Mrs. Tristan Kaplan.

Their first two years of marriage had been heaven. They talked, played, shopped, and traveled to Mexico, Asia, and Europe. They concluded their holiday tour in July two years ago. They had arrived from the Mexico trip and spent a few days with Tristan's parents. The visit she identified as the turning point, when her heaven became a lonely hell.

Tristan refused to tell her what transpired in his

father's office, but after their meeting, she never saw his parents again. On no account had Tristan wanted to discuss the incident. Instead, he and his entourage took frequent trips on his yacht, for weeks and sometimes months at a time. "I need to get away," he'd said.

Georgina slid the shoes under the bunk, removed her dress, and crawled under the covers. She reached over, turned on the lamp, and stared at the ceiling. The memories, good and bad, flowed through her mind, as clear as the water in the Gulf of Mexico.

Everyone probably thought she was mourning Tristan. In truth, she cried for Jake, who was first and foremost in her thoughts. She picked up the jade pendant from the chain around her neck and rubbed the silver love knot between her fingertips.

Jake simply could not have been on that exploding ship. She felt it deep within her soul, he lived. Yet, the tears gushed. If he hadn't been on the yacht, then where was he? Why hadn't he come to rescue her? And the worst question, what if their brief time together was all they had?

****

On the third day of Georgina's captivity, Aleksandr surprised her when he walked into her cabin, leaving the door open. He had a fistful of blossoms and pushed them into her hand. He stood, silent and hairy. She lifted the green stalks to her nose to discover the lavender-tinted blooms were from a rosemary plant. The pungent, spicy scent reminded her of Thanksgiving. Would she be back in Nero by the end of November? The thought of home brought a fresh wash of salty liquid to her exhausted tear ducts.

Georgina used her lower front teeth to pull her lip inward and suck up the tears. She raised her head to thank him when she heard his in-drawn breath.

"You. Come to dinner at seven." Aleksandr turned around and tromped down the hallway.

Georgina stood in the doorway perplexed at his reaction. No Neck Number Two glared. Childishly she wanted to stick her tongue out. Instead she glared and slammed the door shut.

Odious man.

Her limited apparel was the skanky, consistently damp dress, swim trunk bottom, smelling of ocean mist and smoke, and a stolen chambray shirt and cap. A long jagged tear on the right front of the dress showed much of her upper thigh. Inadequate attire wouldn't be an acceptable excuse. No, she would go. She needed to learn how her opponent played the game. Forfeit wasn't an option. She'd win. Aleksandr Styopas would not sink her metaphorical ship.

Georgina had one hour until the dinner bell rang. She drew the dress over her head and let the material rest loose on her hips. In the last three days she had lost weight, and with her smaller frame she shouldn't lose any more. She folded the halter of the dress around her waist and tied it at the back. The chambray shirt went on next; she buttoned and tucked the tail into the waist of the dress.

Not an outfit for fashion week in New York, but it covered most of her body.

She tortured her feet by placing them into the heels. A pedicure was number one on her pamper-list when she finally got to civilization, if she ever got back home. When the long anticipated knock sounded, she drew the door open to find No Neck Number One.

He held the metal portal and waved his hand, indicating she should walk over the threshold.

"What's your name?" Georgina asked. Play number one: always try to make a friend in the enemy camp.

"Viktor." His name sounded like veek-tar.

"Viktor, I appreciate the water and journal."

His face reddened. He clamped his lips together. Either he was bashful or he had been instructed not to talk to her. He led her through the maze of metal corridors. The sound of the underwater pressure made a reverberating noise, like a loud gong being hit by a hammer. They reached one end of the vessel. Since they remained below deck, she didn't know if she was at the stern or bow. She tried to calm the rapid beat of her heart by thinking of Jake. She'd get free and find him.

Viktor knocked on the wardroom door and stepped behind her. She turned her head to ask him about No Neck Number Two when the portal opened.

Her stomach growled at the scent of roasted duck. Her appetite had returned. She threw her shoulders back, stepped over the splashboard, and strolled into the center of the room with an air of confidence. She glanced around the cabin, surprised at the interior. Not only because of the large space, as it was twice the size of her cell, but because the decoration resembled a sultan's tent. The yellow, white, and black colors appeared bright, making the cabin seem like something out of Arabian Nights. The embroidered fabrics were pure and vivid, ranging from linen to satin and silk. Indigo pillows had a darker blue silk cord sewn along the edges.

Oriental carpets with acanthus leaves, spirals, and stars covered the floor. Hassocks and wicker baskets were scattered throughout. Silver and gold gilded pieces of leather panels disguised the metal walls. Additional pieces covered the lamp shades and gave the impression of jewels as light shone through from underneath.

"It's a beautiful room, Aleksandr." She swiveled

around, taking in the opulence. Her fingers itched with the desire to touch the soft fabrics and the smooth warmth of the teak. She wrinkled her nose at the tinny scent of the metal.

"Call me, Sasha." His coal eyes pierced her and exposed vulnerability, a child-like innocence. What a crazy thought; the man just killed her ex-husband.

"I'm Georgina." She held out her hand to shake, to establish an agreement, hopefully.

"George. I will call you George, because St. George is one of our state symbols. You will bring me luck on this voyage as you have slain one dragon. What I can do to make your stay better?" His lips tipped up, brief and unconvincing.

As a photographer, Georgina had learned to notice the details. The little things often overlooked, like revealing hand gestures, head shaking, and divergent eye movement. She kept her gaze on him, but he didn't reveal his thoughts by his actions. No physical clues. Well, hell, she'd have to wing it.

"What dragon would that be?"

"Why, Kaplan of course."

"No, I didn't conquer the dragon." Yes, Tristan had been a beast, but she hadn't slain him. Rather, he won the fight, but lost the battle. She lifted her hand to touch her talisman, the Celtic knot and jade necklace. Tristan's light went out and good overcame evil; well, in this case wickedness overcame immorality. Cripes.

Aleksandr placed his hand under her arm and led her to a round table. Two sets of silver and crystal table settings sparkled on the white tablecloth, bright blue stoneware plates added a spot of color. He pulled back the chair, and she plopped down onto the seat. With a suave look-at-me walk, he rounded the table, held back the lapels of his pin-striped black jacket, and sat down. He wore an Armani suit. She knew because Tristan had owned one exactly like it. The man had good taste in clothing. Aleksandr tipped the wine bottle to fill her flute.

His eyes roamed over her face and landed on her breasts. Shivers skittered across her skin as she sipped a drink of water. She needed to survive and to do so; she would have to play by the captain's rules. Her fate was in his hands. The loss of a past love and the disappearance of her new love caused her great anguish. An image of Jake flashed across her mind. The ache was so fresh and painful she wanted to double over. She held a hand on her nervous stomach, drew in a deep breath, and closed her eyes.

She needed to focus on freedom.

"In regards to your question about needs, I'd like a change of clothing, including undergarments, personal items like soap, deodorant, toothbrush, paste, a brush, and lotion. Necessities." She moved the wine to the side.

"You no like wine?" He scowled, transforming his face into the pirate she believed him to be. The vulnerability had disappeared as fast as his glass of vodka.

"I don't drink alcohol very often. If I'm going to have calories, I'd choose chocolate." She smiled a sweet hint of a smile. To convince him they shared a sense of commonality, she'd found something they both liked—food.

"Ah, here is dinner. Duck, vegetables, and maybe Yakov will have a chocolate dessert." He nodded to No Neck Number One, Viktor. "George wants chocolate. Tell Yakov."

"Oh, that would be wonderful, Sasha," Georgina bubbled. His responsive smile was broad enough to show crooked brownish teeth. The incisors bent over the two in front. They were crowded together, much like her shipmates with the six beds in a small room.

Georgina nibbled at the delicious bird, grilled mixed vegetables, and drank the water. She answered his questions, while inside she mourned lost love. Thankfully, Aleksandr was easily steered to talk about his homeland.

At the end of the meal, Yakov—judging by the white jacket—brought out a chocolate truffle placed in the middle of a spotless plate. She savored the dark dessert, inhaling the rich scent of the cocoa. Aleksandr escorted her back to her cabin. He threw open the door and waited for her to enter. Immediately, she noticed the antiqued white dresser complete with finials shaped like fleur-de-lis on the corners. Cosmetics, bottles, and tubes of various shapes were neatly arranged on top. She walked over and lifted lids to take in the scents. The aroma of raspberries, the floral scents of magnolia and jasmine, and spices spread throughout the room. At the faint sound of footsteps, she anticipated a touch and tensed in preparation for it.

Aleksandr's wine scented breath flowed over the side of her face. She dropped the lid of the perfume, but resisted the urge to turn away. He took a step forward.

Damn, damn, damn.

She stepped away from him and out of her shoes.

"I know you mourn him. But he was not a man." Aleksandr picked up the crystal decanter of perfume and sniffed.

"How do you know he's dead? Tristan's clever. He could have escaped." She sat down on the side of the bed, placed her shoes underneath, and lined them even with the bed frame.

"I make sure he is dead. If you see him again— ghost." He held his arms out to the side of his thin body. His shirt was black and the pin-stripes were a lighter version of licorice. Being dressed all in dark cloth, he more closely resembled the bandit he was.

"He was a man I loved. I need time to grieve." Georgina lowered her head, pictured Jake in her mind, and raised her hands in prayer. Out of the corner of her eye, she watched Aleksandr take a few steps away from her, closer to the door.

His deep voice was calm and as rusty-sounding as the door. "George."

She raised her head. Tears hovered at the edges of her eyes.

"I will give you time, but you will be mine." The door closed, sealing the vow.

When she heard his footsteps tromp down the corridor, she jumped from the bunk and ran to the dresser. It was like a game show, every night something new appeared in her room. How had he found these items on board a freighter in the middle of the ocean? In each drawer, she discovered a variety of clothing, but the most important were the decadent silk undergarments. The price tags were still attached. She rubbed the fresh new material on her face. Oh, how nice the fabric felt. It would be wonderful to wear underclothing again.

She sorted through the items, finding cotton blouses, linen slacks, and a flannel pajama outfit, perfect for the cold nights. Oddly enough they were all her sizes. She grabbed the bottle of shampoo and bath soap and headed for the door.

She expected to find Viktor waiting outside. Instead she found No Neck Number Two's cruel countenance. "I want to take a shower."

"Go," he snarled.

Sour puss. She entertained the idea of throwing him overboard.

He led the way down to the bathroom, entering first, she assumed, to make sure all of the men were elsewhere. The door opened and he stepped away. She heaved a sigh and went inside, knowing he would guard the entrance and her. A few minutes later, she let the android resembling a human lead her back to her room. She had a full stomach, clean body and teeth, brushed hair, and fresh underwear. She didn't write in her journal. Instead she crawled into bed and dreamed of Jake and their future, once she found him. Her heart stepped up a beat and tears clouded her eyes. She would find him.

Georgina woke to the sound of broken glass and a loud thump. She opened her eyes and saw a live matryoshka doll. A tiny, curvaceous woman stood beside her dresser wearing a bright orange blouse, a brown silk shawl, and a full green, orange, and brown skirt. The Russian woman hacked at a halter dress with scissors. Tiny pieces fell onto the floor.

Dazed and confused, Georgina sat up in bed and shook her head. "Who are you?"

Instead of answering, the pale-faced woman, with glittering black eyes, spat at her. Georgina recoiled in disgust. The rusty door squeaked open and Viktor rushed in. He grabbed the woman from behind. She shouted and clawed at his arms.

"What's she saying?" Georgina tucked the covers around her and crawled to the back of the bed until she bumped against the side of the ship.

"You took her clothes and nice things. She says she smells like cabbage soup without her perfume." He hissed as the woman kicked his shins with her spiked heels, and threw her head back against his chest, repeatedly.

"I didn't take anything. Aleksandr did this." Georgina pushed her hair behind her ears and sighed. "Who is she?"

The angry peasant continued to spit and say the same word over and over.

Viktor held her arms near her waist. She tried to raise her slim legs and use her feet to kick. Her long skirt prevented her movements from being effective.

"American bitch. Sasha my man." Little puffs of air and spittle flowed from her mouth.

Her face had a red flush, and her eyes were squinted. The angry scowl made her pretty features look like an old apple. Georgina could tell she grew tired of struggling against Viktor when her legs stopped kicking and her arms rested on his. Then the woman started to cry.

Aleksandr rushed in, panting short bursts of air as if he had run miles. He snarled at the woman and Viktor released her. She pressed the blue cotton top to her face and ran out of the room. Viktor pulled on his lower ear lobe and followed close behind, shutting the door behind him.

"I will replace." Aleksandr fluttered his hands, indicating the clothing and bottles, leaking liquid floral fragrance, scattered throughout the room. "Were you harmed?"

"No. Is she your wife?" Georgina continued to hold the covers close to her chin.

"Nyet. Friend." Aleksandr scratched his beard and nervously placed his hands in his pants pockets.

"Considering her attack on me," Georgina waved her hands at the destruction of clothing and glass items strewn about the floor, "I'd assume you're lying."

Aleksandr hadn't lifted his head.

"If you don't mind, I'll have dinner in my room tonight." Georgina wanted to avoid having dinner with him every night anyway. She needed to concentrate. The dangerous game she was playing just moved up a notch. She had limited time before he'd force his attentions. He had been nice, but she would hurt him if necessary.

"Nyet. Viktor will bring you to dinner at seven." Aleksandr straightened his shoulders. "Clean this mess." He marched out of the room.

Damn, that didn't work. Georgina slid off the
bed and slipped on the shoes. Cautiously, she walked
to the door and opened it a crack. No Neck Number
Two was on guard duty. Great. Her horoscope must
have had a luck meter of zero.

She searched the floor to find a toothbrush and
paste, and cautiously stepped toward the door.
Matching No Neck Number Two's stare, she turned
and clunked down the hallway to the bathroom.

When she arrived back in her room, the glass
had been picked up and the clothing had been piled
on her bunk. She heaved a sigh and discarded the
irreparable garments. Later she would search
through the drawers. She pulled on a pair of
trousers and a plain cotton blouse, and climbed onto
the bed.

Georgina opened the journal and let her mind
escape by placing her memories on paper. Seven
o'clock would come very soon, and she would need to
strategize her next move. By the desperation
flickering across Aleksandr's eyes, she knew he
wanted more from her than clever banter.

Chapter 4

Nero, Virginia
Four months earlier

"Gemma, it was fabulous. I snapped shots, took notes, and interviewed possible recruits. Andy has a great sense of humor. We took a lunch break with another recruiter. Their conversation about drop-lifts made me snore, but I smiled and nodded. He'll like the photos, and I've got great ideas for the article." Georgina held the phone between her cheek and shoulder, and shoved her weekend bag onto the bed. She lowered the phone to the cradle and pressed speakerphone. Piece by piece she removed the clothing from the suitcase.

"Great because I've invited him over for dinner tomorrow night, when you're here."

Georgina paused in the unpacking process. "I'm using the speakerphone, so I must've misunderstood you. Did you set me up on a date?"

"You wouldn't, so I had to."

"Did you just sigh? I'm not a charity case, Gemma, I can find my own dates."

"Oh yeah. What about the hunky neighbor? Have you talked to him since he performed his heroic stunt?"

"I'm going to," Georgina murmured, while stuffing the empty luggage into the closet.

"Procrastination has always been an issue with you."

Georgina cringed at the criticism. "Well, then I guess I'll see you tomorrow night. Seven?"

Her stomach twisted as tight as a sailor's knot. It had been a long time since she'd gone on a date and she was nervous. She was thankful Gemma eased her into one by making it a gathering, instead of a one-on-one.

"Yes. I'm off to take a nap. Congrats Gee, I'm sure you did very well." She paused. "Don't worry, it'll be fine."

Georgina hung up. Another hot, muggy, September night and not a bit of air flow existed in her house. She took a long, cool shower in the refurbished claw-footed tub. The water became a cascading rain, sweet and fresh, rinsing away her fears, her anxieties about doing well with the photograph, and the article. But the healing properties of the earth element didn't wash away her loneliness.

She put on a strapless cotton top, her tiniest pair of shorts, and flip-flops and ran down the stairs. Her fingers snagged a wine cooler out of the refrigerator. She turned the kitchen radio to her favorite station that played a variety of music, and went outside. She walked around the yard, checking on the growth of her sunflowers, herbs, and her favorite pumpkin patch. Her glance naturally went up from the garden to the few stars shining bright, in a cloudless sky. If rain wasn't predicted for the next couple of days, she'd need to pull out the sprinkler.

A gentle breeze picked up. The scent of grilled meat from one of her neighbor's barbeques overrode the smell of the sunflowers and fragrant rosemary, tangy thyme, and sweet basil. She breathed in deeply and snuggled onto the wicker love seat. She placed her drink on the small table, leaned back, tucked her arms against her waist, and watched an airplane's lights flicker against a backdrop of stars. The waning of the moon created a romantic night for lovers, and she was alone. What was up with the melancholy tonight?

"Do you want company?" a voice asked.

Her heart beat a quick rhythm in reply as she thought of bare-chested Jake. She smiled. "Yes, I'd like some company."

He scaled the picket barrier, his white T-shirt, tight against his chest, gleaming in the dark.

"Want a drink?" she asked.

"Sure. I'll get it. Want anything?" His husky voice made her tingle in all the right places.

"Not yet." Well, she might be nervous but he certainly wasn't. He made himself at home and went directly for the refrigerator. A few minutes later the screen door slammed shut, and he was sitting snug beside her.

Snap out of it.

The smell of a man, outdoorsy, with a vague scent of spicy cologne made her crave something. She guessed desire or that something, a connection, men and women had. His presence, a solid force, warmed her, excited her, and made her aware of her aching womanhood.

"Where have you been? Haven't seen you for a couple of days." Jake paused. "Sorry, not any of my business."

"That's okay." She smiled. "I got a job shooting pictures at a Navy recruitment fair." She didn't know if she should be flattered he cared enough to wonder about her absence. "What have you been doing?"

"Dabbling in photography." He breathed deeply and then exhaled. "The night's beautiful. I've been feeling a bit down, thought it would be nice to have company, and there you were."

Goodness, could she have more in common with him than photography? Her lustful wishes? If only.

She moved around on the bench, so she could

view his strong profile.

"I Googled you. There's a Jake Callahan who's an award winning photographer. No mug shot though. Are you the Jake Callahan, sitting right here on my patio?"

"That would be me," he whispered, with a grating tone.

She elbowed his arm lightly. "I'm humbled."

"Lucked out on the awards." He shrugged and took another drink.

"What do you like best, people or landscapes?" She gathered her hair and pulled it back, tucking it into a knot.

"Landscapes for fun. To pay the bills: actors, models, publicity head shots." He continued to talk about some of the more interesting people he had photographed, all the while his fingers stroked back and forth, up and down on her bare arm. His touch was driving her crazy. The tingling all over her body amplified.

Georgina sighed. Why fight it? Jake's voice soothed her, relaxed her. He smelled so good. His cologne was a mix of wood, bergamot, and spice. She leaned against the back of the bench, and he lifted his arm and placed it across her shoulders. His fingers dangled near her arm, would he touch her again? Continue to lead her down the lustdom path?

She tensed. What was wrong with her?

A man's touch was what she'd desired. Now she had her coveted connection, and her first instinct was to recoil. Relax. Enjoy the moment. He's not making overtures, he's simply adapting to the limited space.

She glanced across the table. Of course, there was an empty chair. She lifted the wine cooler and took a long drink. God, quit psycho-analyzing everything.

"Where was it?" He took a drink, placed his

bottle on the table, and turned into her.

"Where was what?" She looked into his eyes but only got lost in their intensity. She glanced away and thought back to what they had been talking about. "The recruitment fair?"

He nodded.

"Newport." She leaned forward to place her now empty bottle on the table. Her thigh bumped against his knee. He didn't move, and she didn't want to.

"Want another one?" he offered.

"No, thank you. My house's hotter than Hades. Do you have air-conditioning?" She glanced over at his house. The yard was immaculately manicured and the faint glow from the stove light illuminated the kitchen. As far as she knew, he didn't have a television or a radio. How could he live like that, without some form of diversion? She needed her tunes, currently Ne-Yo sang about Sexy Love. Her fingers tapped the arm rest in time with the song.

"Only in the bedroom. How's the knee?" Jake lifted her foot, placed her leg on his and rubbed her calf and ankle. A gentle massage. How charming, and he was so very good with his hands. She pictured his fingers rubbing other parts of her body, and those very elements aching with the need to have more, feel more.

She forced herself to answer. "Fine. The bruises are light purple going to yellow and..." She didn't know how to act around a man who made her heart pound as fast as the click of a camera shutter. His stare remained direct. Did he see through her? She glanced at her chest and resisted the urge to roll her eyes. Eighty-five degrees and her nipples were tight. Damn lustdom.

"What's wrong? You stopped mid-sentence." His glance dropped to her barely covered chest.

Oh damn. She crossed her arms under her breasts hoping to disguise her arousal.

No luck. A gleam appeared in his beautiful gray-blue eyes, but he had the good grace to avert his gaze.

"You were, ah, telling me about the article." His hoarse tone tingled through her nerves. The rasp in his voice touched her, made her yearn. An odd fluttering occurred lower in her belly.

She placed two fingers against her forehead giving a salute. "Shots, bound to attract every young man and woman and make them feel patriotic. I expect my pictures will send them in droves to the recruiting office."

He chuckled. "I'd like to see them."

"I used a digital camera."

"Great, I'd love to take a look."

Georgina lowered her legs and propelled off the bench, skirted the table, went inside the house to the office, and removed the camera out of its bag. On her way out of the tiny five foot room she glanced in the hallway mirror.

Yikes!

She detoured into the powder room and grabbed a hairbrush from under the cabinet. Several passes over her hair, she leaned over and sprayed the Chia-pet mass with hairspray. A quick swipe of the lash building wand, a touch of Precious Pink lip gloss, and she didn't appear quite so plain. She lifted her top to mist her skin with sweet summery scented magnolia body spray. A spritz to the back of her knees and ankles, and she was ready to go.

The suck-click, suck-click of her flip-flops on the tile floors bothered her, so she kicked them off. On bare feet she padded toward the patio doors. What was she thinking, showing off her amateur shots? The man was a professional. Granted he did head shots and stills to pay the bills, but the idea of sharing her photos with a photographer of his caliber was intimidating.

From her research she discovered he had had at least two gallery showings, one in New York and one in Washington, D.C. His work resembled Ansel Adams, an artist renowned for light and composition. Jake's artistic eye helped him create an award winning black and white photo of the ocean. The illumination landed on the peaks of the waves and the shadows inside. She tingled with envy as she remembered the image. The exceptional shot allowed the onlooker to experience the agony and strength of the sea. The powerful waves spiked over and captured the radiance within its force. Much like he did to her.

In the Washington, D.C. show, the displays contained head shots of interesting but ordinary people. At first they seemed like casual snapshots, but the enlargements told a greater story. Some of the photos were taken throughout Europe and the former Soviet Union. They illustrated an underlying tension. One poignant photograph exemplified an outwardly peaceful older man, while his eyes gleamed with hatred and fear. Jake could read people with extreme detail. She'd need to be sure to cover her emotions and not let her past be exposed.

Jake Callahan's celebrated art work would make hers look like a kindergartener's finger painting of Mommy and Daddy. Suddenly self-conscious, she stood at the patio door with her camera in hand. He glanced up, eyebrows raised.

She was being silly. Casual. Keep it casual. Stop worrying and enjoy the night. If he criticizes, I'll appreciate his advice because he's famous.

She eased open the door. "Do you need another beer?"

"Just water please."

She placed the camera's shoulder strap on her arm and walked over to the fridge. Her fingers latched onto two bottles of water and a couple of apples. She snatched a bag of pretzels from the cupboard and made her way to the door. Using her rear end, she pushed it open. Nora Jones sang Don't Know Why, her deep, raspy voice spilling out from the stereo speakers. Lord, she had yearnings. Yearnings for something she thought she had and realized recently that she never did.

Jake stood and reached for the water and apples. As he leaned over her, he drew a deep breath and moaned. Low and light, but she heard the inhale. He'd noticed her primping.

Ah, score one for seduction. Did he realize in the few minutes he had been with her she had changed from Pollyanna, next door neighbor, to Diana the huntress? At least, she hoped so. *Go get him!*

He closed the patio screen door. They settled back onto the cushions, and he lifted the camera. "No second thoughts?"

Was the man a mind reader?

"Have at it." She twisted open the cap, and swallowed the cool water, hoping she hadn't made a mistake. Damn, she couldn't read his poker-faced expression. Her stomach muscles clenched. Did he think she was an amateur? Should she give up the idea of a career as a photojournalist? What would she do instead? The house wife gig certainly hadn't worked out.

She munched on pretzel sticks, while he reviewed the pictures a second time. His strong firm fingers pushed the buttons. Say something. Nod. Shake your head. A sigh. A moan. Anything.

"They're wonderful. Creative. When you had the recruiter stand in front of the video you got superimposing without the cross sections. Generally, this type of shot causes a muting or fuzziness in the background. You brought both into focus." He lifted his face.

She connected with his glance and could see he

wasn't giving false praise. Her instincts were quite honed, and her gut told her that he was telling the truth. Maybe she could make it as a photojournalist after all, at least the photography part.

"Which one are you going to use with the article?" He laid the camera on the table.

"The one you were commenting on, with Andy."

"Andy, he's the recruiter?"

"Yes." The tension knots, created because of her insecurities, released and moths flew around her stomach. She touched her hair, pushing a strand behind her ear.

"If your writing's as good as your photography, you'll be busy every day of the week."

"Thanks for the boost in confidence." She smiled. The flutter settled in her stomach. As a professional, his words meant a lot. She craved his respect as a photographer and his embrace.

Jake picked up an apple and bit into the red succulent skin. She'd stared at him while he chewed, slow, methodically, and then took a deep swallow. Never had she thought watching a man eat could be so seductive. The fresh, clean, scent of the fall fruit permeated the air. Nora Jones had finished singing the blues and Bocelli's soft Celeste Aida filtered from the kitchen.

"So, where are you from? I'm guessing New England from the accent?"

"Sorry, Virginia born and bred, sugar. I went to boarding school in Europe, so the accent lost some of its charm." How horrible, lying to a man she was attracted to. What kind of relationship could they have if it started out as a lie? Keep fabricating. What was up with the good and bad angels sitting on her shoulders? Get off, she shouted at them. Regardless, instinct told her to protect herself.

"I'm an only child, how about you?" At least that was true.

"Two brothers, two sisters. I'm the middle child."

He stared at her, as if he knew that she had fabricated. Did she need to work on her facial expressions when she told lies? Being able to detect dishonesty didn't make her a good liar. As soon as he left, she'd do an internet search, and learn how to successfully tell whoppers.

"I wanted brothers and sisters. Didn't happen. Gemma's my sister, and I'm hers, well one of her five sisters actually."

"Are you engaged? Currently involved?"

"No." Nervously, she tugged her shorts down to cover some of her skin.

"Ever been married?"

He was bold, asking her those questions. Was he fishing for certain answers? Did he know more about her than he was letting on? She couldn't read his facial expression. But the last thing she wanted was to discuss her past. She couldn't disclose any information. Tristan would find her. She had to keep rule over her emotions and especially not get involved.

She hitched her breath, and steadied her hands. Stay calm. At the crescendo of Bocelli's Celeste Aida, she reached over, lost control of her bottle of water and spilled the contents onto his pants.

"Oh, I'm sorry. I'm so clumsy sometimes. Here, let me get the towel." She grabbed a beach towel off the back of a chair and pressed the cloth between his legs. Her heart rate, a fast cadence, matched her patting. What had she done?

He halted her hands. She glanced into his eyes. The light from the kitchen provided enough illumination she could see a grimace on his face. Had she pressed too hard? The pain couldn't be a result of her avoidance of the question. He didn't know anything about her, so why would her evasion cause him to react as though she'd taken away his favorite toy?

She was officially a liar. She wouldn't have spilled the water if she hadn't been lying through her teeth. The sense of guilt overwhelmed her. She wanted him to leave and take her shame with him.

"Thanks for the drink. I'll go now." Oddly enough he sounded disappointed.

"Right. Sorry about the, um, accident." She backed away from him and tossed the beach towel onto the chair. Bocelli ended a finale. Braham's Lullaby came into play. How appropriate, so much for romancing the neighborhood hunk.

Jake slowly rose from the seat and shook like someone coming out of a cold ocean. He walked around the front of the house and crossed over to his place. A screen door slammed a few seconds later, snapping shut as fast as an angry dog's jowl. She guessed jumping over the fence was out of the question.

Damn Tristan.

Damn lustdom.

Chapter 5

Aleksandr's Freighter

Georgina sat cross legged on the bunk, engrossed in reliving each moment and recording the memories of Jake. She glanced up as a heavy tread sounded on the metal floor. Viktor stood in front of her. She hadn't heard him knock.

"It's time to eat. Need to go." He glanced at the door.

She resented the intrusion. She wanted to remain in her world of Jake. "I need to find something to wear. Could you give me a few minutes?"

"No time. Boss expects now." He frowned, crossed his arms and jutted a hip.

"Do you really want me to go dressed like this?" He had a perplexed look on his square face. "Five minutes, Viktor. I'll explain to Sasha."

The use of Aleksandr's nickname closed the deal. With a nod of his head, Viktor tromped out of the room, shutting the door behind him.

Georgina went through all of the clothing to find something salvageable. One white silk blouse had missing buttons, but it could be wrapped over and secured with a belt. Bottoms. She found a skirt that had a slice up to her upper thigh. She didn't want to encourage Aleksandr to look at her legs, so she tossed it aside. In the bottom drawer she found a pair of black slacks. Size eight and in perfect condition. The Russian crazy lady hadn't had enough time to shred them.

Georgina slid into the pants and heels. Damn, her only pair of shoes had been destroyed. The heel had been cut, or broken. She'd wobbled down the hallway earlier. She picked through the debris on the floor and found a leather belt. After removing her T-shirt, she put on a front-closure, pale-pink bra and snuggled into the silk blouse. It was heaven on earth to have an undergarment and silk against her body. She would never take clothing for granted again. She twisted her hair into a French knot and secured the mass with a shell encrusted hair pin.

Viktor knocked and opened the door. The surprised expression on his face told her she had achieved her goal. She hoped that by wooing Aleksandr, she could get him to let her off the ship in Norway. She had yet to determine a method of escaping his custody once she got there. First things first, getting him to trust her enough to take her off the ship. Once on solid ground, she'd run to the nearest embassy.

She tripped over the water ledge at Aleksandr's door. Damn shoes. Despite falling inside the room, Aleksandr whistled when he saw her. Hmm, a ship full of men and only one other woman on board. She'd need to downplay the seduction game, or the pirate would seize the maiden.

"Sorry I'm late, I needed to pick through the torn clothing to find something to wear."

She pirouetted. "What do you think, Sasha?"

He whispered, "I think you are beautiful, George."

She smiled, success would be inevitable. "What did Yakov make for dinner? It smells yummy." She walked over and sat down in the same chair as the night before. The licorice smell of tarragon and grilled cheese made her stomach growl and her mouth water.

Aleksandr twitched, closed his gaping mouth,

and glanced over the table. "I do not know. Fish?" The hair of his mustache melded with his black beard.

Maybe she'd overdone it; he didn't appear to be thinking straight. She grabbed her soup spoon. "Do you mind if I start with the vichyssoise?" Cold potato soup was her least favorite food, but the meal was a means to an end.

"Please, do begin." He sat down with a thump and placed the napkin in the V of his shirt. Tonight he was dressed in the grays: jacket, shirt, and pants.

"Have you ever thought about shaving off your beard?" She took a spoonful of soup and placed it in her mouth. The potato cream combination was repugnant, but she chewed and swallowed.

He rubbed his beard and fingered his mustache. "I like beard. My image must be maintained."

"Hmm. I guess. I just wonder what you'd look like under all that fur." She put down her spoon and touched her face, dragging her fingers from one side of her jaw line over the top of her lips to the other.

Without moving his glance from hers, he lifted his glass of vodka and swallowed the entire contents. He touched his beard again. She raised her water goblet and hid a smile.

"What are you doing in Norway? Trading the goods in the hull? What was Tristan buying from you anyway? I guess I'm kind of curious since he traded me for it." The contraband carried on the freighter led to people dying, Tristan's ship sinking, and her being taken into captivity. Oh, yeah, she wanted to know. Curious didn't begin to describe her feelings about the merchandise in the underbelly.

"None of your concern." The scowl was back. "Here, George, crusted fish, fresh, caught today."

He nodded toward Yakov who placed a steaming platter of fragrant fish in front of her. Queasiness erupted, and she didn't know if she could keep the soup down. Relax. Breathe. Think pleasant thoughts. Ignore the fish smell. Think of spicy cologne, gray-blue eyes, and brownish hair.

"Who was the woman in my room this morning?" Georgina swallowed the vomit in her throat, and lifted her water goblet, hoping to wash the foul taste away.

"No one." Aleksandr rubbed the hair on his face while looking into a silver soup spoon.

"I think she is someone. Did you give me her clothing?" She sucked down a bit of the thick broth.

"You needed clothes. Only woman on board your size." He took a healthy sized bite of fish.

For the second time Georgina swallowed the soup. *Only woman on board my size? Are there more women here?*

"Eat."

"Sorry, thinking about a mad-woman in my room, with sewing shears, made me lose my appetite." She picked at the fish, making it appear as if she searched for the tastiest morsel, and finally lowered her fork.

"Not to worry. She will not bother you again." His black-eyed glance went from her countenance, to her hands, to her plate, and then to her face. She lowered her eyelids, rubbed her fingers across her mouth and picked up her glass, took a sip, and set it down.

Georgina lifted a fork full of fish. *Please stay in my stomach.* Please stay in my stomach. Despite her fears, the fish was delicious. Yakov had brushed it with butter and tarragon spice, and coated it in a cheese mixture. Thank goodness white fish didn't have a salty taste or she'd be heading toward the port hole.

"This is very good." She took another small bite, swallowed, and moved the fish around on her plate. "Tell me what your trade is in."

"Commodities." He smiled to reveal the slightly yellowed, crooked teeth. "I provide a freight service for people who need large quantities of highly sought after merchandise that is difficult to obtain."

"Yes. I can tell you're a very good businessman. I'm surprised you didn't keep Tristan's yacht though. You could have made a nice profit from the vessel."

"Tristan did not keep a low profile. The Feds or Interpol were close to catching him. I did not want his ship tracked to me. Easy to destroy. No evidence."

"Will you sell the goods to Tristan's customer now? Oh, and who was the mad woman?"

"I have another buyer. Pay more money." He frowned at her. His eyes became shards of coal. "Woman of no concern." The chill in his voice convinced her to drop the topic.

"How many days until we reach Norway?" She forked up a green bean. The game was easy when the players were equal. Aleksandr was a hardened criminal, so he had the advantage. But she was a woman, and for some odd reason, he wanted a fey fairy instead of the stripper he could have had in Kandi. Had Kandi died on the yacht or could she be the other woman on board besides the matryoshka doll?

"If weather is good, seven days."

Yakov brought out a short, dark cake. Chocolate fudge icing had been drizzled over the top and dripped down the sides.

"Yakov. This is a thing of beauty," she murmured.

His pockmarked face flushed. He placed the dessert on the table and bowed his hairless head. With a quick step, he took his gray and white clothed, boyish, body back toward the door. Georgina watched him, wondering where the door led. Yakov's reflection appeared in the starboard windows, a smile on his face. He probably didn't get very many compliments.

With her stomach rumbling and her nerves on edge, how would she be able to eat the damn thing?

Aleksandr waved his hands toward the baked treat. "Cut. Eat."

Yakov had provided a cake knife, when she had hoped for a sharp blade. If she secured a razor-edged knife could she hold Aleksandr hostage and forced the ship to port? Ha, not likely. She'd stick to the other plan. Play a smart game.

She slid the knife through the cake, lowered a slice on one of the dessert plates, and placed the treat in front of Aleksandr. His eyes widened in surprise. He nodded his head in encouragement. She smiled. Male arrogance was predictable. She imagined thrusting the blade into his pasty hairy body, but she knew she couldn't attack to kill. Besides, his body-guards were a whisper away. She sliced a smaller piece and settled in to eat. With a tiny bite, she let the chocolate rest in her mouth, providing her with a sweet, rich joy. She swallowed and followed with a sip of cool water. So far so good.

"Do you want port?" He lifted a bottle of wine with a label written in what appeared to be Russian.

"No, thank you."

She took another bite and then another. Before long the piece of cake had disappeared, but the sweet cocoa smell remained in the air. Absolute pleasure had been obtained from the scents and the taste. If only Jake were there to share it with her.

"I ate too much." She yawned and closed her eyes to half-mast, watching him to see if he'd let her go.

"I will take you back to your room. First, we need to come to an agreement." He refilled his glass with vodka and took a sip. He pierced her with a stare. The knots were back in her stomach. She clenched her hands, expecting the worse.

"A trade agreement?" She returned his stare.

"I am negotiating man. Talk." A glint of amusement appeared in his eyes. He was having fun. Maybe some decency existed inside that hard shell of a criminal.

"I want to go into the city in Norway and buy some decent clothing. In trade, I'll provide entertainment for the next few nights."

"Entertainment for me alone?" The smile disappeared. His eyelids lowered, but the hint of a smile lingered on his lips. It was a smile she'd seen on Robert's face many times when he looked at Gemma. Georgina usually left shortly thereafter and the next day Gemma told her details about the awesome sex.

"No sex," she sharply replied.

"For now." The words barely escaped his mouth.

Aleksandr agreed too easily. He must have something in mind. Was she fighting a losing battle? Regardless of how fast her heart thrashed around in her chest, the game wasn't over, yet. She held a couple of strategies close.

She rejoiced in the small success. The smile in her head must have been reflected on her face, because he slammed his glass of vodka down with a hard thud on the table.

"If I want, I take." His jaw hard-set, she had no doubts he'd seize what he wanted. This wasn't just a man seeking a woman's company. He was a kingpin to trafficking and a very dangerous racketeer.

The sight of Tristan's burning ship flashed through her mind. "Let's just say that if I ever fail to entertain you, then we'll renegotiate."

"I like a strong-minded woman. I will think about your offer." He nodded and waved Viktor forward. "Take George back to her cabin."

Thankful, Georgina quickly rose from the chair.

She held out her hand to seal the deal. Aleksandr was a criminal and a murderer, but hopefully not a rapist. She waited, with her gaze directly on his face. He stood. His eyes warmed. He took her hand into his, drew it up to his lips, and kissed the top.

She disliked black-haired men, especially gorilla-hairy men. She resisted the urge to shudder and brightened her smile.

"'Til tomorrow." He released her hand.

Steady as she goes. She walked toward the door. A trickle of sweat ran down her back. She'd escaped to play another day.

She glanced over at Viktor. His gaze remained fixed straight ahead. "Viktor, where could I get a pair of boots? My shoes are damaged. They keep sliding off."

"I'll have Mihail repair them."

Damn.

"And in the meantime?" She wanted and needed boots or sneakers.

They had arrived at her door. He opened it, held out his hand, and waited. She removed the heels and handed them over to him. She nodded at No Neck Number Two who stood guard for the night. As usual he ignored her.

No answer had been forthcoming about shoes or boots, so she shut the door.

She would need to find another way to get a pair of footwear. Norway in the fall would be frigid, so she couldn't run away barefoot. The journal peeked from beneath the pillow case. She placed the book carefully on top of the bed. She removed her shirt and black pants and placed them in the dresser. Settled on the bed, she smoothed her hand over the silk of her bra, opened the journal to re-read the last passage, and put off until tomorrow what sort of diversion she would dream up for Aleksandr.

Chapter 6

Nero, Virginia
Four Months Earlier

Georgina glanced out the car window. Thank goodness there wasn't a lot of traffic this late at night, so the trip to her house would be short. She turned toward her date.

Andy the recruiter man.

"Thank you for escorting me home. I'm sure Robert appreciated the break. I would have driven, but they felt a celebration was in order and didn't want me to drink and drive." Why was she so nervous? She spent two days in this man's company and never blathered once. Now, it was as if she couldn't form an intelligent thought and talked like a brainless nit.

Andy drove a dark blue Jag 320 Z. She'd have been more impressed, but she had friends who drove similar vehicles. Frankly, cars were cars. He talked about all of the attributes of the Jag, details of the motor speed per minute, stopping factor, blah, blah, blah. Boring.

His attractiveness was compensation. He was physically perfect. As he talked about the car and then the status of the military, she focused on his profile, his facial movements. He had a beautiful smile and light brown hair, cut short, but not a buzz cut.

Andy had been telling her about a friend on active duty. She stared at him and his handsome, million-dollar smile spread over his countenance.

Unfortunately, she had only partially listened to his story and couldn't comment. Instead, she focused on his peachy, pink mouth and brown eyes, according to the recent issue of Cosmopolitan a man loves a quiet woman who gazes into his face in an admiring way. Was that true? She had borrowed the magazines from Gemma to find out about current dating trends. If the advice didn't work, at least she found out what was in the spring fashion collection.

His smile seemed genuine and dimples creased grooves in his cheeks. Little crinkles were visible around his eyes as they glittered, reflecting the lights from the dashboard. He was attractive and sweet. Too bad he was boring.

She nodded in response and continued to daydream. Perhaps a gal couldn't get everything wrapped into one beautiful package. At least this hadn't been a bad start to dating. She had a moment of confidence until they arrived at her house. A lump clogged off her throat, prevented her from saying anything.

"Are you going to invite me in, for coffee?" He unsnapped his seatbelt.

She swallowed the lump and hoped he wouldn't notice her shaking hands. Her fingers fumbled with the smooth metal clasp as she unfastened her seatbelt. She collected her purse off the floor. Her heart seemed to rise to her throat, adding to the blockage there. Nerves prickled her skin. What now? She was a teenager the last time a man brought her home from an evening out. Damn, she shouldn't have spent all her time on fashion and focused more on the dating articles.

"Sure, after dinner coffee sounds like a nice idea." She breathed slowly in and out. Because she carried a tiny black evening bag, the keys were easy to find. He took them from her trembling fingers and opened the door. She led the way into the house.

Georgina flipped on the switch for the overhead fan and light combination. The room could have been right out of the pages of architectural digest or a home decorating magazine. She was very proud of how well she outfitted the room on a small budget. When they walked into the postage stamp size foyer, he whistled. Her lips lifted on one side. She placed her purse on the walnut entry table and ambled toward the kitchen.

"Make yourself at home, and I'll start the coffee." He appeared to be evaluating each piece of furniture. She flipped on the light over the range and turned on the stereo. A routine. Similar comfortable activity. Something she did every morning, except now it was late at night and she had an attractive man in the other room with a possible future date looming. She opened the patio doors and drew the screen over to let in the late night breeze. Her underarms were beginning to get wet. She grabbed a bag of Seattle's Best coffee from the freezer, hovering a moment to cool her face, and then prepared the brew.

The overhead light in the living room went off and the automatic electric fireplace went on. Oh no. September night, hotter than blazes, and he turns on the fireplace. Cripes, did he want to create a romantic atmosphere?

"Everything okay in there?"

"Yes. The light was too bright. The fireplace is very nice." A whoosh and the glow disappeared. His voice became louder as he moved from the living room into the kitchen. "Where did you find the retro-style furnishings?"

"On the internet. The house was built in the mid-fifties. I wanted the decor to be in line with the architecture."

"I like the furniture. Especially that cool lamp." He came closer to her. His breath flowed over her neck, the small hairs which had escaped her up-do swayed and tickled.

"Um, yes. The lamp looks like something from a sci-fi movie. The tiny little lights make specks on the wall. Freaks me out at night, but I like it."

He placed his arms around her waist. "You smell nice. Not flowery, but spicy. Citrus?" He nuzzled her ear.

"Yes," she softly answered.

She wasn't ready. What to do? And he answered her internal thought.

"I love this song. Let's dance." He hummed Blue Moon.

"Not enough room." She edged away.

He spun her around and grabbed her hand. As he tugged her toward the patio doors, the scents from the freshly painted kitchen and her herb garden perfumed the night air. Snatching the remote to the stereo, he yanked open the screen and pulled her onto the patio. His large smooth hand moved onto her back, his fingers touched her skin where the V of her dress left her bare. He turned up the volume, so loud the dog next door barked until the owner took him inside.

Andy pulled her into an embrace, and they swayed to the music. She glanced over his shoulder to check and see if Jake was outside. No sign. Was that good or bad? She needed to concentrate on the warm, six-foot male holding her close. Andy had a scar on his chin, so fine an indentation it wasn't evident until she was within inches of him. His cologne, a popular scent with supposed ocean fragrances, wafted into her nostrils. He eased his cheek against hers. His rough whiskers braised the side of her face.

She backed away and whispered, "The song's over."

"Let's see what the next one is." He leaned over,

breathed lightly into her face. The after dinner drink of brandy was still fresh on his breath. She lifted her chin, and her gaze connected with his.

She experienced a pull, a moment in time where two souls connect.

The stars twinkled around a full moon, adding the perfect backdrop. He wrapped his arms around her waist and lifted. She balanced on her tip-toes. She heard Magic of the Night from the stereo system, looked into his lust-laden eyes, and knew a split second of indecision.

He kissed her, a sweet gentle touch of lips. His fingers tugged the comb from her hair and her silky waves fell to her shoulders. The clip pinged as it dropped to the cement. She widened her mouth, wanting to ease her wantonness, the ache. She opened herself to the magic, and he deepened it. The song ended, and so did the kiss. He released her, and she eased her heels onto the cement patio. His hands moved from her waist to clasp her hips.

In that brief instant she saw a light flash from a window of Jake's house. She peered into the darkness but could not make out his face or form. An illusion? The light could have signaled he was home and would come out into the back yard. And do what? He hadn't shown an interest in her. Was lustdom restricted to one man? Could she feel desire for the man holding her snug in his arms right now?

"The coffee's done," she whispered as she turned to walk toward the house, her hand still clasped in his. Jake's garage door opened, and his car, with its spurts and bangs, drove away. She led Andy into the coffee scented kitchen.

"Coffee's not what I want. I want you." He hauled her into a tight embrace again and leaned over her, this time he kissed her passionately. Instead of letting her lips linger, after a minute she broke away. The nervousness had returned. Her body wanted to be touched and gravitated toward him. However, her mind wouldn't release the idea Jake had witnessed the lip-lock. The thought of him seeing her kissing another man was strangely disturbing.

"I'm an old-fashioned kind of gal. Never on the first date, and I'm only recently divorced. So I need to take it slow. To ease into a sexual relationship." She didn't plan to step away, it simply happened. Her clit tingled with the need to be satisfied, but her heart had left with the sputtering car.

"Oh. Sorry, I didn't know. I'll help you ease into it." He culled her closer like a puck to a goal. He bumped her hips against his. Her breasts peaked and her nipples touched his chest. His engorgement fit nicely between her legs. Despite what her body wanted, her mind rebelled.

"Like I said, never on a first date. And this isn't even really a date."

He leaned back, hands on his hips. "I see. You're serious." His direct gaze didn't falter.

"Yes, I am."

An uncomfortable silence filled the kitchen.

"Maybe you should go home." Georgina smoothed down her dress and maneuvered around him. Her shaking hands brushed her hair back. She ran to the front door.

Andy joined her in the foyer. He wove his fingers through her hair and placed his large hand at the back of her neck. She raised her glance to meet his. He kissed her, not a tongue down the throat kind of kiss, but a sweet and caressing dedication.

"I'll pick you up on Friday night at seven. Dinner and a movie."

"All right." She lifted two fingers to touch her lips and felt the moisture from his. A single dimple creased his face as he smiled and sauntered out the door.

****

Who could possibly be ringing her door bell at six in the morning on a Sunday? She ignored the blast and tugged the covers over her head. The signal continued to vibrate in her head. Her fingers gripped the lightweight blanket and sheet, jerked them off her body, and forced her legs to move. She slid into her Green Lantern slippers. The fuzzy green house shoes with the plastic image of Hal Jordan, defender of justice, peeked out from under the robe she shoved her arms into. She went in the general direction of the stairs. The dog next door barked maniacally.

"I'm coming!" This better be important. She flipped the two security locks and eased the door open to peek out.

Jake stood on the other side with wrinkled clothes and a snarl. "Hi! Am I interrupting anything? Need to borrow some sugar. I wanted to make sweet tea and didn't have sweetener. Got sugar?"

He rattled so fast; he obviously didn't need more caffeine.

"Interrupting? You're interrupting my sleep." She yawned and opened the door wider to let him in.

His glance traveled to the stairs.

"You said you needed sugar?" she asked, trying to keep the sarcasm out of her voice. She could tell he wasn't even paying attention. So, what was he listening for? Sounds of a lover upstairs? Well, let him snoop.

Her ungraceful pivot caused her feet to shuffle as she made her way toward the kitchen. She lifted the plastic container out of a cupboard and peeled off the lid. The sweet scent of sugar made pleasant tingles in her nose. She glanced over at the untouched brew in the coffee maker left over from last night. Only a few hours old, and Seattle's best, it should still be good. She grabbed a cup off the shelf, filled it, and slid it into the microwave. A quick punch to the start button and a minute lit the display. A sigh and cross of her ankles, she gazed at Jake.

"I like the slippers." He nodded toward the house shoes but kept his gaze fastened on hers.

"Thanks, the Green Lantern is one of my favorite superheroes. I like the understated heroes. Superman, yes he has undeniable muscle, but even he used one of the power rings from the police force of Green Lanterns, maybe Hal Jordan's ring. The power ring could generate energy and be sustained by the strength of will. The Green Lantern used his wits to battle the enemy," she said. "How much do you need?"

He looked like he hadn't slept in days, and he was as jittery as a dragonfly.

"Two cups." He shoved his hands into his pants pockets and rested his hip against the doorframe.

"For sweet tea? You must have a sweet tooth."

She got a large measuring cup from one of the drawers and filled it to the brim. "Besides the Green Lantern had a cool motto, not sure if I'll remember it all, '...and I shall shed my light over dark evil. For the dark things cannot stand the light. The light of the Green Lantern.' Here you go." She set the cup on the countertop, gleaming white sparkles fell over the top.

"I don't believe I've seen a Green Lantern movie."

The timer went off on the microwave. She sighed, pulled her hair back, and twisted it into a knot.

"Comic books are best, although there was a short TV series, I think." She turned to get a spoon out of the drawer. Her hair fell into her face and blocked her vision.

"I need a haircut," she sighed under her breath.

"Why don't you get one?" He moved closer to her and leaned against the counter.

"I can't afford one right now. I have to wait until the fifteenth or until I get a check from the Navy. I'm betting on the fifteenth." She removed the cup from the microwave, blew on the surface, and took a sip. She picked up the spoon and added sugar. Not something she ever did, but the sugar was out and the coffee tasted like the thick nasty remains in the bottom of a pot in a sleazy diner.

He started to dig around in his pockets. "I'll give you the money."

She reached over and halted his hand movement. "No. Thank you, but I'd rather wait. I don't like to owe people." Her voice came out soft, but her nerves were as tight as a bowstring. Her heart beat a quick tandem inside her chest. She shouldn't have added the sugar.

His blood-shot eyes glanced at her face and then down at her hand. She snapped her hand back faster than a broken rubber band. Lust for Jake never rested.

"I did a still for a stylist, so she owes me a favor. Come over at two this afternoon, and she'll cut your hair." Her expression must have reflected her resistance to the idea, because he quickly said, "You won't owe me a favor. You'll be helping me."

Georgina twisted her mouth into a moue, while contemplating the suggestion.

"I certainly don't need a haircut, so you may as well lessen her guilt and help me out," he reiterated.

"If it'll help you, Jake, I'll do it." She smelled the bitter coffee and sipped a bit of liquid and put the cup back on the brown and cream Formica.

"Great. I'm going to take a nap. I'll see you this afternoon."

"Maybe you should, your eyes look like a road

map of the state of D.C. Red lines everywhere." She winked at him while her heart continued to tap madly.

He frowned, rubbed his eyes, and walked out of the kitchen.

"Jake, you forgot the sugar." She grabbed the measuring cup from the counter and raced to catch him at the door. She handed it over, smiling at his forgetfulness. He sheepishly grinned, took the cup with one hand, and flipped open his cell phone.

"Thanks," he mumbled.

She shut the door and jogged up the stairs. After a quick shower, she lounged on the bed and looked through the magazines for hairstyles, biding her time until two o'clock.

****

Georgina strolled over to Jake's house to find a woman hovering at the front door.

"Hi, I'm Georgina." She held out a hand.

"Amber. Where do you want to do this?"

Amber had bleached blonde hair. The part curved over her wide forehead. She wore sandals and brief shorts and her nails were perfectly manicured.

"Around back? There is a table on the patio and an electrical outlet." Georgina pointed to the rear of Jake's house.

"I need to talk to him first." Amber held a black case as big as Georgina's weekender.

"I'll get Jake."

The entrance was unlocked, so Georgina peeked her head inside. He couldn't be found on the first floor so she trotted upstairs and pounded on the only closed door. She rapped three times. Maybe not very loudly, but knocked nonetheless.

She opened the door to find him in bed, bare naked, with the dark blue sheets down around his ankles. Even with the arctic breeze coming from the rattling window air conditioner, his Johnson was fully extended. Compared to her ex-husband's, Jake's penis was long, thick, and bigger than any she had ever seen in magazines or television. She wanted to stroke him. To feel him inside her. *No, can't think like that.* She tried to look away, but her gaze kept returning to his anatomy.

She kneeled on the bed and yanked the blanket on top of him. The mattress gave way as she pressed her mouth close to his ear. "Jake, Amber's downstairs, and she'd like to talk to you. I told her to set up her equipment outside on the patio, so clean up would be easy. Is that okay?"

She rather liked how her voice came out, raspy and sexy.

He rolled over and placed his fingers against her cheek and kissed her. Gently at first, and without taking a breath, increased the pressure with a passion that made Andy's smooch resemble a green school-boy's.

Her stomach muscles clenched, and her lower region tingled, moisture collecting. Cripes, not every man could propel her to the lustdom maze. Only Jake.

She wanted to feel more. Experience more. No, it was wrong. He had to be dreaming and didn't realize who he was kissing. They were neighbors. He had never verbally indicated an interest in her. Yet, her attraction to him could not be denied.

She shifted her nose to the side so the mouths could fit more fully together. Lips so smooth she wanted to outline the edges and imprint their shape into her mind.

Without a thought, she raised her hands to separate strands of his light brown hair. He drew her closer. His penis pushed against her thigh. Unlike with Andy, she didn't pull away. The covers fell between them, lightly shielding the contact. Her body warmed. The heat and the friction from the cloth as he rubbed his thighs against hers created an awareness she had, up to this point, only dreamed about.

He slept naked. She dared not look down at his body again. In her mind, she could picture his firm muscular thigh resting against hers. His tight rear, she had admired on several occasions, flashed through her mind.

Okay, she needed to get a grip. She leaned back and ran her right hand gently over his eyebrow, feathering the hairs. Her fingers touched his crooked nose and migrated until she reached his mouth and pressed her fingers against his lips.

"Jake, it's Gee, from next door. You asked me to come over at two. It's two."

He opened his gray-blue ocean-deep eyes and looked at her for the first time. He didn't appear to be surprised she was in bed with him. Instead, he kissed her fingers and raised his hand to lower them from his lips. He flipped onto his back and released a sigh. His eyelids closed again.

"Sorry. Long night. I'll shower and be right down." His voice was croaky, cold, and distant.

She had offended him. The kiss. She should have stopped her lips from attacking his before it became passionate. As the only alert one, she was responsible. She'd apparently become the desperate divorcee her mother had told her she would be when she left Tristan.

"Right. I'll be downstairs." She hurried out the door before he could see the flush that heated her face.

His house was a tract house like hers with one major exception. He had what appeared to be Goodwill excess as furniture: a brown ratty couch, one chair, cream with coffee stains, and a single table between the two. She jogged to the kitchen and glanced around. What should she do while she waited? The only items that appeared to be new were the kitchen ware. The measuring cup of sugar rested on the counter top. He must have been so exhausted he hadn't prepared the tea before he went to bed. She'd make his tea. She started by making simple syrup with hot water and sugar, pouring the liquid into a pitcher to cool. Tea bags were located in an otherwise empty cabinet. She placed three into a pot with additional hot water to sit and brew. The two would be put together after the tea had finished brewing.

Georgina went out onto the patio. Amber had arranged her styling instruments on a table. She sat in one of Jake's lawn chairs, rocked her foot on the ground, heel to toe, and smoked a cigarette.

"He'll be down in a second. What do you want me to do to prepare?" Georgina asked.

"I need to talk to him alone first, but you could wash your hair. I like to cut hair wet." Her long red fingernails shone in the afternoon sun as she blew rings of smoke into the humid air.

"Okay. I'll go next door and be back in about five minutes. Do you want some iced tea? I have some brewing in the kitchen."

"If it's no trouble." She threw her cigarette onto the cement and ground the tobacco in with her spiked heel. Georgina questioned trusting this woman with her mane, having only met her moments ago. If she cut it too short, or in a wacky manner, the hair would take months to re-grow to this length. She eyed Amber one last time, noting her perfectly shaped locks, threw caution into the wind, and took off at a run to her house.

Although Georgina had washed her hair a few hours before, she went through the process again. She didn't want to disrupt Amber's energy. She combed through her long blondish-brown locks and wrapped a towel around her hair to keep her shirt dry.

She grabbed her cell phone and jogged back over to Jake's house, stopping in the kitchen to mix the tea and liquid sugar. She pulled ice from the freezer and prepared three glasses. A quick scan through the cupboards indicated he didn't have a serving tray, so she grabbed a plate and placed the tumblers on top. It wasn't easy to open the patio door and walk out, but she managed. She set the plate on a chair.

Jake had a frown on his face, making his lips pull into a tight line. His hair, wet from a recent shower, was plastered to his head. Amber twisted her shoe back and forth to pulverize a fourth cigarette butt into the cement. She was, without a doubt, angry.

Had Georgina interrupted something? Maybe a lover's disagreement?

"Ah, if I'm interrupting, I could come back. Or perhaps we should just cancel the cut. Thanks anyway, Amber." Georgina pivoted, ready to cross over the threshold, but stilled when Jake called to her.

"No. I want to help you. Please. Sit. Amber was asking me to take pictures of your session so she could use the shots as an advertising ad. I wanted to have a day off. We've come to a resolution, and she'll get her photographs this time." As he said that last part, he glared at Amber.

"Thanks, Cal." Amber turned her back on Jake and flashed Georgina a grin. "On the stool."

Georgina removed the brown turban from her head and climbed onto the stool. Amber wrapped a dark green satin cape around her shoulders, took the towel, and tossed it onto a chair.

"Aren't you supposed to be taking photos, Cal?" Amber asked sweetly.

Jake's eyes narrowed, but the five-foot-nine woman never flinched. He stalked into the house. Some negative energy existed between the two. Georgina didn't know if she wanted to find the root of the problem.

A few minutes later Jake came out with a Nikon D200 camera. He evaluated the angles, used the light meter, and clicked shots. With ten point two mega pixels and a large LCD screen, the camera was a snap to use. She knew every little graphic detail of the instrument, and her fingers clenched the cape or she'd reach out and snatch it out of his hands. He knelt on the fragrant, dark green summer grass and ummed and aahed. Finally, he took the camera into the house and out of temptations way.

When he came back out, he took a glass of tea and moved a chair into the sun. He made her nervous as he stared. Amber, with her tight lithe model's body, hadn't distracted him. His gaze remained fixed on Georgina. The click-click as the scissors snipped her hair and lulled her into a state of relaxation. He lifted the condensation-laden brew and drank. The muscles in his forearm bunched as he put the glass down on the cement. She was mesmerized.

Her glance connected with his piercing gray-blue gaze. She saw the desire in his eyes, or was it a reflection of her own want?

The sun pierced her skin as her face flushed with heat. A small smile appeared on his countenance. He removed his shirt and leaned back in the chair absorbing the rays. He was undeniably gorgeous, crooked nose and all, and she remembered every single inch of his warm tightly muscled skin. Her fingers itched to touch that hot, hard, body from top to bottom.

Within a few minutes her hair had been shaped and semi-dried by the sudden wind. Amber turned on the dryer and used a brush to whip the Chia into shape. She wrapped chunks of hair around a straightening rod. Several strokes later she unplugged the iron, sprayed a finishing product, and stood back. She cocked her head to the right and to the left. Evidently she was satisfied as she removed the cape and threw her styling items in the black carrying case. Hot iron and all. The girl rushed to the door, clanging her case against the frame in the process.

A few seconds later Amber was en route to the door. "Send me the photographs, and I want the signed release now."

Jake jumped from the chair and put his shirt back on. He pursued Amber. He withdrew an envelope from his rear pocket, and handed the parchment to her.

Okay, if Amber planned to use pictures of Georgina, shouldn't she be signing the release? Or Jake for permission to use the shot? It didn't make sense, but perhaps the document was a contract from a previous shoot.

"Thanks for the hair cut, Amber." Georgina tilted her head back and forth, enjoying the light bounciness of the cut.

Amber turned at the threshold and smiled. "Anytime, Georgina." She sashayed down the sidewalk.

Jake shut the door. Georgina watched Jake's glance sweep from her hair, to her face, and down her body. He tucked his hands into his pockets.

"Where's a mirror?" She couldn't wait to see the results.

"There's a full length mirror in the bedroom upstairs." He jerked his hands from his pockets and entwined her fingers with his. Together they jogged to his bedroom. She avoided looking at the bed. Her body jangled with desire, and his nakedness was fresh in her mind.

She stood in front of the mirror. He posed behind her. Reflected in the glass was a stranger. Internally she didn't recognize the emotions running rampant through her body making her lust after Jake. For twenty-four years she had always worn a pageboy style that brushed her shoulders. After she'd filed for divorce, without time and inclination, her locks grew to resemble Rapunzel's mane. Curly and long, her hair had grown to reach the middle of her back.

Now her tresses brushed her shoulders but had been cut into layers. The weightlessness added volume and drew attention to her eyes. The light hair had been cut away and showed more brown than blonde. She leaned closer to the mirror. In addition to the blue-green color of her eyes, she noticed a vulnerability deep within. She switched her gaze from her image to Jake, who waited behind her, silently watching.

He came closer and placed his arms around her waist. "I think we should celebrate the new you. Will you go to an early dinner with me?"

She glanced down at his hands folded over her stomach, felt his body align itself with hers from behind, and lust intensified to the point it was painful to feel his palms on her without acting.

"Yes," she answered. And more if offered.

Chapter 7

Aleksandr's Freighter

Georgina woke in a cold sweat. During the dank darkness of the night, she had dressed in the magically appearing pajamas, but now they were damp. She pushed her hand against the cabin wall, the buoyant feeling of the ocean noticeable beneath her fingers.

She'd been dreaming. Awake, her current nightmare continued.

The nap had refreshed her. She sat and crossed her legs. She removed the journal from its hiding place and recorded the events that led her to her first dinner with Jake. Georgina failed to notice the time until a knock on the door jerked her back from Nero, Virginia. Regretfully, she rose from the bed, shook off the numbness from sitting cross-legged, and walked over to the door.

Viktor stood with his beefy arms crossed over his massive chest. "Why aren't you ready? Do you know it's seven?"

"Hello. There's no clock in here," she retorted. His grimace bothered her a little. Why was she being angry and mean? Viktor had been decent and didn't deserve the smart remark.

"We'll be late." He frowned and lowered his arms.

"Don't worry, Viktor. Give me a minute to get dressed. I was busy writing my last will and testament." She puffed out her cheeks in frustration. She really couldn't wait to recall the events following her first meal with Jake, especially now that she had to entertain and avert a possible rape from her captor.

Georgina had made a deal with the devil, so she went prepared to win the game. She threw on the black slacks, slid into the chambray shirt, and let it hang outside the pants. A long gold necklace had been broken, so the clasp didn't hold. The Russian woman might have been wearing it when Viktor grabbed her from behind. Regardless, the spoils of war go to the victor, and Georgina felt as though she was the champion in that battle.

The gold necklace fit around her waist, she dropped it over the shirt, and created a sailor's knot to hold the links in place. Her shoes hadn't been returned. She threw on a pair of thick socks, which had arrived in her room earlier in the day. A swift stroke of eye-liner and a dab of lipstick, and she was ready. She snatched open the door.

Viktor had apparently gone off duty because No Neck Number Two leaned against the metal wall across from her room. His cold stare didn't shake her. She'd traveled on the subway station once in Boston and found out from a stranger that people are only intimidating if you didn't meet their stare. The intent look shouldn't be held for a long period of time. Just let them know you're not afraid and then turn away. This method proved to be helpful with No Neck Number Two.

Georgina met his stare with an icy glance and stomped down the corridor. The thick padding of the socks made a thump-thump sound on the hard floor, while protecting her feet from the cold. She could now move through the ship, blind-folded, and find the captain's cabin located on the port side. The side which would also be her exit point if the opportunity presented itself.

Busy planning her escape, the door swung

inward surprising her. Did Aleksandr have sophisticated camera monitoring equipment on this metal tub? Her father had dabbled with electronics, and she knew enough to believe it was illogical. The metal would bounce the electrical waves all over the place, unless he used a plastic conduit in the walls to insulate the wires. She made a mental note to evaluate her room closer when she returned. Chills racked her body. Had he been watching her? She stepped into the spider's web.

"George, you look lovely tonight," Aleksandr said.

Yakov rolled his eyes as he placed salads on the table. She held her hand to her mouth to cover a laugh with a cough.

"You are not getting a cold? I will have another blanket delivered to your room. It will be colder the closer we get to Norway." If Aleksandr wasn't her abductor, she would have appreciated his caring attitude and soft, romantic, accented voice, but he was and she needed to keep his evil blackness in mind.

"How close are we?"

"The currents have been our friend, and we are now only a couple of days away."

"Wow, they have been friendly. The current shaved off quite a bit of time." Georgina's mind raced to find ways to manipulate him into taking her onto land. To the city. To freedom.

"Come. Sit." He grasped her arm and tugged her toward the table. He propelled her chair away from the china setting and pushed her into it. She teetered back and forth, and hung onto the arms to keep from falling over.

"I guess I haven't got my sea legs yet." In reality she didn't know why she couldn't maintain balance. Nerves maybe?

Focus Gee. You need to get through tonight

without a close encounter of the worst kind. Entertain. Be jovial.

"Tonight..." He paused and rubbed a finger along the cuff of her shirt at her wrist.

"Yes?"

His black eyes, so dark the iris blended together with the pupil, made him appear demonic. She tried to soften hers, to make them dreamy. In boarding school, the coeds on her dorm floor often would practice using their bodies in seductive ways. When you only got together with the male species once or twice a year, a girl went prepared. She had been voted the one with the best dreamy-eyed look.

She obviously hadn't lost the ability, because he squirmed in his seat. Back off now. Find the balance to keep him sexually interested but at a distance. A fine line for sure.

Aleksandr rubbed his jaw with his bronze hand. "Tonight, I will honor your request. If you can entertain me, I will give consideration to taking you into Norway."

He smiled and his eyes had that sultry look. He expected her to lose, the game and her womanhood.

She licked her lips. Taken aback, she noticed he had trimmed his beard. It was a mere scruff. Shivers ran down her back. If she lost, he would be all over her like a bee on a flower, sucking everything out.

Fake it. You did often enough with Tristan.

She fabricated a smile. "Wonderful. Tonight I will need a deck of cards and poker chips or anything that could be used as currency." She widened her grin to a true smile. Let the game begin. Losing was not an option. She would not forfeit her body. Freedom would be obtained.

****

Three hours later she'd accomplished her goal. She thought.

"Do you want to fold?" Georgina asked after his

fourth straight win.

"Nyet." Aleksandr threw down his cards. "You let me win."

"No, I didn't. The river favors you tonight."

To her dismay, he didn't seem to believe her. He frowned and scratched the scruff on his face.

"Sasha," she reached over and touched his arm.

His head lifted so fast she could hear the snapping of the muscles as they rubbed together. She withdrew her hand and shuffled the cards.

"Why don't we invite the guards and Yakov to join us? More people, more money for you to win. Think of it as a bonus and greater challenge for you. I'll be the dealer." She lowered the deck to the table top, looked in his face, and blinked a few times. Slow seductive blinks.

Aleksandr's slashed brows and keen eyes watched her. She felt like a criminal in an interrogation room. His dark glance hadn't moved from hers.

"Viktor!" he shouted.

Viktor ran out from behind the kitchen door, his great bulk and height making his movement awkward and comical with the bright silk fabrics in the background. He looked like Baby Huey walking through a china shop as he ran into the table, causing the dishes to clink and rattle.

"Get Nikka, Yakov, and Mihail. Bring money."

"Nikka's guarding Magda."

"Bring Pedro then."

Viktor ran out of the room. Aleksandr divided the poker chips into four piles. Georgina inhaled the jasmine scent in the room and mentally reviewed the rules in her head. She'd made intentional plays so Aleksandr would win. Now, she'd need to follow the rules or create her own version.

Within minutes the men stood beside the table.

"Hi, guys." She looked at each of them for a

potential ally. Viktor and Yakov were the two possibilities, but Aleksandr was a clever man. It would be imperative to be aware of her actions and limit her suggestions. At all costs, she couldn't favor Viktor.

"Sit. We play game. Texas Hold 'em." Aleksandr waved his hands toward the chairs. Each man had a stack of poker chips in front of him. Blue, red, black, and white chips stood out like colorful confetti on the white table cloth.

"Who knows how to play Texas Hold 'em?" Georgina asked.

Viktor and Mihail nodded, which left Pedro and Yakov to be educated. If needed, she'd claim the rules were Virginia Hold 'Em.

"The shuffle, the deal, the blind. The two players to the left of me, Viktor and Aleksandr, post the blinds. Meaning they put money in the pot. The amount is determined by Aleksandr." Georgina shot him a smile. "The first blind will be Viktor, who puts up half of the minimum bet, the second blind, Aleksandr, puts the full amount in the pot. The next round, Aleksandr will be the first blind and put in half the amount. Yakov will be the second blind, he'll put in the full amount, and continue around the table. Any questions?"

She looked at each pair of eyes, and they seemed to understand as there weren't any blank stares.

"Like many poker games, the players can call, raise, or fold when it's their turn to bet. After the first round of betting takes place, I'll burn a card. A burn is when the first card is tossed away. The next three cards are flipped up. This is called the flop." She illustrated by tossing one away and turning three cards over. "Round of cash to the pot by the players who want to remain in the game. I'll burn card and place another face up; it's the turn card or fourth street. Another round of betting, card burned, and a fifth card is face up. This card is the river or fifth street. You make your bet using the five cards face up on the table and the two cards only you know about, the cards in your hand or face down on the table. Does everyone know what card combination wins in poker games?"

All the men nodded.

"Well then, let's play cards." She paused and lowered one eye lid in a seductive wink. "And remember to tip the dealer."

Aleksandr was second only to Yakov. Either Yakov learned quickly or his math skills were sharp from years of memorizing, altering, or creating recipes. Pedro was out of money after the first hour and left. Viktor had half of his funds remaining. The burn was a method to prevent cheating; however, for this game she would look at the first and last card. She could burn the top or draw from the bottom. Once again, boarding school weekend activities helped her adapt. She played the game her way.

She refilled the cups, keeping the cold vodka flowing. "Put in your blinds, fellas."

"You don't drink vodka, George?" Viktor asked in his deep resonant voice.

Aleksandr turned his black eyes toward her, like a vulture waiting to pick up the bloody remains.

"I don't drink alcohol. I prefer chocolate." She smiled into Viktor's glistening eyes and then shot her glance toward Aleksandr.

As teens, Georgina and Gemma would borrow a horror tape from one of the teachers, Miss Margot Wicket, her name as formal as she pretended to be. Wicket's collection was vast. She had all older movies like Sammy Terry, Twilight Zone, and X-Files. Gemma loved Mulder. Hmm, Robert resembled Mulder. Aleksandr's black eyes reminded Georgina of the Sammy Terry character who introduced the fright night movies. Unnerving and evil.

"Ah, yes. Chocolate." Aleksandr turned his attention back to his cards.

Viktor put in the full amount to draw him down to a couple of thousand. The first round went fast. All three remained active. She knew Aleksandr had an ace and an ace was the burn card. She burned from the bottom of the deck and placed an ace of hearts, a jack of spades, and a two of diamonds face up on the table. Viktor squirmed in his seat. She looked up to see Yakov scrutinize each player and pierce her with a poignant look. Glancing down at the cards, she forced herself not to fidget.

While the guys stared at their cards, Georgina snuck a peek at the burn card and the last card at the bottom of the deck. Another two and an eight.

"I'm all-in," Viktor stated. He reached up to scratch his nose. A dead give-away that he was trying to bluff. The nose scratch had been used every round, and he was zero for six.

"I will take the bet." Yakov pushed in the paltry amount and sat back in his chair.

Aleksandr sipped his vodka and pushed the money into the pot. His intense stare made her sweat. She wiped her palms on her slacks, burned the top card, and flipped the turn.

It was an ace.

"I fold." Viktor rose from his seat and headed toward the room from which Yakov always appeared.

"I will walk George to her room, so you can retire Viktor," Aleksandr said.

Viktor stopped mid-way and turned with a grimace, transforming him into a blond-headed Arnold Swartzenager. "No trouble. I'm on duty."

"Nyet. Take a rest for a couple of hours."

Her stomach clenched, and her palms were now dripping with sweat. She thought Texas Hold 'em would be a way of keeping Aleksandr busy. Did he know? Did he realize she'd allowed him to win? Had she sacrificed her queen for nothing? Checkmate? This dangerous game of chess done? Game over?

Viktor glanced at Georgina. The heat rose up to his cheeks. She lowered her head. The flush on his face wasn't because of vodka, as he hadn't been drinking. Viktor had overheard Aleksandr and her earlier conversation, so he knew the outcome. She would be Aleksandr's entertainment tonight. Viktor ambled toward the hallway door while digging in his pants pocket. He withdrew a twenty dollar American bill and with a wink handed the money to her.

She smiled her thanks and tucked the bill into her rear pants pocket. A quick gather and shuffle of the cards, she sighed. "Place your bets, gentlemen."

Two hands later Aleksandr pushed his stack of chips to the center. "I am all in."

Yakov picked up his cards, glanced over at Aleksandr, at the flop, and to meet Georgina's gaze. He scratched his jaw line. "I'll match your bet and call."

Georgina breathed deeply. The bottom card would assure Aleksandr's win. She tapped the top card and glanced at the men. They both returned her glance with an expectant stare. She discarded the burn and flipped over the river. Jack of hearts.

Aleksandr turned over the ace of spades and a five of clubs.

Yakov exposed a jack of clubs and a queen of hearts.

"Three jacks win the pot," she whispered.

Yakov gathered the chips and separated them into color groups.

Aleksandr handed over the cash. "Congratulations, Yakov. About one million rubles." His dark eyes turned to Georgina's. "Fifty thousand American dollars."

Yakov chuckled and stood up from the table. "Thanks, Sasha. I'll have good time in Norway. Da." He withdrew a crisp hundred-dollar American greenback and handed the bill to Georgina.

She accepted the money and graced him with a broad smile. Freedom would be hers, but at what price? Georgina glanced over at Aleksandr, and her breath caught in her throat. A grimace and a narrowing of Aleksandr's eyes made her hands tremble as she gathered the cards. Now, she had to play with the hand she had dealt herself.

Chapter 8

Nero, Virginia
Two Months Earlier

Jake's heart beat strong and steady against her shoulder blades. Georgina's pro and con list last night proved to her that she wanted Jake. Not Andy, or any other man, would satisfy her needs. She desired someone who cared enough to notice when she wasn't home. A guy who mowed her yard without telling her he did or asking if she needed it done. She wanted a man who arranged a hair stylist to come to his house at the last minute, on a Sunday. Georgina yearned for this man whose heart beat strong against her back.

Her glance locked with his, reflected in the mirror. Their hearts pounded at a rapid rate, his at her back and hers marching to the same tune. The image of his hard body, naked in the bed, invaded her mind. The memory of his tender lips pressing against hers made her heart escalate to the limit. His spicy scent. Crooked nose. Perfect ears. Sinewy arms. Sweet mouth. She was totally immersed in the lustdom maze and only Jake could lead her out.

His big hands gripped her hips, but he held back as if he wanted to pat her head like a child who had done a good deed.

"Why did Amber call you Cal? Is Cal your nickname?"

"Yes, but I'm Jake to my family." He kissed her cheek, sighed, released her hips, and patted her backside. "Go put on a dress, and I'll take you to a special little Greek place. I have to make a couple of calls, so take your time."

"Okay." Georgina shot him a broad smile, and strolled back over to her house feeling beautiful for the first time in years. She extracted her cell phone from deep within her shorts pocket and speed-dialed Gemma.

"Hi, big mamma. Guess what? I got my hair styled, and it looks great. Go to your PC. I'll take a digital and send the picture over." Georgina entered her house.

"I can't wait. I haven't heard you so excited about something in months." Gemma's labored breathing as she moved through the house came through the phone connection. "Okay, I'm here. I'll get into my email account, while you take the shot. I'll put the call on speakerphone. Let me know when you're ready."

Georgina lowered the phone to the desk and picked up her camera. She looked into the hallway mirror, clicked the tiny button to open the shutter, turned her back, and punched the button. She placed the camera on a highboy, lined the shot, set the timer, and walked to stand in front of the silvery surface of the mirror. A bend of her knees and she posed. The camera flashed. Within seconds she downloaded the pictures to her PC and attached them to an email.

She grabbed the receiver. "Gemma, I've sent them over. Let me know when you receive them." She brought up the mirror reflection picture on her PC and dabbled with it in Photoshop.

"Got it, Gee, I'm opening the image now."

Georgina took the phone and trotted upstairs. She searched through her closet looking for the best dress for this lunch.

Gemma squealed. "I love it. I was so tired of your other hairstyle. I'm glad you changed it. A darling cut. How was last night with Andy? Did you get a good night kiss?"

"Yes. He invited me out Friday." She snatched a dress from the closet, placed the hanger over her neck, and twisted to and fro in the full length mirror. The green silk would work.

"You don't sound excited."

"Jake asked me out for an early dinner, and I want to find the perfect dress. What do you think of the jade-green spaghetti strap?"

"Next -door-hunk Jake?"

"Yes. Gemma, he rocks my world."

Snickering came from the other end of the phone as Georgina bent to get a pair of heels from the closet floor.

"Well then, I guess the jade-green dress is perfect." Gemma coughed lightly. "What about Andy?"

"I'm going to cancel. Oh, I'll be nice and go to the base tomorrow to tell him in person." She stepped out of her sandals, removed her shorts, and started unbuttoning her blouse. "I need to go. I'll call you later and tell you how it went."

She opened her underwear drawer and searched for sexy undies.

"Call me regardless how late it is. If I'm napping, tell Isabella to wake me."

"I will. Take care of my god baby." Georgina disconnected, changed into the dress, stepped into the leg-enhancing heels, and rushed downstairs. She opened the door. Her breath caught, and her heart raced as fast as a lawn sprinkler. Whoosh, zap. Jake wore a button-down oxford and black pants. She admired his taste in clothing, the cyan shirt made his eyes more blue than gray. Dashing. Gorgeous. Why couldn't she think in sentences when Jake was around?

He inhaled and slowly exhaled. Her gaze met

his. She smiled. He grinned, held out his hand, and she placed hers within his safe, firm grip. Yes, this seems right.

Jake led her to his car, opened the door, and waited while she snuggled onto the bench seat. He settled behind the wheel.

She rubbed her hand over the surface of the leather. "What kind of car is this?"

His face brightened. "A Thunderbird."

"By the tone of your voice, it must be something special."

"It's a classic and as old as my father. He refurbished the car and gave it to me recently." He inched his finger pads around the steeling column.

"Do you think it'll get us to the restaurant?"

He squinted to give her the evil eye. "Are you insulting my ride?"

She laughed. "Nope. I think it's, um, cute, but the poor car sounds like it's begging to be put out of its misery."

"It's a classic. " He didn't sound angry, but she wasn't planning to walk miles in her Jimmy Choos so she changed the subject.

"Where do your parents live?"

"The Midwest, northern Indiana."

"I've heard good things about Indiana, up and coming in the communication field. Do your brothers and sisters live there as well?"

"My older brother, Peter, married with three kids, is a corporate attorney in Indianapolis. My older sister, Elizabeth, is a museum curator in Chicago. She recently became engaged to an investment banker named Joel. My younger brother, Henry, is attending Yale. And the baby of the family, Emily, is a senior in high school." He chuckled. "She thinks she wants to be an actress."

"How lovely. Your parents must be very much in love to have such a large family." Georgina was envious. Her parents barely tolerated each other and as even as an only child she lived away from them more than with them.

"Yes, they are very much in love." He elaborated about how his parents met and growing up in the Midwest. Before she knew it, they were pulling into the parking lot.

The Greek restaurant was on the outskirts of Calumet, a sixty-minute drive from Nero. The older brick building had a charming red tile roof. The dark interior would be lit later by wicker-wrapped bubble-bottomed green wine bottles with candles stuck in the top which also decorated the tabletops. Late afternoon, the candles remained unlit. They were escorted to a table with a plastic green and white checkered cover and chairs that wobbled.

Georgina opened the menu and reviewed the choices as Jake selected a wine. A goblet of iced water was placed in front of her, and she took a sip to ease the dryness of her throat. Would the beverage ease her nervousness or should she wait for something stronger? The scent of sugared almonds and garlic made her aware of her hunger. Her stomach growled very unladylike.

"What looks good?"

You. "Everything." The garlic and tomato smells coming from the kitchen were making her salivate. "What do you recommend?"

"It's all delicious."

The waitress, Marta, came back with a bottle of wine, airing in a container.

"Our specials today are calamari, a baby squid batter fried for seven dollars, and Septsofar, spicy sausages flavored with red wine, orange, and leeks, a family recipe," she winked, "all for eight dollars. May I start you off with a pita platter?"

"Order for me, let me get to know you through the foods you like." Georgina cupped her chin on her upturned palm with her elbow resting on the table.

"We'll start with stuffed grape leaves with goat cheese, not the beef or pork, and Cos for a salad which are Romaine leafy greens." He stared at her like he wanted confirmation the order was okay.

"Leafy greens, sure, love them." She nodded.

"And cuttlefish." He shot a glance at Georgina. "Sound okay to you?"

The waitress cocked her head, waiting.

"Yes, that's perfect," Georgina answered.

"Chamomile tea or Greek Frappe Coffee?" the waitress asked.

"Tea, please." Georgina smiled and lowered her hand. Her elbow stuck to the plastic and made a suck noise as she moved.

"The lady would like tea, and I'll take the coffee. We'll look at the dessert menu, later." Jake handed the menu back to Marta, and she bounced off toward the kitchen.

"So, what is cuddle fish? Something you want to hug instead of eat?"

"C-u-t-t-l-e. It's like a squid. Has ten arms, eight short, two longer in order to capture its prey." He winkled his ten fingers.

"Okay, now I have too much information. Feel like I'm personally acquainted with the critter. Don't know if I can eat something I'm so familiar with."

He chuckled deep in his throat. "Don't make a decision until you taste it."

A tip of the bottle and their glasses were full again.

Georgina leaned forward and whispered, "Tell me about Amber."

Jake laughed and raised the flute of red wine to his beautiful lips. She envisioned kissing his mouth again. The imprint of his body had been etched on hers. Her lower region hummed with a new awakening. She took a large swig of her wine. The drink didn't help, the ache intensified as he stared at her.

"Ah Amber, a hairstylist extraordinaire and an aspiring actress. I'm sure she'll get a lot of time, on stage." His voice held a hint of sarcasm.

Had a joke been contained in the statement? If so, it was beyond her understanding. How could an aspiring actress acquire fame in Virginia? Shouldn't she be located in New York to be on stage?

"An actress, huh? Well, I wish her luck. Can I be nosy and ask why you're taking stills?" Georgina settled back into the chair.

"They pay the bills. So, what's your preference? If you were given the perfect career opportunity what would you choose?" He swirled the wine in the glass.

"Freelance photojournalism. Maybe a long term contract with the New York Times."

"Did you get the article about the recruitment fair finished today?"

"Yes, I'm going to deliver it to Andy tomorrow." She pulled apart a breadstick and placed the savory garlic piece in her mouth.

"The corporal who lives across the street told me you moved in a few months ago. She said you refurbished the entire house in a few weeks. Did you decorate houses before you became a photojournalist?"

"You could say that. I enjoy decorating. Why did you move to Nero?" She wanted to avoid discussing her move to Virginia and her past. To distract him she leaned forward, allowing the soft fabric of her dress to show off her breasts.

"Work. I had a contract offer and needed to be in range." He cleared his throat and took a drink of the pale red wine.

"With a business, museum, magazine?" She placed her fingers around her water glass smearing water over the smooth tumbler, a stroke up, a stroke down, and gazed into his eyes. Lustdom was making her act outside her comfort zone, do things to attract his attention.

"Uh, huh. Do you want some more wine?" The poker face was back. Why would he avoid answering her simple question?

"No, thank you."

He topped off his wine. "What brought you to Nero?"

She promptly forgot about his avoidance of her question, when he replaced the bottle in the bucket and settled onto the chair. His face had a strange look. He reached over and moved the water goblet away from her hand.

Georgina laughed out loud. He was onto her and didn't want to be doused with water again. "I came to Nero to be near my best friend, Gemma. She's family. I'm going to be a godmother, and I take the responsibility seriously."

"Congratulations." He lifted his flute, and she tapped hers, the clink of crystal rang through the air.

Their food arrived. Casual conversation bantered back and forth while they ate the delicious Greek meal served family style, meaning the food was placed in large patters set in the middle of the table. Each person took as much as they desired. This concept was new to her and she liked the method.

Jake told amusing stories about his family, and Georgina forgot for a brief time that she was in Virginia to hide away and disappear. She let her guard down and enjoyed the evening and the date.

****

Georgina stood at her front entrance fidgeting with her keys, not wanting the night to end. Andy had asked to come in after their date, but Jake apparently didn't feel compelled to do so.

"Would you like to come in for coffee?"

He hesitated. No choice, she inserted the key into the lock and twisted it to the right with hopes his alter-ego would click simultaneously with the barrel.

Georgina had been wired since the afternoon and that kiss. Granted, Jake had probably been dreaming, but she had benefited. She removed the key, opened the door, and turned to face him.

He took both hands out of his pockets. "I should get back. I have projects due."

The dark shadows of the porch hid his face, so she couldn't guess what he was thinking, as if she could read his facial expressions anyway. Ha. He lifted his hand. Was she getting a handshake? The magazines hadn't prepared her for this, for a handclasp at the end of a date.

"Georgina, I need to tell you..."

Her glance shifted from his raised hand to his eyes. "Yes, Jake?"

"Oh, hell," he muttered and wrapped his hand around her neck and drew her close. He kissed her with the same passion he had exhibited earlier in the day. She curved her arms around his trim waist. The keys clanked against each other and created a tiny musical chime.

She lifted on her toes, inhaled the scent of the after-dinner mint, and leaned into his kiss. Hesitantly, she stroked his mouth with her tongue and inserted it inside the warm cavern. His tongue touched hers, and like an electrical lightning bolt, she felt the charge.

Jake must have felt it too, because he jerked back. With regret, Georgina moved her hands from around his waist and with shaky fingers plopped the keys back into her handbag.

"Good-night, Jake. Thank you for arranging the

haircut and the wonderful dinner."

He nodded and pushed the door open for her to enter. She walked across the entranceway. She wanted more, didn't he?

"Good-night, Gee. I had a great time today." His raspy voice came across the threshold, making her yearn for that something she still couldn't describe.

She sighed and closed the door. Georgina looked through the security hole to watch him walk away. Throughout her life the important people always walked away. To her surprise, Jake remained on the other side. She pulled the knob on the door. She'd tell him she wanted him to make love to her. A simple twist and tug she'd ask him to let the storm free, take her, right there, right then.

"Lock the door," he growled.

Georgina flipped the lock, secured the chains, and marched upstairs. She needed stimulation, a solution to the deep ache filtered through her mind. Could she climb onto the clothes dryer, with lopsided heavy garments inside, to vibrate her excited vagina? The down comforter probably needed to be washed and dried. She changed into shorts and a camisole top, gathered whatever heavy items she had, and carried them downstairs. As she loaded them into the washer, her cell phone rang.

"Hello," she barked, frustration zinging through her body.

"Georgina Kaplan?" the muted deep voice asked.

Her heart stopped beating, and her lungs failed to provide air.

"No. Wrong number," she choked out.

She pushed the end button hard enough to shut the cell down. How had he found her? She had a pay-as-you-go cell phone listed under George Grey. Damn. Her hands became slick with sweat and the receiver slipped to the floor, clanging as it banged against the tile and then a thud marked its resting place alongside the wall.

Georgina had to get rid of the phone. With a key identifier, the device could lead anyone to the location of the cell and to Nero, Virginia. She flipped open her laptop, booted, and waited for the search engine to load. She ran upstairs, grabbed a sweater off the padded hanger, and slipped it on. Her shorts fell to the floor. Her palms were sweaty, but chills racked her body. She slid into a pair of khakis.

On hands and knees she searched the bottom of the closet for a pair of sneakers. She tugged the shoes into place, tightened the strings, and ran back downstairs. She plopped onto the chair and started typing. Bingo. A postal branch was three miles away and closed in twenty minutes.

She snatched the phone from the floor, grabbed her handbag off the entry table, and raced to her borrowed Mercedes Coup. Focused on her destination, she hadn't seen Jake standing in the driveway, until she looked in her rear view mirror. Georgina couldn't explain where she was going or her intentions, so she ignored him. She turned on the headlights and threw the car in reverse. He jumped out of the way as she sped by. She broke the speed limit getting to the post office branch.

Her heart beat as fast as the keys as they bounced against the steering column. She pulled into the postal center's parking lot. The place looked deserted. Please God, let it be open. She pushed down the acid in her stomach, secured her handbag, and shoved the phone within.

Inside the building, she scanned the envelopes in racks on the wall which were available for purchase and grabbed two padded plain yellow packets. The cell phone fit in the smaller packet. She labeled the outside with her Boston address, pulled the white tab, and pressed it closed. She placed the sealed one into the larger packet to check the size. It was perfect. She labeled the larger packet with her solicitor's address and took both envelopes to the slate counter.

"May I help you?" a heavyset blonde-haired woman asked while she lifted her glance toward the clock. Her hair had been wrapped so tight into a knot she didn't have any creases on her face. Her eyebrows had been drawn with a pencil and created the only visible expression.

"Yes, please. I need to get this posted tonight. Overnight to Boston." She found talking to be difficult with acid laced cuttlefish lodged in her throat.

"Okay, you made it just in time. Truck leaves in ten minutes."

"Thank you. Please put surface mail postage stamps on this smaller one." Georgina held out the package.

"Do you want to insure it?" The clerk hefted the envelope up and down while carrying the package to the scales.

"No, thank you." Georgina glanced at the clock. If the phone's lost, all the better.

Georgina took the pouch from the woman's hand and placed the smaller stamped envelope into the larger one. She wrote out a quick message and sealed the casing.

"Okay, ready to go." She handed the padded yellow container to the clerk.

"You'll need to put a return address on the outside." The clerk frowned and held out the envelope. Her lips were drawn so tight they resembled her line-drawn eyebrows.

Georgina wrote her parents Boston address in the corner. "You're sure it'll go out tonight?"

The postal worker raised a black eyebrow. She held out her callused hand. "That will be fourteen thirty-eight."

Georgina dug out her last twenty from deep inside her handbag. A large black man came in from a room behind the counter. He glanced up, nodded, and loaded white square containers onto a cart.

"Mick, here's another one." The clerk threw the stamped package into a white mail bin.

Georgina slid the money onto the slate. "Keep the change. I appreciate your help." She smiled a sincere smile despite the food lodged in her throat. Her sneakers squeaked on the gray linoleum floor as she sprinted out the door. She ran to the nearest bush and threw up the contents of her lovely dinner. She remained in the bent position for several minutes.

"Honey, are you okay?" said a soft southern female voice.

Georgina glanced over to see the clerk from the post office. She clutched her purse close to her side and was leaning down to look into Georgina's face.

"Yes, sorry. No offense to the government." She nodded toward the now dark building. "Dinner didn't sit well."

Georgina straightened and lifted the edge of her sweater to wipe her mouth.

"Could you be pregnant?" Her eyebrows were slanted down.

"Only if it's an immaculate conception. Thank you for asking. I'll be okay." Georgina wiped her hands on her pants. On unsteady legs she waddled to the car. The clerk took off at a fast clip on the dark sidewalk.

Back inside the car, Georgina leaned her head against the steering wheel. Realization struck her hard and fast, and her stomach muscles clamped around the cuttlefish sending another round to her throat. The nightmare wasn't going to end. Tristan would never let her go.

Jake was waiting on her doorstep when she

arrived back at her house. Georgina sat in the car and looked at him. She would give up her trust fund to be able to tell him everything and lean on him for comfort and support. Impossible. Tristan and his murdering ways had to remain a secret.

She dug a piece of mint flavored gum out of her bag and popped the sugary treat into her mouth. She slid the shoulder strap of her purse over her arm and opened the door. The lies would begin now.

"Hi, neighbor." Suddenly hot, she pushed the sleeves of her sweater to her elbows.

He jettisoned off the porch step, his brows contracted, his lips compressed. "What did you think you were doing? Drive like that and you'll end up in the morgue."

His annoyance didn't lighten the mood.

She tried to move past him. He reached out and touched her arm.

"You're cold and clammy. Are you ill?"

She pulled the sleeves of her sweater down and inserted the key in the lock. "Good-night, Jake."

"I thought we were friends?"

His voice sounded forlorn. She pressed her head against the wood of the open door. "I don't feel well. I'm sorry, but I need to go to bed."

Point-blank he whispered, "Tell me. Gee, trust me."

She must have heard him wrong. "What?"

She swayed with the yearning making its way to her heart. Oh, how she wanted to confide in him.

"Go on upstairs. I'll make some tea and bring it up to you." He followed her into the house.

She dropped her bag on the table, and much like an old woman, used the banister to pull her weight up the stairs. Once in her bedroom, she removed a pair of baby-doll pajamas, with tiny purple flowers printed onto the cloth, from the dresser and shuffled into the bathroom. She brushed her teeth while the water in the shower heated to a scalding temperature. The steam rolled out, and she stepped behind the curtain. She scrubbed her body until she thought the old layer had been removed and nothing remained, but new, stronger skin.

She came out of the bathroom. A cup of tea waited at her bedside table, and Jake lounged on the chair near the window. Tiny fireflies skittered across her stomach. If only she could let him in and have him hold her.

"Do you want to talk about what happened tonight?" he ran his hands through his beautiful, light brown hair.

"Not really. I'd like to rest." Georgina couldn't look into his face, meet his storm cloud eyes, and see the disappointment about her lack of trust. She wanted to scream, it's not lack of trust, its fear, Jake. I care about you, but I dread what could happen if you knew the truth. You would be a target.

"One question then. Is it Gemma? Did she lose the baby?" Jake's voice held trepidation, a worry that beat a tandem into her heart. God, his concern was for her and her friend.

"No, Gemma is holding strong." She took a sip of the too sweet tea. "Thank you, for the tea."

"You're upset. I don't want to leave you. I'll sleep on the couch tonight and tomorrow maybe you'll tell me why you ran out tonight and came back ill." A bit of anger was mixed in with the sweeteners.

She kept her gaze on Jake. He rose, walked over to the bed, lifted the sheet, and waited until she slid her legs under the covers. He didn't mention the wet straggly hair that once again resembled a Chia pet.

"Gee, what am I going to do with you?" He sighed and kissed her forehead. Not waiting for the answer, he turned out the light and left through the open door.

She closed her eyes, willing her body to relax

and her mind to become vacant. Aware of the noises downstairs, she listened as he opened cupboards, searching for blankets. He must have found them in the hall closet as the lights went off. A few minutes later she heard him speaking in low tones on the telephone.

Safe, with Jake nearby, she continued to have haunting dreams of Tristan. She shuddered. In her heart she knew he was close, too close.

Chapter 9

Aleksandr's Freighter

Georgina strode down the corridor with Aleksandr, the echoes of their footsteps ringing in their wake. "Aleksandr, you had fun?"

"Da." His silence bothered her. What should she expect? He'd lost a lot of money. He breathed deeply, keeping time with her steps.

In front of her door she stilled and turned into him. Whenever she used his nickname, Sasha, she'd been able to accomplish her goals. "Thanks for walking me to my room, Sasha. I'm glad you had a good time tonight. I've an exciting game planned for tomorrow night."

She held up her hands and counted fingers. "We'll need at least eight people and ten dice. Bunko is the name of the game."

She shoved her hand out to shake his. He looked down and instead of touching her hand, he rubbed his fingers along his jaw line. The bristling of the short hairs sounded loud in the hallway.

No Neck Number Two shifted his feet, drawing her attention. Shivers ran down her neck as he smirked. He creeped her out. Viktor said he would be on duty tonight, so where was he? How could two men, resembling each other enough to undoubtedly be related, have such different characters?

Georgina opened the door, stepped through, and turned to close it. "Night, Sasha." Aleksandr stopped the door, slid through the opening, and snapped it shut.

Damn. Her heart picked up pace.

"I thought you had a good time playing Texas Hold 'em?" Georgina took a few small steps backward and picked up the jade necklace hanging heavy around her neck. She rubbed the smooth warm silver between her fingers, hoping it would give her strength, willing the symbolism of Jake's love to give her courage. The necklace became her Green Lantern ring of power, but she needed Jake nearby to recharge the energy.

"I did." He took a few long steps forward, grabbed her around the waist, and moved his hands up to cup her breasts. He tugged her body close. His breath smelled of peppermint.

"Then, what is this?" Georgina pushed his hands away and jumped backwards. Forced to stop when her back hit the dresser, she shoved him. He didn't budge an inch. She took a step to the side and opened her mouth to stall him. Think of something clever to say.

He moved forward, placed one hand on the side of her face and one on her waist, drew her head close to his, and slobbered a kiss near her mouth.

She tried to scream, but he moved to the left, and his tongue slid between her lips. Georgina lifted her knee. He lowered his hand from her face to her leg. She adroitly moved her cheek.

"You're drunk. While I appreciate the pass, you should probably crash in your room."

Aleksandr shifted and zoomed again. She swiftly shifted her head, and his forehead hit the hard wood of the dresser with a clunk. She sidestepped and danced to his other side. However, the pencil box of a room didn't give her much opportunity to out-dance the aggressor.

"George," he slurred. "I want you so much."

She slid past him again, but he grabbed the necklace wrapped around her waist. Off-balance, she fell onto the bed, landing cross-way. The back of her legs hit the sharp edge of the bed rail. The sting to the back of her knees wasn't as sharp as the pain in her chest when he landed on top of her. He forced a hard kiss. His tongue invaded her mouth; the taste of alcohol was strong. The coarseness, the vigor, and the aggressive movement of his tongue made her gag. She pushed against his shoulders and used her elbow to jab his throat.

"No," she sobbed. Fear took over. Protect. Light overpowers evil. Do not lose control. Reason with him. "You promised. You're a man of your word."

"Nyet." He pinned her shoulders to the bed. She floundered around like a fish on deck, twisting her lower body. She brought her knee up, trying to connect between his legs. He rolled to the side before she could damage his private parts. He released her arms.

She didn't want to be raped. The last man to touch her was Jake, who she loved. She would be soiled if Aleksandr raped her.

Aleksandr rolled her from the side and climbed on top of her. He snapped her necklace belt and the two pieces fell from her waist. He held her arms over her head and jerked her pants and underwear down with a quick snap. She rocked back and forth, trying to dislodge him, and in an attempt to keep his fingers away.

His black haired hand moved down her thigh. His zipper slid down, sounding louder than her panting. She felt the cold metal touch her skin. The soft material wrap around her thigh.

God, please don't let this happen. Please protect me.

Georgina twisted and clawed with her fingers, trying to scratch his hands. She threw her head forward hitting his nose with her forehead. The thud sounded like a crack in the small room. His and her heavy breathing added to the nightmare.

Her heart batted against her chest. Aleksandr reared and with the small slice of freedom she pushed him off the bed. He fell to the floor with a thump. She jumped off the cot, pulled her pants up with one hand and ran to a corner of the room. What would he do next? With all of the new furniture she couldn't go anywhere. She was trapped. Her mind raced to form a plan.

He put his hand to his forehead. He drew it back and looked at the tips of his fingers. She didn't see any blood. As he rolled to his feet, she cringed and pressed closer to the wall. He frowned. Her heart continued its erratic beat. Heat flooded her face. Could she continue to fight?

She didn't have the strength but lifted her head and glared at him anyway. The same fierce look her mother used with her father. Her father retreated to his library every single time. At thirteen, she had practiced the expression in her mirror. Now she used the sneer on Aleksandr, hoping she would have the same results.

A drunken lust-filled smile crossed Aleksandr's face.

Damn, the glare didn't work. It never worked when she tried to use it on her mother either. He walked toward her. She touched the Celtic knot on the jade necklace and then put out her arms in a defense mode. At the last minute, he turned toward the door. Shocked, she stared at him.

"Tomorrow night. Be ready. I will not drink. You will be mine." He stumbled and placed his hand on the door to keep from falling. He shot one last glance at her, a look of longing crossed over his face. Was it sympathy or too much alcohol that had prevented her rape?

The door shut. She fixed her pants, rushed to the only chair in the room, and wedged the back under the doorknob. Made of lightweight wood, she hoped the chair's counterforce would work in her favor.

Only a forklift would force her out of the room. Dry-brushing her teeth, she spit the liquid into the trash can and fully dressed climbed under the covers. She removed the journal from inside the pillow case and placed it under her head. She drew her legs into fetal position and cried. Large fat tears soaked her pillows and clogged her nasal passage. Her throat felt raw from trying to restrain the sobs. Her stomach ached from the contracting of her muscles. She clasped her hands to keep them from shaking and put them between her tender, bruised thighs.

"Jake, I need you," she whispered. The jade necklace slid to press against her cheek.

Chapter 10

Nero, Virginia
Two Months Earlier

The front door slammed shut and footsteps sounded on the hardwood floor. Georgina vibrated with excitement.

"Hi, honey. How'd your day go?" Her southern accent and verbiage had gotten stronger, deeper, and richer than the tea. The wooden spoon clanged against the glass pitcher as she stirred in the sugar water.

"Good, how about yours?" Jake leaned against the kitchen counter, one knee crossed over the other and a sexy grin on his face. His gray-blue eyes shone with humor.

"Fine. I spent time with Kist." Early in the summer, Georgina had planted a small vegetable garden beside her herbs. A neighbor, Kist Jorgensen, an eighty-year-old retired Navy Chief Petty Officer, provided guidance. A lonely old guy, he was more than happy to teach her how to prepare the ground with natural fertilizers, the proper way to plant the tomatoes, lettuce, peppers, carrots, and pumpkin. They had forged a friendship.

Jake smiled and reached behind him. "I have a gift for you. A client who creates unique jewelry couldn't pay for an advertising spread, so I had a necklace designed with you on my mind."

He popped open a teak box to reveal a pale green jade pendant with silver filigree embellishment nestled on cream velvet.

His beautiful fingers removed the pear shaped necklace. The large end was the size of a dime. The silver wrapped around the fat end in a basket weave with a Celtic love knot at the center.

"May I?" At her nod, he slipped the chain around her neck and snapped the clasps. "It has a safety clasp as well, so it won't fall off."

She felt his warm lips on her neck and turned into his arms.

"I love the gift, Jake. I'll never take it off."

"That's what I'm counting on," he murmured.

She twisted to look in the black framed mirror to see where the pendant rested on her chest. The Celtic knot and the gift in general made her heart swell with adulation for this man. Her stomach vibrated with a need. Maybe tonight he'd fill that void and make love to her.

She wanted him to say, "I count the hours until I can make love to you."

And she'd reply, "Why count, I'm ready now." She'd grab his hand and pull him up the steps. Perhaps they'd make slow intense love on the stairs, no, the edges would hurt. They'd make it to the bed; he'd rip her clothes off because he couldn't wait to claim her. He'd spear her with his hard, massive penis, and she'd get her groove on...finally.

Instead, he told her about his day, catching a photograph of a little boy with a sling-shot. He didn't know they made them any longer. Georgina half-listened while imagining what could have happened if her daydream had come true. The end of the lustdom maze continued to elude her.

****

A grueling lust-filled month passed, and the routine continued. Tonight, Jake arrived at sundown with a bunch of calla lilies and white wine in hand. He placed the bottle on the kitchen counter and handed her the flowers.

111

"You're going to spoil me, bringing gifts to me." She sniffed the delightful fragrance of the lilies.

"Want to go out for dinner?" He grabbed her around the waist and tugged her close to his muscular hard chest.

"I've a chicken dish ready to go into the oven. I'll keep it in the fridge if you have your stomach set on something else."

"No, love, your cooking is, ah, something special." He glanced over at the casserole.

She narrowed her glance. "Is that a compliment or should I take a cooking class?"

He released her and pulled out a corkscrew from a drawer in the kitchen.

A deep inhale of the sweet tropical scent of the flowers, and she dropped them into a crystal bowl shaped vase. She tapped the vase with her finger, a housewarming gift from Gemma and Robert. The crystal chimed at her tap. She added water and set the bouquet on the table.

"I've only compliments," he popped the cork out of the wine. "Shove it into the oven, and we'll go sit outside to enjoy the last bit of fall."

"Sounds like a plan." She flipped open the oven door, slipped on oven mitts, and placed the casserole inside.

The man was either a creature of habit, or he didn't want to be seen with her. Every night, they'd dine at an out of the way restaurant or she'd try her culinary skills. Sometimes she hadn't read the ingredients correctly and the food wasn't the least bit tasty. But he ate the poor fare and didn't say a word.

Jake grabbed wineglasses. She slipped off the oven mitt and carried the crudities: celery, carrots, snap peas, and peppers. Carrie Underwood's voice bellowed from the radio about a cheating boyfriend. They placed the flutes and appetizer tray on the table and sat on the bench.

"Other than Kist, what else did you do today?" Jake handed her a wineglass, lifted a lock of her hair and smoothed the strand out between his fingers. He carried it to his nose and sniffed.

"Oh, I visited with Gemma, took multiple photographs of her advancing pregnancy, shopped for the baby, and the nursery. No financial photojournalistic opportunities. Other than the dog and garden shows, a few Navy recruitment events will be coming up in the next few weeks. Robert rescued me once again." She sipped her wine and set the flute down on the table.

"What about the military guy? Do you see him?" He moved his hand to her shoulder and tugged her closer.

"Andy?"

He nodded.

"I think we're working toward a friendship. A new Navy Recruiter, a glamorous redhead by the name of Teresa, has a desk beside him. Rumor has it, they're dating."

"Good, I don't want him interested in my woman." He kissed her.

My woman! Joy bubbled throughout her. Did this mean they would finally have sex? Had she reached the end of the lustdom maze? She wrapped her arm around his neck, twisted so her chest met his, and kissed him. He moaned. His tongue touched hers, a light exploration at first. She welcomed his thorough search and seizure. She moved her leg over him to straddle his lap, settling onto his arousal. His penis tempted her. Teased her. The prize was a zip away.

"Gee, the alarm," he warned.

She was drunk with sensuality, wiggling on his lap and kissing his face. "What?"

"The oven's alarm is going off." He groaned and

unseated her. She plopped down onto the bench seat and shook her head. He stood and went inside. The patio door to the kitchen snapped shut. The buzzer stopped its obnoxious beep. Akron sang, "Don't Matter" loud and clear. The romancing for the night was over.

****

The next day, Georgina replayed the entire scene to Gemma. She looked around the room while Gemma ummed and aahed. The nautical navy blue and white decorated office suited Robert. The masculine brown-toned furniture fit his personality and Georgina's rear very well. A framed American flag took up one entire paneled wall.

Gemma held onto her rounded belly. "Sex is out of the question in the Sheraton house. Sorry. No solutions from my corner."

Georgina smiled and opened a fresh page of the notebook and settled into Robert's squeaky leather chair. She ran her hands over the teak surface of his desk, so soft the wood felt like Silkstone, warm and smooth. She inhaled to get a whiff of the earthly timber.

"Change of subject. Your family should arrive tomorrow, and I've decided on the theme for the baby shower. Want to hear what I've thrown together?"

"Bring it on." Gemma sat down in the taupe leather club chair opposite the library desk and lifted her swollen ankles onto the footstool.

Georgina used the web to add minutes onto the pay-as-you-go cell phone, which was registered in Gemma's grandmother's name. They used one of Gemma's credit cards from the days when she was single. To add on minutes, Georgina purchased a card at discount store and paid cash, so the phone couldn't be traced back to her. A few keystrokes to enter the specific identifier code and almost immediately one hundred minutes added to the phone bank.

"Bob the Builder. I have an entire backdrop with Bob and his life-size mechanical trucks and tractors. You should see the cake. It's based on Built to be Wild, the newest Bob the Builder DVD. It's a western. At Bailey's Costume Store, I purchased fringed vests and cowboy hats. I think your sisters will like them."

"Oh, Georgina. Robert will be so surprised." Gemma laughed, and her belly shook with mirth. "No one has ever been able to get away with calling Robert, Bob, except you. I think he tolerates the nickname because of our relationship."

"The sister thing?" Georgina laughed.

"Right, we are sisters after all." Gemma heaved a breath. "My cheeks hurt from laughing."

****

The next day Georgina stacked china cups on the silver platter. She glanced over to see Gemma escorting her last baby shower guest to the front door. A quick scan of the room and she found who she was seeking. Jake and Robert stood near the windows eating white cake and adamantly talking.

She met Jake's gaze and held it. He answered Robert's question, but maintained eye contact with her. Twinges jerked her stomach muscles into binds. He touched his finger to his lips. She air kissed him in return. His jaws tightened, and his eyes fired with lust. She grinned and arched an eyebrow. Jake winked, and sipped punch from his Bob the Builder cup.

Georgina swung by with the tray in hand and overheard them discussing piracy on the high seas. During the baby shower, they were closed away in Robert's office watching *Pirates of the Caribbean, the Curse of the Black Pearl*. The debate must be a result of the movie. She planned to watch the DVD

115

later. A girl's got to love Orlando Bloom swinging around a sword and Johnny Depp with an earring, tight pants, and a swagger.

Gemma waddled in, her beautiful womanly glow lighting up the room. Her hand rested on her lower back. "I'm exhausted. Let's sit and talk about," she glanced over at Robert, "the gifts and who brought what to the house." She winked.

She must have heard some juicy gossip. "Sure, Isabella can finish gathering the dishes. Is she here?"

Gemma lowered to the sofa and patted the seat beside her. "I think Robert volunteered for clean up duty. Let's spend some time alone while my sisters, the naggers, are out."

She smoothed the brown satin top and retied the taupe, already perfect, bow.

"I talked Gunnery Sergeant Lawrence into giving your sisters a quick tour of Nero and then the naval base. He volunteered to take Arabella to see Norfolk tomorrow." Georgina chuckled at Gemma's surprised expression.

"I can't allow that. My baby sister's too young to be alone with Mark Lawrence. Lawrence of Arabia is what the book club members call him. Why he's old enough—"

"They're the same difference in age as you and Bob." Georgina placed the tray, holding two cups of blue punch and two slices of white cake, on the coffee table and plopped down on the couch.

"Well hell." Gemma slid a furtive look over towards Robert.

Georgina glanced at the guys. Robert frowned and resumed his conversation. Jake grinned.

Gemma rubbed circles over her expanded belly and nodded her head toward Robert and Jake. "Who knew those two would have so much in common?"

"I didn't! Hey, did I show you the necklace Jake

gave me?" Georgina pulled a silver chain from under her collar and held out the pendant.

"Fabulous, good quality jade. Not to dark, not to light. No striations. What does the silver embellishment represent?"

"Not sure. I think it's a Celtic love knot, but I don't know the origin. I'll do a search tomorrow." Georgina tucked the jewelry back inside her blouse. "Gemma, I think I'm in love."

Gemma snorted.

"I mean real love. The forever type." Georgina pulled out the pendant and evaluated the rosette. It looked different today.

"Uh, huh. What are you cooking for your handsome boyfriend tonight?" Gemma asked.

"He is adorable isn't he? I think I'm going to try a beef roast with the last of the vegetables from my garden." Georgina had found simple, delicious meals and recipes online and continued her attempts at cooking. She smiled at the memory of Jake walking through the door last night, sniffing the savory chicken and decadent apple pie.

"Do you think I'll ever get used to cooking and not get burnt?" Georgina turned her hands over and showed the old burns and recent burns. "It doesn't really matter, I guess, when I see the look of bliss on Jake's face. Trying to figure out a recipe and the minor skin burns are worth the effort."

Gemma rolled her eyes and chuckled.

Georgina tapped her chin. "Maybe I could create a by-line titled, Dating, the Art of Seduction through Cuisine."

Her evenings consisted of trying to discover the way out of lustdom and into Jake's bed. He led her on a merry chase through the maze, and she followed him this way and that way. But she was losing patience; she was near the end of her frustration and wanted to claim the prize. Despite her best efforts, he refused to have sex with her.

"Wouldn't hurt. Write up a proposal and send it off to the newspapers and magazines." Gemma bent awkwardly over her knees and snatched a glass of punch off the coffee table. "He never questioned the night you rushed to the post office and puked all over the bushes?"

"No, I thought it was odd, at first, but then I was grateful he let it drop. It shows he cares enough to support me, without question." Georgina removed one high heel and placed her leg under her.

"About the support, how are you doing with the physical side of your relationship?" Gemma lifted both eyebrows and her dark brown bangs lowered, playing hide and seek with her eyes.

"I need to up the stakes. He continues to generate a heat. The passion's there but seriously Gemma, I must have sex." Georgina picked up a mint from a crystal dish to suck on.

"Do you think he wants to wait until marriage? Some men are like that nowadays, according to my book club that is." Gemma rubbed circles on her sides, or at least where they used to be.

"God, I hope not. I expect to hear from Mr. Sinefield any day now, about the divorce. I certainly don't want to jump into another marriage, just to satisfy my lust. Do you think I'm sexy enough?" Georgina looked down at her body. Her breasts weren't as large as Dolly Parton's, but they were decent. She always got stares from men.

"You have an hour-glass shape. Old fashioned, but some guys like curves." Gemma, normally, was model thin.

"And?" Georgina wanted affirmation that she was sexy. She'd only slept with one man, and he had multiple affairs. What if she wasn't good in bed? How would she know?

"Of course you're sexy. If I wasn't pregnant with

my husband's baby, I'd be all over you."

Georgina narrowed her eyes.

"Seriously!" Gemma burst out in laughter.

Georgina glanced at the men, who stopped talking and with raised eyebrows stared at them. She joined in on the laughter.

"Thanks, doll, I'd be all over you too." She slid on her shoe and rose from the sofa. "We should go. I need to stop at the pharmacy and pick up more aloe for the burns."

"It's early afternoon. Rain's expected. We haven't talked in such a long time. You spend all your time with Jake." Gemma whined like an exhausted child.

"You're worn out. Please go rest before the horde comes back and sucks out all your energy. Besides, we talk every day." Georgina knew that Gemma would be fine. The baby, even if he didn't go to term, would live. He had passed the critical line of survival.

"I'm not tired and my sisters will take up all my time next week. Sit. Talk. I'll help you think of ways to get Jake into the sack." Gemma defied the comment by yawning, but her hand quickly covered her mouth.

Georgina leaned over and kissed her cheek. "Go take a nap, big mamma."

****

Georgina reached over to turn off the buzzer on the oven, which was competing with Rascal Flatts, "What Hurts So Much." She hummed along with the music, a nice beat, and the words were profound. Wanting something so much it hurts. Oh, boy, could she relate to that.

Jake walked through the door and sniffed the air as if to determine the night's menu. To her great delight, he walked over to her and snuffled her neck, ear, cheek, and hovered over her lips.

"I like this portion of the meal best," he murmured between nibbles.

He kissed her. Not a sampling, but a head-rushing, hard and slow kiss. A smooch that made a woman want to forget about the hours of labor over a hot stove, pull her man up the stairs to bed, and ignore everything but him. They'd stay in bed until the smoke from the burned dinner reached their nostrils.

Maybe tonight was the night. Her luck meter for the day indicated five stars. Was the end of lustdom near? She desperately wanted to stop the ache.

"How was your afternoon? Any good photographs?" She licked her lips, savoring his taste.

"Some great shots of my love's face. I'll show you later if you like?"

She pressed into him, a full body slam. "I'd like."

He backed away a pinch.

"Hungry?" she asked, trying to cover the pain that racked her body at his withdrawal.

"You betcha. I'll go wash my hands and set the table."

Jake had stayed in Nero the last few days. She loved it when he'd stayed in town for his photo shoots. More often than not, he would travel and be gone for two or three days at a time. When she asked about his trips, his response was almost always, "Couldn't get an inspiration if it bit me in the rear." Georgina would sympathize and fluff his hair, kiss his forehead and caress the side of his face.

She shouted toward the powder room. "Tonight we're having roast with fresh vegetables from my garden." She lifted the apron from around her neck. How could she make him see her as a woman in need of love?

"Kist thought the pumpkin was a waste for ground space as it needed to be on a mound, but I refused to forfeit the fruit. I love the fall season and can't wait for the orb to magically morph into a delectable pie or simply decorate my front stoop." She turned up the radio volume to hear Rob Thomas sing about not being lonely 'no' more.

"But when Kist came by today, he told me the pumpkin blooms could be picked, soaked in salt water, dipped in egg batter, rolled in flour, and fried into a crunchy treat. I think he was hinting around that he wanted some. I plan to try frying up some tomorrow, and I'm going to invite him over. Are you interested in a sample? Will you be around at noon?"

She washed her hands and slapped on a layer of lotion. She removed ceramic plates from the cupboard. The floral trim on the dishes reminded her of her wedding china, which she had left behind when she fled. A feeling of regret about her past stole some of the joy from the evening. The dishes clanged together as she placed them on the table.

"Can't, I need to be in Lynnhaven at nine tomorrow. Dinner smells good, but not as good as you." Jake stepped up behind her and nibbled on her ear, worked his way down her neck, and eased her blouse and bra strap to the side, baring her shoulder. Thank goodness she'd unfastened the first three buttons on her blouse. He captured her waist. She turned and he kissed her directly on the lips. "I love seeing you in the kitchen, preparing a meal. So homey."

Cripes, maybe he did want marriage first. Moaning deep in her throat, she slid her hand between his shirt and his back. She touched the muscled cords and worked her fingers around to his front, sliding the shirt up. He accommodated and helped her remove the plain blue T-shirt. She rolled her tongue over the peak of his nipple and sucked lightly to feel it tighten beneath her mouth. His heart beat strong and steady under her lips.

Seconds later, her white blouse had been

unbuttoned. He lifted her face with his right hand. His other continued to touch her waist, lightly stroking his fingers up to her rib cage, exciting her more. Her glance connected with his. She moved her hands down to his belt. She pulled back the leather end and tugged it tighter to release the silver notch. Freed, she pulled the belt from the last loop. It slithered to the floor. She unsnapped the brass button and unzipped the barrier between her and the prize.

The heat warmed the lotion on her fingers, as she slid her hand under the waistband of his briefs. Jasmine scent floated through the air. She pulled the band back. His eyes went from drowsy to liquid fire, the gray-blue igniting her soul.

He broke the kiss and stopped her hand before her fingers touched the stiff, large spear she desired. A crack of thunder sounded, so loud panes of the patio door rattled.

A storm was coming.

Georgina let go of his briefs and looked away from his lust-laden gaze.

"Why?" she whispered. The need she suppressed choked her throat. Maybe she wasn't as desirable as she thought. She wouldn't kid herself; she knew men were able and willing to have sex with any female with working parts. Why had he stopped?

Surely he wanted the release as much as she. She remembered the soft touch of his hands against her skin. When he escorted her down the park walk the gentleness of his fingers on her waist, or when they sat on the bench outside and watched the stars appear, he'd reach over and draw swirls on her arm. Sometimes, a poignant glance across the table would make her pulse slow and her throat to close off with joy. When they talked with Robert and Gemma, one of them would finish the other's sentence.

Nuances of a relationship.

The love she experienced with Jake made her heart swell against her ribcage. She didn't deny he could have another woman somewhere else, but she doubted he did. He desired her as much as she wanted him, and this contradiction of his withdrawal confused her.

"Why, Jake?" Her voice cracked. Her hands didn't know where to land and fluttered in front of her. She didn't care if she came across as weak.

His rejection hurt.

Tears clouded her vision.

She backed away and held a hand to the lowest button of her blouse. Then she got angry. What gave him the right to dominate all her time? He discouraged her from dating other men by monopolizing all her time and discarded her himself? Not one single indication from him led her to believe he didn't care for her.

He rubbed his chin and dragged his hand, the very hand a moment ago made her skin tingle, through his blond streaked hair. He didn't appear to want to answer.

Fine.

"You should go. I guess we want different things from this relationship." She grabbed his discarded T-shirt and threw it, his woodsy scent filtered through the air.

"Gee, you don't understand..."

"Then explain it to me." Her voice rose with a fury equal to the wind blowing outside. "I don't need a commitment from you. What do you want? It's evident what I want." Damn. Her voice continued to be raspy. She blinked back the tears. She would not cry. *Be strong.*

Her chest hurt with closed-in sobs.

No, her pain came from unrequited love. She loved Jake, and her self-esteem couldn't handle the rejection. The tears pooled on the edge of her eyes.

She sniffed, pulling the water back into the abyss of her lonely heart.

"Don't. Please, don't cry." Jake's voice was husky as well. He surrounded her with his arms, with his kindness. It was beyond her understanding. He was so sweet and, yet, when it came to intimacy he pushed her away.

The rain started pounding on the cement patio and bounced off the sliding doors. The suddenly dark interior wasn't dispelled by the fast upbeat song playing on the radio, Christina Aguilera's "Lady Marmalade." Bereft, Georgina clutched his back. She found a man she wanted to share herself with, and he kept her at a distance.

She straightened her shoulders, twisted out of his embrace, and walked over to the patio access. One of the hardest things she had ever had to do in the past two months was to slide the glass door on the runner. The metal crashed against the frame. She looked down at her bare feet and watched the rain splatter on the floor. The fresh clean scent of the downpour overrode the smell of the roast meat and vegetables. His shoes came into view at the edge of the exit.

"Georgina, please allow me to explain. It's not that I don't want you, because I do. My god, how I do. I just can't."

He pressed against her, she could feel his large engorged penis seeking her sex. She couldn't listen to any more. The pain in her chest had to be released. Maybe he had a wife somewhere, because he certainly could rise and fulfill her needs.

"Go," she croaked. Johnny Lang's "Second Guessing," belted out from the radio. God could the music this evening be a better fit for the outcome?

Not looking at him, she watched his black loafers as they took the rest of the man through the opening. She pushed the door shut. Her neck stiffened. She straightened her back, and made a direct line for the refrigerator. She changed course, shot her index finger to push the button to shut down the oven, flipped off the radio, and grabbed the bottle of wine from the counter.

Georgina Grey Barrister walked away: away from love, away from desire, away from Jake, and toward loneliness. And she would convince herself she'd be all right with that.

She jerked the unfastened blouse from the waistband of her shorts. As her hand lowered the light switch, the sliding door whooshed opened. Pivoting, she started forward and stopped.

Jake shut and locked the door. He threw his T-shirt on the chair. The stove lights created blue and green crystal prisms in the raindrops glimmering on his firm bare chest. She released a sob and opened her arms to accept him. He reached her in two strides

He kissed her, a long and hard kiss, almost as if in desperation. Her heart full in her chest, pounded strong, making her pulse beat as fast the rain pouring down outside. The desire deep down in her lower abdomen rose, and she returned the kiss, power-packed with unspoken love.

He broke the connection. "I want you. I need you. Obligations be damned."

She considered asking for clarification, but God as her witness, she wanted this man and would sacrifice her dignity whatever his obligations were. He lifted her into his arms, nestling her like a bouquet of flowers. Her head rested on his left arm, and her legs hung over his right wrist. The bottle of wine banged against his shoulder. He looked at it, then at her with a question in his eyes.

"We might need a thirst quencher later," she whispered. She hoped they would have a need for liquids later. Much later.

He smiled, held her close, and walked toward the stairs. The man was in terrific shape because he carried her up the stairs and to her brass bed without a pause. He kicked off his shoes, hesitated, and then gently lowered her to the chenille bedspread. She reached out to him and touched the drops of water on his hard chest. He leaned over her. Rain drops fell from his hair, onto her face, her neck, and the top of her nearly bare chest. She giggled.

He shook his head and the rain splattered over both of them. She put her hands on his face, brought it down to hers, and kissed him with an unleashed passion. A recklessness she didn't know existed, until now, and only with this man. She lifted her upper body off the bed to touch his nipples with her tongue. He lowered the sleeves of her blouse, a slow reveal of her skin. Her front-closure black bra caused him to falter. She placed her hands on top of his and guided them from her shoulder blades to run over the top of her breasts and down to the clasp. A snap and her breasts were released. Her hands moved down to his belt-less jeans, and she unfastened the brass button.

She snagged the zipper, lifted her gaze to meet his, and lowered the fastening inch by inch. Her fingers glazed over his tight stomach and his hips as she gradually worked his jeans down over his trim butt. The pants dropped with a soft thud to the floor. He inhaled. She smiled and pulled at his briefs, extending the band over his enlarged cock. They dropped to the carpet. He rolled his hands under her butt and eased her shorts and panties off.

Anticipation made her breathing quicken, faster as she glanced at him. She had seen his nude body, but this was different. His body was flushed and engorged because of her. He wanted her. She flashed him a make-love-to-me smile, full of seduction and promise.

He made a growl, deep in his throat, and straddled her body. His staff jutted out toward her, seeking a place of excitement. A tight, wet place. A place to settle in for a stay. She lifted her shoulders off the bed and wrapped her arms around his back. He brought his head down to hers, and her tongue entered his warm, sensitive cavern. She pushed her tongue in and out, a rhythm much like the pace she hoped to experience farther down her body, soon. The tingling became more pronounced as his fingers caressed her stomach and inched it down toward the curls blanketing the entrance.

"Jake, please. I need to feel you inside me."

"Foreplay. I want our first time to be special." He kissed her, slowly, hungrily, a contradiction, but exciting nonetheless. He inserted a finger or two, and her juices flowed faster and wetter. The smell of musk infused the air.

She whispered, "We've had foreplay for the past two months."

Her breasts felt swollen and her nipples ached, needing to be touched. As if vocalized, he leaned down, kissed one, and then the other. She groaned. He moved his hand to her face. He lowered his chest to touch hers and appeased the ache. Their hips touched. His penis was at the juncture, and she urged him forward by pressing closer. Her lips opened and the head of his cock rested at the precipice.

"Protection," he murmured.

Her fogged brain didn't connect with what he asked. She was at the end of the lustdom maze and wanted nothing more than to celebrate the victory, enjoy the prize. "Protection?"

"I don't have a condom, do you?"

Ordinarily she wouldn't have had one. "Nightstand, the top drawer."

He leaned over and jerked open the drawer. He

held the package, waved it. "Orange neon, glow in the night?"

Georgina chuckled. "Gag gift from Gemma. Need help?" She reached down, sliding her fingers over his tuff of curls until she made contact with his penis. Her palm touched his silky hard softness. She stroked his firm large cock.

"So not necessary," he hissed. He ripped open the packet with his teeth, extracted the pliable rubber and quickly rolled it on. He kissed her using a slow-hard burning pressure. Then, to her relief and joy, he entered her.

She lifted her hips and joined in a primal rhythm. The climax built, and she clasped his shoulders tight. The pace quickened. Her breath shortened. Shattered. She felt shattered. Never had she experienced this magnitude of joy before. The build up started, a rush, a wave of sensation moved to her breast to making them ache again, and then to her head, where an explosion occurred.

He lowered the lids of his eyes and licked his lips, turning her on further. He pushed harder, stronger, and faster. The cords of his neck stood out. His chest touched her aching nipples, easing the pressure.

He moaned, "Gee, my love."

And she shattered once again. A simultaneous merging occurred, as a crack of thunder sounded outside and a bolt of lightning illuminated the room.

He unlocked his elbows and lowered his body to rest on top of hers. His chest pressed against her breasts, his wonderful erection snug inside her.

"My God. I knew we'd be good together." He kissed her lips, a brief, love-to-love-you kind of peck. She moved her face to rest in the crook of his neck and shoulder, sniffed the woody, ambary fragrance of his cologne, mingled with the scent of the rain and musk.

"I'll move in a minute," he said.

"Don't. Stay on top of me for awhile, if you don't mind."

His chuckle erupted from his chest and flowed out of his mouth, blowing tendrils of her hair into her face. He rubbed his skin against hers creating a friction, electricity.

"Don't mind at all." A few seconds later, he rolled over, placing her on top of him. Her curls fell forward onto his body. His hands filtered through her hair strands. "This haircut, it emphasizes your beautiful turquoise eyes. You're gorgeous."

She knew she wasn't beautiful and relied on her keen intelligence to make herself interesting. Except for her eyes, she was ordinary. She disconnected from his hard cock, rolled over to his side, and closed her eyes to imagine that his statements were true. At this moment in time, she did feel gorgeous. And better yet, she had an aptitude for sex.

"Damn."

Her eyes flew open. The annoyed expression on Jake's face made her redirect her gaze downward. His encased shaft glowed orange except at the top where flesh and thick semen were exposed. The rubber had broken and the best swimmers had escaped.

"Don't worry. The egg isn't close to dropping."

"I'll pick up some quality non-glow-in-the-night condoms."

"So, we'll do this again?" She chanced a glimpse at his face.

"Of course. That is, if you want to?" He was on his side, his flexed muscle popping out from his arm as he rested his head against the palm of his hand. His fingers slid down over her side and settled on her stomach.

"Oh, yes." She had been holding in her breath to the make her hip bones pierce through the skin and her stomach concave, but after his statement she released the air. Sex was good.

"But not until I get reinforced protection and maybe some of that roast if it's still edible."

She grinned. The way to his heart and the prize in lustdom was through food. Who knew?

He rose from the bed and leaned over her. His lips hovered, and she closed the distance to connect her mouth with his. "You'll let me know?"

"Know?"

"If we've created something even more exciting from what we did a few minutes ago?" A quick peck on her lips, and he headed toward the shower.

"No worries." She smiled the dreamy smile of a sexually satisfied woman.

Chapter 11

Aleksandr's Freighter

Georgina woke up to the tainted foul smell of heavy breathing. She turned her head to see who was puffing air in her face and felt the warmth of a steel blade biting into her throat.

Damn, this trip kept getting better and better.

She glanced out from the side of her eye and noticed the handle of the knife, silver with ornate scrolling. She swallowed and the dagger moved with her throat muscles, cutting into her skin. It looked like the butter knife she used at dinner last night. Regardless, the dirk was pressed against her skin, and if strength was behind it, she could have her jugular vein sliced.

"Where is Sasha?" Onion scented breath flew over her nostrils. Her first instinct was to bring her arm up to cover her nose. But she always burrowed down in the covers, so she was wrapped in a cocoon and body movement was impossible. The pressure from the knife lessened. She peeked at her captor and closed her eyes again.

Psycho-slut strikes again.

The live matryoshka doll straddled her. She was trapped, with a woman bent on revenge pressing on her full bladder. How in the world had she slipped past the guard?

The limited air flow made her voice sound hoarse. "Hi, Magda. I hope you left the few vials intact on the dresser. I don't expect much, but shampoo and deodorant are very important to me."

"Smart mouth. Where is my man?" Magda bent over, narrowed her eyes, and applied pressure to the knife, cutting into Georgina's throat.

Georgina blew out a breath and turned her head a pinch, the knife went with her. The crazy woman didn't even ask how she knew her name. Egocentric. A good thing; she would use it. She dealt with a few egos in boarding school. Work with them, pad their idea of self importance, and great things could be accomplished.

Magda's breath smelled like more like beans than onions. Nonetheless, the stench was a very bad odor. The sloshing of the water against the hull of the ship reminded Georgina she had needed to use the restroom.

"He stumbled out of my room last night about midnight. Ah, Magda, could you move the knife? It's making talking difficult."

Magda threw the blade. The metal pinged off the side of the dresser and fell onto the floor, sliding under the bed. She lifted one leg over Georgina's inert body, dropped to the edge of the bed, and sobbed into her hands. Georgina rose, placed her back against the wall, and quickly looked to see if any other obvious weapons were within reach. Nothing was visible.

"You're wearing my bathing suit," Georgina said. Early dawn and as cold as a Virginia Christmas and this woman wore a bikini. Not a bit of sun shone through the peep hole of the port window.

Magda twisted her face, spread her fingers, and muttered. "Mine. You cannot have."

Georgina didn't bother to point out they were stolen items. "Fair enough, but how did you get it?"

"Why do you want my Sasha?" Magda moved her hands from her face, revealing the tears as they rolled down her plump cheeks.

Georgina sat up straighter on the bed and crossed her legs. The facilities seemed farther and farther away. She cautiously patted Magda on the back, quick little reassurance taps.

"I don't want your Sasha. I've a man of my own, whom I love."

A fresh stream of tears ran down Magda's face. She croaked out, "He does not want me."

"You don't know that. Maybe you're not making yourself noticed. A businessman," Georgina tried to think of Aleksandr as an entrepreneur instead of what he really was: a pirate, a thief, a possible rapist, and a definite murderer, "likes to be entertained. They grow bored quickly and desire variety."

"I will not share my man with others." She threw herself at Georgina, with outstretched arms. Whether Magda intended to hug or scratch her eyes out, Georgina didn't know. Others? Once again, she questioned if other women were on board the freighter.

Georgina stretched her arms, palms out, and crunched further back into the corner. "Whoa, there. I know what you mean. I don't want to share my man either. We have that in common. How about if I give you some tips? Pointers you use later tonight so Aleksandr will stay with you."

"Why would you do this?" Magda sat back on the bed with a thump as she hit the wall. She used the backs of her hands to wipe away the tears.

"I'll trade information with you. You'll tell me about things."

"No. You cannot take more of my clothes." Magda squirmed on the bed. One leg was thrown over the other, and she crossed her arms. She uncrossed her arms, and then her legs. If she bounced one more time, Georgina would be doomed to sleeping in a wet bed tonight.

"I don't want your clothes," Georgina said. "First lesson, you need to calm down. You've a very short fuse. Be more relaxed and don't get excited about the least little thing."

Surprisingly, Magda took a deep breath but narrowed her eyes. "What do you want to know?"

"When did you get the clothes? Did any of the people escape the burning yacht? For these answers, I'll share a sex trick with you: the Dance of the Seven Veils. Do you know this movement?"

"No." Magda sounded like a petulant child, not having the best toy and wanting it.

Georgina met her glance without flinching.

"It's a dance of artistic expression, using scarves and the bathing suit you're wearing. The burlesque has such a seductive swing your man won't let you out of sight...for days, months. Rather years." Georgina gave her a smile, hopefully a convincing, I'm-telling-you-the-truth smile.

"Da. I want to learn this dance." Magda scooted to the edge of the bed, stood, and placed her hands on her hips.

"How did you get in here?" Georgina looked around. The chair that had blocked the door was missing.

"Nikka let me in," Magda said. Georgina assumed Nikka was No Neck Number Two.

"We need to toss items around the room. Please just throw my shoes or plastic bottles. Don't break anything else." Magda's confused expression made Georgina sigh. "He only let you in to cause me harm. If he thinks we're helping each other, he won't let you enter the next time. We should scream, too."

They shrieked and Magda threw bottles and the heels repeatedly around the room. Georgina leaned over to whisper in her ear. "I must use the restroom. You go to your room, get seven long or large scarves, and return. I'll teach you, but first I need that information."

Magda grunted. "The crew went to fancy boat—"

"You mean Tristan's yacht?" Georgina's heart raced with fear, but ultimately hoped that Jake was alive.

"Yes, when Sasha was talking to the American man and you came on board in your whore dress and high heels. We could take whatever we wanted from the ship."

"And?"

"You will get more after you teach me dance."

Georgina nodded and screamed one last time. With a flourish, Magda stalked out of the room, slamming the door behind her. Georgina searched under the bed for the knife and found it near the bedpost. She stretched until she grabbed it. The knife had a thin line of blood on the edge. She reached and touched her throat. Damn.

She gathered her toothpaste and shoes from the floor. She folded a shirt around the hygiene items, knife, and covered her neck with a torn skirt. Her guard would think she'd been injured. She ambled out of her bedroom, with her eyes downcast, but watched him.

Nikka, No Neck Number Two, typically didn't make any facial expressions, but his eyes glittered with joy. Bastard. He wouldn't get away with this. On her way to the facilities she realized that if Nikka was her guard today, then Viktor would be her watch tonight. Viktor could be manipulated.

Much like the bathing suit on Tristan's yacht, Georgina carried her underwear into the shower with her. Every other morning she washed the garments and the silk dried within hours. It was a sad state to go from randomly purchasing one hundred dollar lingerie to protecting grungy ones. She relieved her bladder, completed her bathing ritual, tore the skirt into strips, and tied one around her thigh, strapping the knife to her skin.

Her mind raced with the knowledge that Aleksandr's crew went over to Tristan's ship, before the explosives went off. She tried to suppress the belief, the glimmer of hope that Jake had survived. He might be alive. He could be on this ship, a captive, like her. They would find each other again—if she could escape.

****

"Look, you've got the basic idea and you're pulling the scarves off in a nice, even rhythm. But if you want him to be so pleased he'll do anything for you, then you'll need to gyrate a little more. Your rear's smaller than mine and should look very nice shaking in front of his face. So swing it." Georgina hoped Magda would get the Dance of the Seven Veils conquered and soon. She had been working with her for over an hour. The routine was simple.

"Let me show you." Georgina tucked a few bits of cloth at the neck of her blouse and in the band of her pants.

"Magda, take your scarf and wrap it around your head and across the lower edge of your face. The only thing showing should be your eyes. Let your eyes express the lust and the love you have for him." Georgina coughed back the repulse she felt at envisioning Magda and Aleksandr together in sexual congress.

Magda very effectively wrapped the scarf around her crown and lower across her face. She tucked the end under to secure the material in place.

"Now, think lustful thoughts about how much you want to touch his body." Georgina wrapped a veil around her crown and across her mouth. Her eyes and nose were the only portions of her face showing.

"Think of how much you enjoy being with him. How much you want him to touch you, to kiss you,

136

and to stay with you through the night. Think of these things while you're dancing and little by little, removing the scarves." She moved one of the cloths to be tucked into her pants pocket.

"The last piece removed should reveal your womanhood. Begin at the top and work down." Georgina slowly drew the scarf from her blouse, waving the brightly colored orange, pink, and red dotted cloth in the air. She gyrated to and fro, as if a snake were being charmed from its basket. "You want your inner arms to be the center of attention when you're waving the material. Turn your wrists toward him and release the scarf with your finger and thumb, allowing the silk to float to the floor."

Georgina released the veil, and with a gentle turn of her wrist she curved around again to face Magda.

"When you are ready to expose your jewel, you might want to seductively move closer to your man and slide the scarf over his face, arm, and lower regions." Georgina had used kohl to darken her eyes, and she opened them dramatically to illustrate how the eyes could be used to enhance the body movements. "When you draw the veil off of your waist, untie the knot slowly, and peel it open like a banana. Make sure you stop and move your wrist outward and then continue."

"What is this jewel? Do you have diamonds attached that you show him?" Magda's neck flushed and the rosy glow moved to her face. Her voice held hints of anger and jealousy.

"No, Magda. The jewel is your vagina. I guess treasure would be a better word."

If Aleksandr was horny, and the last Georgina knew he wanted to have a full mast, she needed to find a method of him getting relief, without her body being the vessel. She didn't trust Magda, but the woman wanted Aleksandr and he wanted sex. They were a perfect fit.

Granted, for some reason he wanted sex with Georgina. Maybe it was the challenge of obtaining the unobtainable. Or because she was American or perhaps he had a love interest that resembled her and he was acting out his desires. She could go on and on with different scenarios. Point being, she would not fill his need. Georgina wanted Aleksandr to find Magda's jewel tonight. If Georgina's luck meter remained high for several nights, Magda would dance and Aleksandr would be busy.

"Do you have any bracelets you could put on your wrists to draw attention to them?"

"Da. Tell me story again. Maybe it will help." Magda picked up the scattered scarves.

"Bracelets will add a musical tone like chimes." Georgina lowered her face veil, blew out a breath, and settled onto the bed. "The legend of Salomé is about faith and trust in your man. At a celebration of Herod's birthday, the young and beautiful Salomé—"

"Me." Magda smiled from cheek to cheek, brown eyes glittering with excitement. She wrapped a scarf around her hand.

"Yes, for this situation you are Salomé. She danced for Herod, his lords, commanders, and all of his men. She pulled off each of the seven veils in turn, until she was wearing little or nothing." Georgina paused, stood, removed her scarf, and draped the material around Magda's upper arm.

"And he was so happy with her dancing he told everyone to give her, ah, whatever she desire." Magda lowered the cloth from her face. She tilted to her side with her elbow propped on the bed and cupped her cheek with her palm.

"That's right, Magda. You'll perform the Dance of Seven Veils in a little while, and Aleksandr will promise you whatever you want." She got off the bed and backed away. "One more time."

Magda must have been thinking x-rated thoughts, because she danced a seductive striptease. Georgina recalled the rest of the story, Herod had been considered an adulterer and Salome asked for the head of John the Baptist, because he spoke out against the union. She'd keep that portion of the story to herself. Georgina didn't want to put any ideas into Magda's spiteful head.

Magda finished, and nothing but the little Band-Aid of a bathing suit was left. Georgina hurled a bottle of peach scented lotion and two shoes at the wall. Magda smiled in appreciation.

"We haven't screamed for a while," Magda said.

"Scream and then tell me what I want to know. You've made the dance so seductive you won't be able to walk tomorrow."

Magda lifted a dark eyebrow and her eyes dilated.

"You whore! You not go near my man. I kill you first." Magda's voice had a hard edge, as if she meant every word she said.

Georgina narrowed her eyes.

Magda let out a piercing scream, which vibrated off the metal walls as she leaned over to pick up a scarf. In a lower voice she said, "People on fancy boat could come with us or die when ship went boom. Most wanted to come with us. This why shipmates are cramped into tight space, and we eat only beans and rice. You get chocolate cake. Everyone know this and they hate you." Magda had gathered all of the veils and proceeded to the door.

"Sasha did this," Georgina hissed and tilted her head back. She lowered her voice. "I didn't ask to be here." She waved her hand to encompass the room.

Magda shrugged her shoulders and cleared her throat.

Damn. Magda's opinion didn't matter, but

getting off the ship did. The deceptions continued.

Magda wadded her scarves into a bunch, opened the door, and tossed a bottle of perfume. The fragrant, jasmine and vanilla scented liquid inched down the wall. As she opened the exit wider, Georgina witnessed the first smile to ever appear on Nikka's face.

A short time later, three taps sounded at her door. Dressed for dinner, on time for once, she opened the door to find Viktor holding a bowl. Steam escaped from under the loose lid.

"Aleksandr will not be able to have dinner with you this evening." He lowered his head appearing to focus on his shoes. "He is sick."

Viktor lifted his head and held out the bowl. She took the crock and pulled off the lid: beans and rice. Georgina laughed in her head. The crew certainly had an odd sense of humor.

"Where's Yakov tonight?" She set the beans on the dresser and tucked the tight T-shirt into the band of her pants. The movement drew his eyes to her chest. Okay, one point for large breasts.

"He has been given a night off." Viktor shifted to look dead ahead, instead of into her eyes.

Oh hell, wars weren't won unless action was taken. "Viktor, I've been cooped up in this room all day, every day, for about three weeks. I'd really like to take a walk on the top deck to see the sun, before it gets too dark."

"Nyet. Not leave room except to see Aleksandr."

"If he's sick in his room, he won't know, now will he?" She presented him with an innocent wide-eyed smile she hoped would convince him to let her have her way.

"One quick trip around the top deck. Do not talk."

Giddiness overwhelmed her. She would look for Jake and get some fresh air. Deep down she had the feeling—no, she knew—Jake would have contacted her if he was alive and on the freighter. However, she pushed her doubts aside. Only hope remained.

Jake was alive and she'd find him. And she'd ask him about the conversation she overheard on Tristan's yacht. Why exactly was Jake on that ship? Was he involved in the trafficking? Her stomach churned in fear. Could he be a pirate hoping to steal the contraband from Tristan and Aleksandr? Had she been a pawn in a game she hadn't realized was going on?

She slipped on her heels and wrapped the chambray shirt over her T-shirt. She rushed out of the door and waited. Georgina would let Viktor lead the way. It was difficult to relinquish control, but she wanted Viktor to feel as if he was simply taking a captive pet for a walk.

Georgina wanted to photograph the large ball of orange as it sat low in the sky. At the top of the stairs, she closed her eyes and simply breathed the fresh sea air. The brisk cool breeze refreshed her rather than chilled.

From what Magda said, the ship was full because of the additional crew from the Turquoise Eyes. With a crowded lower deck, she wasn't surprised that crewmembers loitered above. Activity was everywhere. Several men swabbed the deck, their back and forth motion keeping in rhythm with the waves. Two men with caps pulled low over their foreheads were polishing the pulleys, hatch wenches, and bollards. Their brown cloth gloves slid the oiled cloths inside and out. Groups of four and five crew members sat around and played cards or threw dice. The large freighters primary use was for transportation of goods, not people. Men were in every corner, nook, and along the railing.

Her head bobbed left and right, face to face, trying to get a glimpse of Jake, praying for a sighting. The men were all dressed alike, in blue jeans, chambray shirts, oilskin jackets, and stocking caps. Some of them added distinctiveness by wrapping a bandana around their crowns or throats.

Georgina was confident she would recognize Jake by his body shape alone. They had a metaphysical connection. She would feel his presence if he was on the ship. She craved a live visual of his face, the longish light brown hair, gray-blue eyes, and crooked nose.

A shudder ran through her body. Jake might not be alive. Would he think she was on Tristan's yacht when it went up in flames? No, don't think that. Jake had to be on this ship. She envisioned the joy she would witness on his face when he saw her strolling above deck.

She caught her heel on an exposed bolt and fell forward. Viktor grabbed her arm to prevent her from hitting the metal surface. Her thoughts were brought back to present as she heard the catcalls.

"Watch your step, missy."

"You trade your soul for pleasure, whore?"

"She went from one captain's cabin to another."

"You can spread your legs for me."

"I'll share my beans with you, princess."

Russian phrases were also voiced. She didn't understand, but the intonation led her to believe they weren't telling her to have a nice day. Block out the comments. Perhaps the imprisonment in her room wasn't punishment after all. She heard men pass in the hallways and laughter late at night, but she didn't realize they could have been discussing her, laughing at her. They thought, wrongly, that she came on board by choice and requested special favors. Could it be that Aleksandr kept her in her cabin for protection?

Viktor held her arm, and they completed a full circle. She wasn't a coward. The crew could think what they wanted. She stopped and leaned over the railing. Having been below deck and trapped in a small square, writing in a journal, made her stir crazy. She truly appreciated the cool breeze coming off the ocean. Yet, the joy of the fresh sea scent had been tainted, and now she breathed in the brine of the murky water.

Three whales majestically arched above the water to slice back into a wave. Their black and gray bodies glistened in the setting sun. The mammals' graceful rise and fall allowed them to keep pace with the vessel and the rate of her heart.

Jake wasn't on deck.

"Why do you cry? Because of the men?" Viktor asked as he stood beside her. He leaned his elbows on the rail and bent his blond head. Her glance met his.

"I'm not crying. I'm responding to the beauty of wildlife in their natural habitat." She lifted the edge of her shirt and wiped her eyes.

"What do you say?" His expression was confused, and she didn't have the wither will to help him understand. She stared at the deep blue ocean.

"Nothing important." Jake wasn't among the crew. She tried to wrap her mind around the fact that he might be dead. No, she wouldn't give up. They'd be together. Her karma couldn't be so twisted as to not allow them happiness.

"You didn't find him."

She pivoted to look at Viktor. Dizziness invaded. She lost her balance and had to grab the railing. To respond she would be admitting she searched for someone and put Jake in danger. Did they know? Was Jake on the freighter? Had he asked about her? Who could she really trust on this ship?

"The men talk. The man you look for disappeared on boat, before our crew went on board to clean."

"Don't you mean to pirate? To claim the spoils of the war?" she retorted.

Viktor had a wide-eyed look of humiliation on his face and turned away. Guilt. She felt so much guilt. He was considerate and compassionate. The first time she could have thanked him for everything he had done for her, and she snapped at him.

It was evident she hadn't changed in the last few months. She continued to be a replica of her mother, arrogant and bad-tempered. Today she'd change, grow into a better person, and become more considerate of others.

She touched his thick, muscular, arm with her hand and glanced into his eyes. "Viktor, I'm sorry. You've been kind, and I'm grateful. Thank you."

"Come. Time to go back." His gruff voice didn't reveal if he was angry. She couldn't lose her only ally. The challenges had become overwhelming. How easy it would be to simply give in. She'd sit in her cell and let whatever fate befall her instead of fighting constant battles. Was that the best choice though? Was that what a person of light would do to overcome the darkness of evil? God, she had had such a lonely childhood.

Stars speckled behind her eyes, and her stomach heaved. She leaned on the rail and lowered her head. Viktor took a hold of her arm and helped her down the stairs. The truth materialized and struck her like the Nordic wind chafing her skin. Tristan knew she was sleeping with Jake. Tristan had prepared to give her away as a gift to Aleksandr. The tan. The dress. The pieces of the puzzle fit together. She had believed Kandi had betrayed her. Kandi wanted to marry Tristan and would have done whatever foul deeds necessary to get him. Instead it was Tristan who played her. He knew about her and Jake. So, what had Tristan done with Jake?

Georgina had been duped.

She'd lost a game she hadn't realized she'd been playing.

Tristan understood she had told the truth. She had a new love, and he couldn't handle what he considered a betrayal. He called her cell phone, waited for Jake to leave, and arrived within minutes afterwards. Tristan had known that Jake was her lover all while they were on his yacht. Her breath panted out and her heart beat a quick cadence as fast as the thump of footsteps on the metal deck.

What about Gemma? Was Tristan's threat to Gemma all a lie? He had her key and knew she was pregnant. Was Gemma safe now that Tristan was dead?

Back in her room she gathered her toiletry items and went to the restroom for her night-time absolution. Victor didn't talk to her, nor did his glance meet hers as it had before. She may have lost her one supporter in a thoughtless expression of words.

Later, settled into bed, she flipped on the light, picked up her journal, and breathed normally for the first time in several days. Georgina would think of the positive. Jake was alive, and she'd forgive him for not telling her the truth. The thought alone renewed her hope. Now, she would become aggressive in her efforts to be free. She reached down to feel the butter knife strapped to her thigh. Norway was only a day away.

Chapter 12

Nero, Virginia
One Month Earlier

Georgina held the telephone to her ear and played with the packets of condoms on the bedside table. Not a neon one among the bunch. She experienced the thrill of capriciousness and recklessness to have a stack of sexual protection in her bedroom. Tristan had insisted she wear a diaphragm, which gathered dust in the bedside table in Boston. They'd never been skin to skin, always a barrier existed between them. How would she feel with Jake's skin, his hardcore, pressed inside of her without the rubber substance between them? Maybe, if they were to become a couple, she'd check into birth control pills. She wanted to be with him, naturally.

"I'm here Gemma. I'm sure Bob doesn't think you're fat. You're carrying his son, his heir, the future Sheraton, in your body. I heard him call you Madonna." She looked down at her cell phone that vibrated and danced to the edge of the bedside table. Her fingers barely snatched the tiny device before it tittered off the edge.

"That's right. He has his princess on a pedestal. Gemma, I'll call you back, because my cell's ringing. Actually, I'll call you much later, because I heard the shower shut off. My man is fresh and clean, and I'll need to check behind his....ah, ears." She laughed in response to Gemma's giggles. "Love you. I'll be over this afternoon, and we'll measure the mound."

Unknown. The incoming number hadn't registered on her phone. Her heart plummeted. She hadn't checked her luck meter today. Her forecast could very well be one out of five with five being good.

Georgina answered with a whisper. "Hello?"

"I found you, despite your efforts to get away."

She dropped the phone. Her breath caught in her chest and a pain entered her heart. Tristan! If he found out about Jake, he'd hurt him. Kill him. Fear and anger merged together. Pull it together Georgina. Her strength grew stronger.

As she bent down to grasp the cell from the floor she heard the bathroom door open and looked over. It appeared to be closed.

"Tristan, how did you get his number?" She rose from the bed and walked over to the window. The sun was high in the sky. She closed her eyes and leaned against the cool window pane.

"Your mother. She wants us to get together, so do I." He softened his voice, reminding her of their dating years. Sweet. Considerate. Fake!

"My mother? Well, I'll change the number, and she won't know the new one."

"I know where you live," Tristan insisted.

"You're assuming she actually knows where I live." Georgina tried to laugh, but shivers ran down her body. She backed away from the window.

"I'll find you." Tristan's low controlled voice chilled her to the core. She pushed the end button, closed the cover, tightened the belt on her robe, and rubbed the frost from her arms.

She sensed Jake's presence before he spoke.

"Are you okay? Your face's pale. Who was calling?"

"I'm fine. It was a wrong number. Rude person." She turned into him and pressed her face against his neck, her heart catapulting with renewed fear. The

147

fresh scent of the citrus scented soap, the dampness of his skin, and the rhythm of his breathing comforted her.

She needed to be honest with him. How could she tell him about Tristan? She was a liar. Would her deceit show in her body language? Her love for Jake overrode her fear of Tristan, right? He never spoke of a future, not a month from now or even tomorrow. Their relationship was a day to day thing.

She struggled to overcome her vulnerability, which was entangled with her anxiety. She didn't expect a commitment after such a short time, but a hint would be nice. If he said, "Next month I'd like to go over to the Smokey Mountains," she would know he wanted a future. Or "Tomorrow night let's plan to go to a movie," she'd be ecstatic. But plans were never made. There were no discussions of a future together, ever.

Jake wrapped his arms around her shoulders and closed the gap between them. He sighed. She felt his chest constrict, like he planned to use the air to say something but released it instead. Within a few minutes he pulled back and used his fingers to lift her chin. She looked into his eyes. He had an indescribable expression on his face. Once before she had déjà vu, that he knew, not just a knowing intimate connection, but almost as if he was familiar with everything about her. But that was impossible!

He kissed her. It wasn't the lust-laden lip-to-lip she experienced an hour earlier, nor was it the sweet I'm-home kind of kiss. The kiss presaged trust; she should have faith in him. She wanted to burst out in nervous laughter. There was a song about lying lips, and hers burned with lies. *Tell him. Tell him now.*

"Jake..." She'd confess before she lost her nerve, but a distant chiming interrupted. "Is your phone ringing?"

"Yes. I need to answer. Family." He rushed over

and picked up his jeans. His firm stalwart fingers removed the cell phone from the pocket. He answered without a greeting. "Give me a minute. I'm not getting good reception."

Jake circled his hand to indicate he was going downstairs. Georgina watched him slide into his jeans, zipping them as he left. She released a heavy breath, put her own cell phone back on the table by the condoms, and went into the bathroom. A discussion about her past, which influenced her present, would be postponed until tonight.

Then Georgina would reveal everything and see if what they had together would last. She debated how to approach the topic of her past while she showered. She stepped out of the tub and tugged on a soft cotton robe. She wrapped her hair turban style, grabbed her moisturizer, and shuffled into the bedroom.

The first thing she noticed was that the bed was made. Next, a small piece of white paper was in the middle of the dark green cover. She snatched up the note. Her heart leaped with joy. Her very first personalized message hand written by her lover. She dropped the towel and finger-combed her hair.

Gee,

I must go. Sorry about leaving a note. I'll see you later tonight. We'll have dinner out. Plan on eight or nine at the latest.

The closing line was illegible and had been crossed out.

Jake

She swirled around, her white robe flowing out like Cinderella's ball gown. Her heart beat a quick melody as she pressed the note to her chest. "He made plans. A spur-of-the-moment man, but he set a future date."

They had a relationship with communication. She sat on the edge of the bed and pondered this new dimension of their affair. Basking in the glow of a cemented bond, a thought nagged at her. Why couldn't he decide on a closing?

"What're you mooning over?"

"Tristan!" Her head shot up and her heart stopped its happy cadence. Dread and panic set in. She knew without a doubt her future would be altered. Her hands began to sweat. Think!

Georgina flinched, clutched the white piece of paper, and lowered it to blend in with her robe. Her ex-husband, Tristan, stood in her bedroom doorway, glaring at her with flashing eyes and fierceness. She wanted to crawl under the bed. Her glance dropped down at the note. He must not see it. She flipped her wet hair with one hand and balled the message the with other. Gently, she dropped the note to the floor, and stood. She took a step, kicked the paper under the bed, making the move appear as if the long length of the gown had stuck under her foot.

"What a surprise. How did you get in? Why don't you wait downstairs? I'll get dressed and join you." Her fists pushed his chest, forcing him to step away.

He held out a spare key, the one Gemma kept with a laminated picture of fetal-baby-Bob as the holder.

"Where did you get that?"

"I think that's obvious." He held Baby Bob's image between his fingers.

"What about Gemma?" She bit her lip to keep the tremble hidden.

"She's safe, for now." His eyes glinted with malice.

"There's coffee." Her voice forced hard words in sharp bursts of air and nodded to the door. She wavered, terror making her knees weak.

He gripped her arms and held her steady. "I'll wait here." He nodded toward her body. "I've seen you naked."

"We're divorced. You don't have the right to look at me naked any longer." Her heart beat erratically with the thought that he held Gemma hostage or at worst, had killed her.

He pressed forward, forced her to move backward. Her robe caught on her heels. She stopped when the back of her legs butted into the bed.

Tristan picked up one of the shiny packets from the night stand. He waved the condom in front of her. "I see you're doing someone."

"I'm making an engagement gift basket for a friend." Lies simply flew out of her mouth with the greatest of ease. Although, it may have helped to have a basket in the area, any kind of bin, as his glance scanned the tiny room.

"Yes, well, the divorce papers are not valid." With one hand he jerked her close and leaned his head down to kiss her.

"You didn't sign them?" Georgina instinctively fell back, pressed into his arm, and forced herself to still. Once, not long ago, she had loved this man. Currently, she didn't trust the liar, but she wanted to live.

She had proof stowed away in a safe bank vault certifying Tristan was dangerous, evidence he killed an innocent man. Despite all of this, their marriage lasted three years. He had been her first lover, and until recently her only lover. She regarded his visage, a worn and lined face. Tristan had seen too much, indulged too much, and had taken too many risks.

"Give me a kiss, and I'll give the papers to you." He wrapped his hand around her neck, catching her hair and squeezing hard enough to make her fear he would cut off her airflow.

She shook her head and lowered her glance, refusing to let him see her fright.

"The only way you'll be free is to have the signed papers," he snapped.

She shivered and controlled the tremors flowing through her hands. Georgina conjured up the happy times they shared, a dapper handsome man escorting a timid debutante to her first ball, their wedding day, the honeymoon, and when they shared a home. The memories of his happy-life-is-for-the-taking attitude flooded her. She reached up to meet his kiss and felt a sting. She glanced at her arm. Tristan pressed a syringe into her skin. She lurched away, but not soon enough. Dizzy.

Georgina met Tristan's glance. His ice-blue eyes didn't waver. No smile appeared on his lips. Black invaded and took her into an abyss, a vacant seemingly lifeless cold space.

****

Georgina dreamed of shooting stars, camera shutters opening and closing, and water hitting the edge of a pool. Where was Gemma? Had they fallen asleep by the pool? Why wasn't there a breeze? Her eyelids were heavy, and her eyelashes had crusted together. She pried them open with her fingers. She lay on a bed. Above her was the low ceiling of a ship's cabin. She angled her head, squinted, and glanced around to see a table, a bench, and a small door. Hopefully, the teakwood panel led to a bathroom.

Her legs wouldn't move. Mentally, she tried to make them shift. What was wrong with her legs? Her heart beat erratically. She checked out her other appendages. Arms were sluggish but mobile. Head and neck—normal. Okay. Maybe her lower limbs had fallen asleep. Think. Lift up.

Hands stable on the bed, she propelled her upper body into an upright position. Her breathing became labored as the memories flew back into her mind.

Tristan had drugged her.

Gemma. What about Gemma? Was she safe?

Georgina surveyed her robe, which had a small smearing of dirt on the lower hem, as if she'd been dragged outside. She lowered her head to rest on her hands. God, no wonder her legs refused to work. An obstacle, but it could be controlled.

She threw the robe aside and wrapped both hands around her left leg, closest to the edge of the bed, and forced it over the side. She took a deep breath and glanced around. Small and unfamiliar. Was she on Tristan's yacht? If so, then she was in one of the little cabins. The room had three feet by five feet of walking space. If she could get the other appendage over, she could balance between the limited furniture and the walls to get to the commode.

With a deep breath, she lifted her right leg over the side, a silver dollar size bruise spread from her heel up to her ankle. She leaned forward. The propulsion sent her head first into the table. She grabbed hold with both hands. Her rapid breathing slowed as she caught herself.

I can do this.

She anticipated tingles and sharp, pin-stabbing sensations as she put her weight on her feet, but nothing. Had she been paralyzed? Her stomach rebelled as the fear broadcasted outward.

She used both hands, heaved herself upright, leaned against the table with one hip, and moved the right leg forward a few inches. She tilted a hip and shifted the left limb forward. Just a little bit further, and she'd find out what was behind door number one. Sweat beaded on her forehead. The few feet she traveled equaled to a marathon as her breath came out in ragged pants.

The bed was her next safety net. She grabbed onto the end and dragged her legs, first one and finally the other. A few more inches and she would be at her goal. Bent awkwardly over, she moved the left foot. Like an old-fashion black and white cartoon, she fell. Before her head could connect with the floor, soft, strong hands grabbed her arms and lifted her upright.

"You've a couple of hours until the Special-K wears off. You should've stayed in bed." Tristan's jubilate voice punctuated the moment. She wanted to take her fingernails and rip off his smile.

"I'm not amused, Tristan." *Please let my legs work soon.* "I need to use the facilities." She nodded toward the door. "Is that a bathroom?"

"Yes. You won't be able to get settled without help." The bastard widened his grin.

She forced down her anger, controlled her flaring nostrils, and swallowed the spittle instead of sending the slime through the air.

"I'll be fine. Help me get inside and then leave." She twisted her upper body, so she was beside him instead of against his chest. This action forced her legs to cross over each other. He picked her up, carried her into the bathroom, and stood her upright in front of the toilet. His white polo shirt worked free from his slacks. Face to face with him, an inch away, she was so very angry she could have bumped her head into his. To do so would have been a mistake, because she didn't know what to expect. She didn't know if she'd ever be able to walk again. Tristan had successfully made her dependent on him.

"Leave now." Her mouth tasted foul. If nothing else, the vile odor should have chased him out of the confined space.

"I'll give you privacy. Knock on the door, and I'll

take you back to bed." He smiled, his dimples making dents on his cheeks. He appeared to love every minute of her helplessness.

She gave a slight nod.

She relieved herself and reached over to wash her hands in the Barbie size sink. Her fingers struggled to reach farther and opened the medicine cabinet. A toothbrush fell out and landed in the sink. Using the tip of it, she pushed out a tube of paste. With limited energy, she scrubbed her teeth and tongue getting rid of that horrible taste. She tried to peer into the mirror, but couldn't move over far enough to see a reflection. Her image wasn't important. Mobility in her legs: important. Her future: very important. Answers: critical. Georgina knocked and hoped for an explanation.

"Ready?" Tristan bellowed from the other side.

"Yes." She gathered up the ends of her robe to prevent a mishap.

He opened the powder room door, lifted her, and carried her into the main area. She plunked onto the bed, and he turned and strolled to the exit.

"Wait. I've questions," she screamed.

"Sleep. I'll be back in a couple-of-hours, dear wife." He continued out the door.

If possible she'd have grabbed anything handy and hurled it at him. She couldn't sleep. Fury raged inside her, and the fear of loss of leg function made her queasy stomach heave and roll. Tristan wasn't stupid cnough to kidnap Gemma. The military would have been all over him. Hours later she glanced at the porthole. The background had changed from blue to black. The door squeaked open. Tristan had returned.

He had a porter in tow. The Hispanic man held a large tray laden with decadent smells of roasted meat, pungent broccoli, and steamed potatoes with tangy mustard and the fragrant earthy smell of tarragon in a Hollandaise sauce. The waiter set the tray on the table and lifted the lid from the plate. Tristan waved him away. The man quickly left, shutting the door behind him. She speared Tristan with a death-to-you glance and the obnoxious viper chuckled in return.

"Do you have feeling in your legs?"

"In the last few minutes I've had the urge to kick, but no muscle control yet. Will I regain mobility? Did you guess on the amount of drug to give me? Am I going to be in a wheelchair for the rest of my life?" She tried to keep her voice light and non-threatening. As of this point in time she didn't' know what he wanted from her. Her toes tingled, but she wasn't going to tell him.

"It should wear off within the next two hours. You've regained control of your arms." He made it sound as though she should be happy with what she had that worked.

"Yes." She couldn't think clearly. The smell of the food was driving her crazy. Several hours had passed since she had eaten, and sex with Jake burned a lot of calories. She glanced at the fare and noticed the Hollandaise sauce with the little green speckles. Her nose was right.

"Are you hungry?" Tristan took two steps to arrive at the side of the bed.

"Must I beg?"

"Georgina, your humor has been tainted and nothing but sarcasm spills from that gaping hole."

She closed her mouth. It had been hanging open. He pulled her legs to the side of the bed. Except for the robe she hadn't been covered. Underneath the housecoat, she was naked. She forced her upper body into a sitting position, tugged the robe closed, and thanked God when she felt tingling from hip to heel.

"If you could help me stand upright, I could twist and land on the bench." The smile she plastered on her face conflicted with the chill in her voice.

"I'll do no such thing. You're my wife, in sickness and in health. I'll carry you." He picked her up and hoisted her onto his hip. The robe fell open, dragged along the floor and became trapped under her as she toppled down onto the padded surface.

"Thanks." Her most ardent desire was to say, "We're divorced. I'm not sick. I don't have use of my legs, because of you." But she didn't know what he wanted or the rules of his game, so she would play it his way, for now. She tugged the sides of the robe together.

"How did you get the key to my house?"

"From Gemma of course."

She bit her lower lip. "Did you hurt her?"

"You know me better than that. I love your friend. Even when she's big as a whale."

Georgina's heart stopped beating. "You wouldn't be able to take her with the military so close. You couldn't."

"I guess you'll have to do everything I ask of you to protect your friend and her baby." He flipped a piece of her hair behind her ear. "I'd hate to see her lose another one because you wouldn't cooperate."

She stared at him. Was he telling the truth? Not willing to put Gemma in danger, Georgina became complacent.

They had shared many meals together in the past, but this had to have been the most bizarre. There was only a bench and the bed, so he sat beside her. He laid the napkin on her lap, handed her a fork, and placed a citrus salad in front of her. Her favorite type of salad, with the jade green spinach leaves, walnut pieces, and bits of orange. The citrus smell revitalized her a tiny bit. She lifted a fork full to her mouth, stilled, and lowered the utensil.

"Why aren't you eating?" Georgina looked into

his lying face.

"I've a late dinner scheduled. The group." He twirled a spoon with his fingers.

Oh yes, the group. She wondered who the femme-de-jour was on this trip. "Considering the drugging earlier, you'll understand why I'd prefer you eat some of the food, before I place any morsel in my mouth." She slid him a smile.

The blasted man laughed a wide-open whoop, and his beady little eyes glittered. "Of course. You've developed a suspicious mind."

He took the fork and lifted the salad to his mouth. He chewed, swallowed, and handed the fork to her.

She dived into the salad. "Who's on the ship with you?"

"The usual, Craig, Arne, Augusta, and Kandi." The last name was mumbled.

Georgina decided to ignore the Kandi reference and jumped onto the name that sent shards of pain to her stomach.

"Craig, the thug who came to our Boston house and held a .38 gun to my side, demanding to know where you were? That Craig?" She reached over to pull the potatoes and roasted meat, beef she thought, closer to her. She speared a chunk of broccoli with the dinner fork and held it up to his lips. He opened, she fed him the bite, and he chewed.

"How do you know it was a .38?"

"He told me. 'I'll shoot you with this .38 if you don't do what I tell you.' I can identify a .38 among many different gun types."

Tristan lifted the wine glass and sipped. "That was a misunderstanding. He didn't know you were my wife, or he wouldn't have treated you that way. Craig's a nice man when you get to know him. Good to have at your back."

Georgina sliced a piece of meat from the middle,

butchered the beef really, but she didn't trust him. She slid the cross section from the middle and another from the edge onto the fork. She propelled the loaded utensil toward his lying mouth and waited.

While he chewed she continued, "A representative of the FBI and DEA didn't have nice things to say about him. They thought his character was shady, murderous, and of course a threat to people in several countries."

Tristan narrowed his eyes, and she could swear real daggers flew from them. She calmly cut into the meat. The beef's spicy seasonings made the flavor quite good.

He stiffened, grabbed her right arm, and a piece of steak went flying across the room. "When were they there?"

She wanted to reply sarcastically about his verbal skills and lack of table manners as well, but her mind wrapped around the stabbing she had witnessed.

"Six months ago."

He stood, muttering incomprehensible words underneath his breath and stalked out of the cabin.

Damn, she should have had him try the chocolate cake before he walked out. The evening she filed for divorce and disappeared, he'd left her in a state of distress, or so she thought. The entire scene played out in her mind like a bad movie.

She had arrived home late from her last night class, excited to celebrate graduation by calling Gemma. Tristan waited for her, accusing her of holding him back from life. He placed his hands around her neck, and squeezed until she couldn't breathe. Tristan acted odd, like a man on drugs, his eyes with large irises darted back and forth. She attempted to pull his fingers away and talk, but his cell phone rang. Releasing her neck, his hand fluttered about in space like an absent minded professor waving his hand in frustration. Without a word he abruptly left.

She stuffed her hair under a Red Sox baseball cap, grabbed her digital camera and followed. Instead of driving to the yacht club, as she expected, he drove to the docks. The smelly, lobster fossilized seedy docks. Excitement and fear created goose bumps on her skin. This was what they discussed in several of her classes, investigative reporting.

Her roiling stomach clued her not to proceed. She should have listened to her body's reaction. Instead, she forced the shivers to recede, slid the camera over her shoulder, got out of the car, and locked the doors. Double checking to make sure she had secured them.

Georgina followed on foot, sidestepping a beggar who leaned against a lamppost. She bypassed men and women hovering around a burning trash can, and crept closer. Tristan glanced back, and she slid between two large odorous men with tattoos and black leather do-rags wrapped around their heads. Short enough, she passed for a boy. Annoyed with her presence, they jostled her away. She remained in the shadows of a line of ships docked along the south pier and waited.

Tristan talked on his cell and continued down the pier. The clang of the bells, marking the lines, sounded hollow and ominous in the darkness. He had acted like he was at home in this god-forsaken area. Had he been there numerous times before? The shadows of the ships allowed her to follow closely behind. He stopped at a disreputable looking boat, barnacles crusted the bottom and the paint had chipped off the railing.

Georgina slipped behind a barrel. Tristan whistled and the running lights on the boat blinked off. The alarm brought a large dark-skinned man from the underbelly of the boat. He joined Tristan on the wharf. They moved toward the end of the quay. She wasn't able to see or hear, she had to find out what their conversation was about.

She held the camera to her eye and zoomed. Furiously she took shots, not caring about the quality. Both men had looks of fury on their faces and shoved each other. Tristan, off-balance, stepped backward. He removed a small oblong object, pushed a button and the silver glint of a blade flew out. Tristan slid the knife across the man's neck and lowered him over the side of the dock. With a grasp she stopped shooting and her feet gave way under her. She sat on the rough wood of the pier.

Georgina lowered the camera to hang around her neck and shook so hard the barrel moved a fraction of an inch. Holding her breath, she clasped her arms close to her chest as Tristan moved past. She forced her breathing to steady, gathered her moxie, and ran back to her car. Her hands trembled when she unlocked the doors, climbed inside, and removed the camera from around her neck. She leaned her head against the steering wheel and digested what she'd witnessed.

A knock on the window brought her head up. Her heart stopped. She couldn't clearly see through the glass. A beggar came closer and held out his hand. Her heart pounded in her throat as she lowered the pane a crack and threw out a twenty. He picked the bill up, looked at it, and shuffled away.

She recalled fastening the seat belt and starting the car. She drove for hours, making plans to disappear, or so she had thought. It had been necessary to stop at her Boston house to gather money and clothing, but she ditched her car and boarded a bus for Nero, Virginia.

****

Georgina opened her eyes to see that she hadn't

shifted from the bench. The food tray had been removed and a tiny scrape of black was in its place. Damn, she had hoped it was all a nightmare. The stabbing, the kidnapping, it had all happened. She wiggled her toes. Good. Nerves and life. She flexed her calves. A charley horse pinched her calf. The pain, while excruciating, was welcome. She bent her knees and had to balance by holding onto the table. Her mobility had returned but cramps shot through her muscles. She massaged and pounded her calves with her fists until the knots lessened.

Upright, she glanced at the piece of black fabric. The cloth was the size of a beverage coaster. She wrapped two fingers around the material, holding it in front of her. A minuscule bathing suit, complete with a thong bottom. She wouldn't wear it, threw it back onto the table, and noticed the note.

Georgina put on the suit, and join us on the top deck. T

Unsteadily she hobbled to the built-in dresser. All the drawers were empty. Like a circus character on stilts, she made her way to the bathroom. Behind the mirror were all of the essentials from her previous trips on Tristan's yacht. What were expiration dates on deodorant and toothpaste? It didn't matter. She needed to feel clean.

Thirty minutes later she made her way to the top deck, wearing her dirty bathrobe over a skimpy bathing suit. She hadn't a choice but to wear the suit, there weren't any other clothes in the room and she had to have a level of protection, even if it barely covered her. Her layered, wet hair blew in the wind, drying into ringlets faster in the ocean wind than if she had used an electric dryer. She clapped her jaws together and approached Tristan.

"Where's the umbrella?"

"Good morning, Georgina. You're not using an umbrella on this trip. You always look like breakable porcelain. You're going to get a tan." He kept his eyes focused on the newspaper. How long had they been at sea? Had she been out of commission for two days? The paper had to be an old one.

"I'll get skin cancer. You know how sensitive my skin is to the sun." She braced both hands on her hips, her elbows jutting out as an act of defiance and to keep her balance.

"We all have to die of something. At least you'll look good. Take off the robe and lay down. You're still recovering."

"No."

"If you take the ratty thing off, you keep it. If I have to remove the damn thing, it goes into the ocean." His eyes remained focused on the newspaper. Not one page had turned.

She tried to pierce through the large dark sunglasses to get an idea of what he was thinking, to no avail. His voice remained monotone. Damn.

She shrugged out of the robe and with jerky motions placed the stained material on the top of the lounge, within reach. Aware that conversation of the deck hands had stopped, she turned around to look at her audience. Tristan had taken off his sunglasses, and she wanted to swing her bare, white, rear in his face.

"That necklace will make an imprint. Take it off." Tristan stated.

Off seemed to be his favorite word today. A snide remark about imprinting hovered on the tip of her tongue when she heard a screech, stomping towards them was a red-haired harridan. Georgina smiled. Ah, now she'd meet the femme-de-jour.

"Georgina, this is Kandi, Kandi, Georgina."

"That's Kandi with an i. Tristan, I've told you at least a billion times to introduce me as Kandi with an i. It's my moniker." Her voice was high-pitched. She talked out of the side of her mouth. How could she do that? The left side of her lips remained tight together and the words came from the right side.

Georgina rolled her eyes. Did Kandi even know what moniker meant? Georgina smiled and snuggled down onto the lounge, face to the sun, and ears closed against Kandi with an i.

"She's wearing my bathing suit. I just bought the black one and haven't worn it. You gave it to her?" A screech owl had a better tone of voice.

Tristan had replaced his sunglasses and held the paper in front of him. "She needed something to wear. Where are the clothes I picked up for Georgina in China a few weeks ago?"

Georgina lowered her eyelids trying to block out all of their encounter.

Kandi sealed her trap very quick because she softened her voice. "Well she does need something to wear while she's with us. I'll check for the clothes when I've time, honey-bear."

Yeah, like that's going to happen.

"Thanks, love," Tristan said.

Georgina kept her eyes shut and shortly thereafter heard the distinct sucking and moaning of a couple being intimate. Great. Her luck meter had to have a low number today. If her number had had been high, maybe the gross sex fest would never have occurred.

There are different types and levels of retribution, and she knew she was currently in her own personal revenge hell. Tristan the devil, kidnapped her, forced her to get sunburned, while wearing a thong and now this. She didn't care what he did with his personal life, but he was offensive to be intimate in public and force her to listen, to bear witness.

A short time later she had to turn over,

regardless of how embarrassing it would be to reveal her rear. She could not handle the heat. The front side of her body smelled like fried chicken. She could remain with her front exposed and let her skin become a bubbling mass of water blisters, which eventually would become like tanned leather, or turn over and let the other set of cheeks fry.

She rose from the lounge, pulled the robe into a ball, and laid back down using the material as a pillow. Her skin stuck to the lounge cover. She anticipated a painful lift off the next time she moved, but she wasn't going to stand around with her butt cheeks exposed.

She glanced over at the man closest to her as he scrubbed the deck, to see if he was staring. His tongue hanging out wouldn't make a difference, she just needed to know. From the back he looked like Jake. Impossible. She must be getting sun stroke. Could that happen in two hours? The man turned his head toward her, and she gasped.

My god.

Chapter 13

Aleksandr's Freighter

"George, are you awake?"

She squeezed her eyes shut. Please let this nightmare end. Exhale. God willing she could keep her control for one more day. She'd convince him tonight to take her into Norway. Her frown converted into a smile, she lowered the blankets and turned to face Aleksandr.

"Good morning. You're up early?" Oh man, bad terminology if he hadn't had sex last night.

"Great night." He rubbed his hands together in a gleeful way.

"You're feeling better then?" She forced her countenance to appear concerned. Mentally, she celebrated. The Dance of the Seven Veils had worked.

"Ah. No. Thought I was getting a cold, did not want to sneeze on you."

"I appreciate the consideration." She moved her legs off the side of the bed. The black pants were wrinkled, but safe. She held the blanket to her chest and his stare focused on her breasts. The tank top had twisted and the sexy pink bra showed.

"I heard you tour top deck?" He pierced her with his lustful stare.

"Yes. I needed some fresh air." If necessary, she'd remove the butter knife attached to her thigh, stab at the nearest flesh, run like a mad woman, and jump ship. They were a day away from Norway. If she didn't suffer from frost bite, maybe a ship would pick her up.

"Let me show you ship. Very proud of it." He slipped his hands into the pockets of his black wool pants, and rocked back and forth. Heel toe, toe heel. The black turtle neck sweater stretched across his expansive chest as he breathed.

"I'd love that, Sasha." She threw the chambray shirt over her tank, pulled the heels from under the bed, and slid them on. She jerked the blanket off the cot and threw the ugly green cloth over her shoulders like a shawl.

She walked through her cell doorway and waited for him in the hallway. He took her arm into his.

"Lead the way," she said and glanced around. "Viktor isn't with us today?"

"Nyet." His mouth close to her lips, he breathed peppermint into the air. He moved his hand from her forearm, to put around her waist, and guided her through the lower deck.

"Seaman's cabins are smaller inside. Captain's cabin is a suite. Now, ship owners are turning freighters into cruise vessels." Aleksander spat onto the deck floor. "Need transportation vessels, not la-de-da ships. This solid dependable freighter. Built in Canada, nineteen seventy-six."

She gasped. "Will we sink, cruising across the Atlantic and North Sea on an antique ship?"

He shrugged. "Don't worry. Vessels like this last years. This cut through frozen water. Can travel the thick ice of the North Sea in January."

"Would I survive in the water this time of the year if we were to sink?"

"Not to worry pretty head. No sink."

He stopped at the staircase and waited for her to ascend first. Was he being a gentleman or seeking to see her behind? The early morning sun blinded her, and she shielded her eyes. The chill of the Nordic wind took her breath away, but she rejoiced in the clean open space. He came along side of her and pressed her arm to move her onward. Surely none of the men would say cruel things to her with Aleksandr at her side.

"This vessel carry twice its weight. Transports bulk of international trade." He guided her into the navigation room. "Steers like yacht. Here, take wheel."

"No thanks." She backed away and looked through the glass to see large violent waves headed straight for them. Cringing, she pulled the blanket tighter.

Outside again, she looked toward the helm. "It's not a very pretty vessel."

"Da, it is, um, eye-sore." He laughed at his own joke.

She smiled at him and inhaled the brine of the sea and the clean smell of the sun. When they finished the round on the top deck, Georgina found the courage to ask. "So what is in the hold? What did Tristan lose his life over?"

Aleksandr shot her a glare and rubbed his beard. The scruff was gone; the curly black hairs were back in place. Several silent minutes later he led her down two flights of stairs. Her heart quickly picked up speed, pitched and eased like the waves she had watched a few minutes before. If she had angered him, he could leave her down here. Magda could dance using the seven veils, so he had no reason to keep her alive. The short, dark corridor beckoned her and frightened her.

Georgina reached over and touched his arm. "Sasha, it's scary down here. I can't see them, but I hear the scurrying of little creatures. Please let's go."

He stared at her. She didn't have to force a frightened expression, her body shook with waves of fear. Norway was a day away. She'd be able to escape if she got to land. Don't get trapped in the hold because of curiosity.

"Da." They turned around and went up the flight of stairs. She sighed in relief. He glanced at her and smiled. On top deck, she turned to go back to her cabin. He grasped her arm and swung her around to go in the opposite direction.

"Nyet. Time for lunch. Come."

Damn, it wasn't getting easy to get out of going to the captain's cabin. She'd play his game, do what she must to survive. This mantra continued to loop in her head. Yakov had plates, with salad, set out on a linen table cloth. Georgina restrained a laugh.

The table had been set with her wedding china.

"Pretty table setting." She touched the porcelain, the silver, the crystal. Tristan must have cleaned house after she left, and put her china on his yacht. The son-of-a-bitch knew the tableware was important to her. It had been a wedding gift from her beloved grandmother. The dishes kept her grandmother alive in memory.

Rot in hell, Tristan.

"Sit. Eat." Aleksandr sat down across from her. Without a choice, she pulled out the opposite chair and lowered onto the hard surface. She removed the blanket and let the material rest on the back of the chair.

"Wine or vodka?" He held a bottle in each hand, labels facing outward so she could read them.

"Wine's fine, thank you." He filled her goblet to the top and handed it to her. She held the glass aloft. "Cheers."

"Cheers," he repeated and clicked his short glass to her crystal.

"Aluminum."

"Excuse me?" She set the untouched wine on the table.

"I sell aluminum in Russia. Malleable light metal. Good electrical and thermal conductivity.

169

Resist oxidation." He finished his vodka and refilled the glass. Was he spouting an ad?

Ah, the goods from the trade agreement. "Not guns. Drugs? No silver or gold?"

He shook his head.

"A metal that has an atomic weight of twenty-six?" she asked. His face crinkled and his dark bushy eyebrows drew together. He looked at her like he didn't understand how her mind worked.

Her mind buzzed, that was how it worked. He killed people for a light-reflecting metal that people wrap their foods in. She thought of a Green Lantern comic about Russians using aluminum helmets as guerrilla tactics against invasive attacks. The image of Aleksandr with a tin foil hat listening in radio frequencies tickled her. They were all about spying, but the helmets seemed like a conspiracy theory.

"I must ask, Sasha, why is aluminum a hot commodity?" She picked up her salad fork and pushed the anti-pasta around on her plate. The crooked short noodles slid smoothly from side to side. The fragrant vinegar-based Italian dressing agitated her nostrils. The clinking of Aleksandr's silver fork against the china plate irritated her. Her wedding china. Priceless. God, Georgina, get past it. Focus.

"Money. Greed." He had eaten all of his pasta and tore off a slice of the garlic loaf. He handed a piece to her.

She accepted the bread. The soft, white and yellow fragrant yeast squished between her fingers. "I don't understand."

"George, you smart woman. Think about times. Gas prices high. Petrol less available. Aluminum used in airplanes, ships, and snowmobiles. It makes craft lighter and uses less fuel. In near future, it will be the metal of choice for all energy saving alloy products."

Yakov brought in the main course, a wheat noodle dish with chick peas, and served it.

"Thanks, Yakov. I love your cooking."

Yakov smiled and a flush of color, the same hue as her red wine, flowed from his neck to his face. With a silent bow, he returned to the kitchen.

Aleksandr coughed. She met his gaze. "The seven-thousand alloy has a zinc and copper added to make strong and lightweight. This aluminum is most expensive."

Georgina tried to digest this information along with the black mustard seed and ginger. Tristan bought it from Aleksandr. When did Aleksandr get it? Did the US government know about this when the FBI came to her house on a witch hunt? Rather, traffickers hunt.

Aleksandr interrupted her thoughts. "George, your food is getting cold."

"Sorry, Sasha. I guess I'm not very smart after all. I can't see why people died over Reynolds Wrap." She used a silver butter knife to cut off a piece of a long noodle.

"I do not know this...Reynolds Wrap. I do know I will be very rich man after tomorrow." He smiled. If he'd had on a suit jacket, she could visualize him sliding his hand under the lapel like Napoleon.

"How was Tristan going to transport the aluminum? His yacht could not have held the weight in the hold."

"Part of the trade was for me to transport goods to purchase location. My bonus was to keep you as my—companion." His eyes dilated. He moved his hand and clasped hers in his large hairy paw.

She jerked her hand from his. To cover, she grabbed her water goblet and drank a long sip of water. The movement tipped the scales from romance to antagonism. He backed off to refill his glass with vodka and tore off another slice of bread.

"Sorry, mustard seed stuck in throat." She added a cough and a raspy hint to her voice.

He didn't say anything. She reached over, touched his hand and drew little circles. "Now, you'll have money and time to take me shopping for clothes. When should I be ready to go?" She pasted a Marilyn Monroe happy-birthday-Mr.-President smile on her face.

Chapter 14

Tristan's Yacht
One Week Before Trade

Georgina stared in amazement. Jake Callahan held his glorious index finger up to his perfect lips. The sense of relief slowed her heart beat. Realization struck, and she was paralyzed with fear.

His life would be in danger if Tristan found out they knew each other.

Both of their lives would end if Tristan discovered they were lovers.

The brass railing had been polished to a shine, but Jake hadn't left the area. He continued to steal glances at her. Probably because her exposed body was as red as a rooster's craw. The urge to cover up her exposed rear kept her nerves on edge. She stared at him, trying to get his attention and pass a message.

She leaned up, pulled her robe in front of her, and twisted around to look at Tristan. "I've second degree burns on both sides. May I go to my cabin, now?"

"Yes. You won't be any good to me with water blisters all over your skin." He sighed.

"Third door on the left, correct?"

"Right, I don't want you wandering around the deck. Tomorrow, you may be able to use sun screen." He never lifted his head from the lounge, but continued to absorb the cancerous rays.

"Tomorrow?" Georgina failed to keep the horror out of her voice.

"Yes." His tone was firm.

"Where are we headed that provides so much direct sun this time of the year? Florida, Fuji?"

"Not any of your business. Only two more days of sun. Use sun screen." Tristan sighed and turned over onto his stomach. Kandi jumped up and smoothed lotion onto his back.

"Great. My skin should make a nice pair of moccasins by then." Georgina rose from the lounge and with great care drew the housecoat over her reddened skin, giving her a moment of cooling. "I'll need clothes and aloe."

"No," Tristan sharply replied. Kandi sat back on her lounge and watched like a rat contemplating the spoils after the kill.

"You want me to wear a bathing suit all the time?" From years of practice, she kept her face neutral and ignored the intense blazing pain and tightness from the burn.

"You have a robe. You'll either be in your cabin or here on deck with me." He scooted off his lounge chair, lifted his drink off the table, and sipped his tea, or more than likely, Long Island Ice Tea.

"You're a sick bastard, Tristan." Georgina gathered the material around her. Legs tight with the burn she slowly made her way to her room. Her goal had been accomplished. Jake knew where to go, third door on the left.

She was a part of whatever game Tristan had planned, and she didn't want Jake involved. As she passed by the man at the bar, she caught a glimpse of his name badge. Arne. She glanced up to see him absorbing the information as well.

"You there, polishing the rail. Go to my cabin and get my sunglasses. You'll have to search for them. I don't recall where I put them," Arne shouted, sounding haughty and superior.

Tristan withdrew a pack of cigarettes out of his

pocket and moved to the side of the ship beside Jake. He tapped the pack onto the rail, until the shift of cylinders caused a stick to spring out. He laughed and kicked Jake. "He's talking to you."

Jake rose. Georgina jogged down the stairs. Jake followed and flagged her into her cabin. She did and then peeked out the door to see him go into another room.

Georgina went into the shower and quickly and gently washed off the sweat and top layer of skin. She jumped out of the stall, wrapped a towel loosely around her, and stepped out of the bathroom. Jake was standing there, strong, and vibrant. His light brown hair had gotten lighter pretty fast in the sun, highlighting his gray-blue eyes. His crooked nose was a symbol of normalcy for her.

"Jake," she said in the wispy breathy voice she knew he loved to hear. He called it the Marilyn voice. She had showed him her happy-birthday-Mr. President skit, which had lead to some untamed sex on the couch, on the table, in front of the fireplace, and on the stairs.

He drew her into his arms. The heat from her skin was more pronounced when connected with his warmth.

"Oh, love," he whispered. To her delight, he kissed her. When she wrapped her arms around his neck, her towel dropped. She hissed at the pain of his hands connecting with her sunburned back.

Jake lifted the towel and wrapped it around her, which prevented pressure on her burn. He kissed her slow and long.

A kiss of a thousand nights.

A kiss of faith, of hope, of renewal and unbound love.

"Why are you here? How did you know about Tristan? I tried to keep him a dirty, little, horrible secret." She touched the hair above his lip. "You've grown a mustache."

He pushed a strand of her wet hair behind her ear. "Do you like it? Get your lotion, and I'll put it on your back while I explain."

"Oh, yes." She went into the bathroom and grabbed the bottle of moisturizer. He took the container from her. He touched her arm to turn her around, and she dropped the towel. The cooling liquid would ease the tightness and the constant burn.

"Please stop moaning," Jake said. "I need to talk to you about a plan, and I can't think straight with you naked in front of me and sexy." He continued to apply the salve. "I found your bedroom empty. Your purse was in the corner. The bathroom light was on and my note crumbled under the bed. I called Robert told him about the situation and gathered information. A few favors from the local law, and I found out the Turquoise Eyes was docked. I paid a porter to take a week off and came on board." He skimmed the lotion over the top of her shoulders and moved lower.

"Did you talk to Gemma?" Her stomach muscles clamped and tightened.

"No, just Robert."

"Was Gemma there?"

"I don't know."

She couldn't tell him about the threat to Gemma. How could he help anyway? "Is Tristan suspicious about the change of staff?"

"At first, yes, but he doesn't appear to care about who serves his food. Besides, I told him Stephan was my boyfriend, and I knew everything about the yacht."

It was difficult to let him rub the lotion on her burned rear, wanting him the way she did. She turned into him and lifted her arms around his neck. "I love you, Jake. I want you to know that, in case we can't get out of this mess."

He leaned down and kissed her cheek. "We'll get out of this, Gee. I promise you, as long as I'm alive, I'll fight to get you free."

"How?"

"Still working on the details. I promise you two things." Taking his free hand he cupped her chin and lifted her face.

"Yes," she whispered.

"I'll get you off this ship, and we'll be together." He glanced down at his watch. "I've been gone for a long time. I gotta go."

He kissed her, a brief touch of lips, opened the door, and glanced both ways. Silently he slid into the hallway. Georgina peered around the corner of the partially opened door to watch him jog up the stairs.

Tristan stood at the top of the stairs. "Hey. What the fuck took you so long?"

"Had trouble finding the glasses. Didn't want to mess the place up, took my time." Jake reached behind him, withdrew the sunglasses, and handed them to Arne.

"Excuse me." Jake shoved past Tristan who knelt low on the stairs. Looking for her?

Georgina gently shut the door and drew on her robe. Rapid taps on the entry sent her heart to bump against her chest. Jake had returned. The beats skipped, what if Tristan saw them? Had he seen Jake leaving her room? She tightened the belt on her robe and cautiously opened the door.

"Kandi, how sweet. Please come in." Georgina didn't think Kandi caught the sarcasm. Georgina jumped to keep her bare toes from being trod upon.

"I need help."

Georgina could not have been more shocked by the statement coming out of the woman's mouth. "From me? You've got to be kidding?"

She looked down at her dirty robe. In the past,

people came to her for witticisms and money. Kandi couldn't pull off the witticisms, and Georgina didn't have access to money. What could she possibly want?

"Yes." With a huff she stomped over and sat down at the table. "I'm sorry. I know you don't have any reason to want to help me."

Georgina slid over to the bed, sat on the edge, and crossed her hands in her lap. Even the backs of her fingers were burnt, and she only had an inch of moisturizing lotion left in the bottle. Kandi smelled like coconuts and almonds of moisturizing sunburn-protecting oil. Bitch.

"I'm pregnant with Tristan's baby," she blurted out.

Georgina kept her head lowered. She didn't want Kandi to see how much this announcement hurt her.

Shortly after Georgina and Tristan walked down the aisle, she begged him for a baby: someone she could love and would love her unconditionally. He was never ready. Now the marriage was over, and his mistress was having the child Georgina had craved. She wrapped her arms around her waist and tried to hold the pain wracking her body within.

"What do you want from me?"

"To take a pregnancy test. I told him I wasn't pregnant, but he suspects. Tristan wants me to prove I'm not trying to trap him into marriage. I know you don't love him. You haven't kept in contact," Kandi uttered.

Georgina's head shot up.

"You don't, do you? Love him and keep in contact with him, I mean?" Kandi asked in her little-girl voice.

"Kandi, he was my first love, and I'll always have feelings for him." Hate foremost. "I don't want to be in contact with him. I'm not married to him."

"Yes, I know. I overheard your conversation, and I found the divorce papers. So, will you do it?" She was biting her lower lip as a teen would, waiting for permission to go out on Saturday night.

"I don't believe you should hide the news from him." Georgina's emotions were raw. She'd had difficulty carrying on a conversation about Tristan's betrayal and babies with her stomach muscles contracting with pain.

"He doesn't want children. If he finds out, he'll make me get rid of the fetus. I need another month or two, and then it'll be too late for an abortion. He'll adjust. Tristan will learn to want our baby. Please help me, as a woman to another woman. You can't be pregnant right?" Kandi's hands covered her face, her chest rising and falling with the uncontrolled sobs.

The pain rose from Georgina's stomach to cause her heart to catch. The ache was unbearable. "Let me think about it." She glanced over to see the woman's tear streaked face. "Maybe I could think more clearly if I didn't have to sit in the direct sun."

"Done." Kandi wiped her tears with the backs of her hands and rose from the bench. She withdrew a plastic cup from her robe pocket and set in on the table top. "I'll need the sample tomorrow. I want you to pee in this container and give it to me."

"Don't you have an instant test I could take myself?"

"It's not that I don't trust you, Georgina. I need to take the test in front of Tristan. You understand, right?"

Georgina could see by the unhidden smile that Kandi had gotten what she came for. The tears stopped as fast as a child who got the toy she wanted.

"I'll consider your request." Georgina slowly lifted off the bed, walked to the door, and held it open.

Kandi flashed a confident smile and sashayed through the doorway. The thin azure silk cover-up flowed in waves behind her, leaving her strong floral scented perfume in her wake.

The next morning Georgina urinated in the cup.

****

Georgina hadn't had an opportunity to talk with Jake for two days. One of Tristan's staff members seemed to always be hovering nearby. Yesterday, when she went onto the deck, Kandi insisted Georgina have protection from the sun and sit under the umbrella. This may have appeared odd to others as Kandi was a woman who presumably didn't give a damn about anyone but herself. Even Arne sent Georgina a questioning glance. Odder still was that Tristan agreed without argument.

Jake walked into the sunlight, and Georgina's heart exploded. She used her hand to shade her eyes, glanced his way, mesmerized by his broad shoulders and tan chest. Her gaze held his, while he tugged on a T-shirt. She had clubbed her hair at the back of her head and out of the way. Her neck felt hot. She dropped her gaze and squeezed a quarter size amount of sunscreen lotion out of the plastic and placed the tube on the table. Quickly lowering the oil-dripping hand to her breasts, she massaged the liquid in slow circles on one mound down in the valley between them and onto the other bosom. The slightest shift and her nipple would pop out from the skimpy material. Her movements were cautious, but she wanted to cover every exposed inch of her burning skin. Another generous squirt from the tube and she wiped slow circles over her stomach.

An intake of breath drew her eyes away from the task at hand and to Tristan, who had placed his sunglasses on top of his head and watched her with widened eyes. Georgina told Kandi she had feelings for him, and she did have hate and anger. What did

Tristan have in mind for her? He was a shark and would take a bite out of any little fish along the way. He would expect her to be a minnow, but she had become a barracuda in the past two years. She reverently hoped he'd underestimate her.

The wind blew the scent of Kandi's floral perfume to their cluster of chairs before she actually arrived. She threw a blanket over a lounge, removed her bathing suit top and settled into her nest. Kandi grabbed the bottle of lotion, lowered her sunglasses, and stared at Tristan.

Georgina's mouth gapped open, staring at the woman. She shut her mouth, rotated her shoulders to ease the strain of duplicity and settled onto the lounge, which was on the opposite side of Kandi. Georgina glanced at Tristan to see his focus wasn't on her, nor Kandi exposing her silicone enhanced breasts, but on Jake. Tristan brought his piercing stare back to Georgina. She raised her eyebrows in question. He replaced his sunglasses and rested against the lounge.

"Tristan, where are we going?" Georgina asked.

"We're going to catch a current, baby, and fly north."

Great, she got a flippant answer. It didn't really matter, though, since she had faith that Jake would get her off the ship. She settled underneath the umbrella and let the warm ocean breeze flow over her. She dreamed of her lover and contemplated how to get the photos of Tristan killing a man to the FBI.

Georgina pretended to be asleep on the lounge. Jake carried his bucket and mops to the lower deck near the staircase. Kandi had taken her little-girl voice and left. Tristan was at the edge of the ship, leaning on the rail and animatedly talking on a portable VHF radiotelephone.

Jake twisted around, so his back was to the group, and swabbed the deck. He banged the mop against the bucket as he started down the stairs. Her eyes flew wide-open, and her glance met his. She looked over at Tristan, who continued to talk on the phone. She pulled on her robe and followed at a slower pace. Jake placed the bucket and mops in a utility closet. When he turned, she took his hand and pushed him inside. The door slammed shut, enclosing them into total darkness.

Georgina heard a rustling near the floor. She rubbed her naked foot against Jake's lower leg and touched an obstruction at his ankle. He carried a weapon. A gun by the hard metal feel of it.

"What is that?"

"Four inches of stopping power. Gee, not a lot of time. I'm working on a plan. Tonight meet me, aft, around eleven, I'll have a boat ready to take you to safety."

Concentration was difficult with his sexy scented closeness. She burned with hot desire, wanting him so terribly. She kissed his neck, nibbled on his ear, and finally her lips fused with his.

He could give her a baby.

He pulled away. "Please focus. We don't have much time." He put his hands on her shoulders, lowered them toward her chest. As quick as the flicker of a snake's tongue, he drew them away. His hands migrated toward her tan exposed skin, the oil made her skin slick and his fingers sailed right over the swell of her breasts tantalizing her. She craved to have him touch them. Her nipples peaked as the ache surrounded them.

"I want you." She shifted her hand from his shoulder and caught a falling broomstick.

"Shh. Be quiet. I need to tell you..."

She connected her lips with his.

Jake reached over to take the broomstick from her. "I want to tell you I'm with the—"

The door flung back on its hinges. Jake

maneuvered her behind him, shielding her, and reached for the gun at his ankle.

"What the fuck do you think you're doing?" Arne reached around Jake and jerked Georgina out of the closet. "Run back to your room."

How stupid! Instead of listening to Jake she attacked him like a wanton woman, a Kandi. She twisted and planted her feet solidly to the floor. Her body pulsed with panic. She sent Jake a worried glance.

"Go, Gee. I'll see you later tonight." Jake pushed the broomstick against the wall and shoved his hands into his pockets.

Tossing a glare at Arne and a glance at Jake, she ran back up to the top deck. She could overhear them talking, although their words sounded mumbled, and then not at all. They must have relocated to a secluded corner near the stairs. She dropped low to the floor, duck-walked over to clandestinely grab a silver ice bucket off the bar and tip-toed down one level of stairs.

The staircase was only used by the staff, so she didn't fear being found by Tristan or Kandi. They wouldn't lower themselves to be seen going up or down the servants' passageway. Georgina held up the reflecting silver and caught sight of Jake and the side view of Arne. She crept as close as possible, sat down on the stairs, held up the bucket, and listened.

"Damn it, Jake. You'll blow the whole operation. Two years of surveillance, near misses, and you blow it for a snobbish bitch." Arne pushed his finger into Jake's arm. Jake stood solid.

"Watch what you say, Arne." Jake snapped back. "I understand your anger. We're close to finishing the case, but you're talking about what's mine."

Mine. What does mine mean?

"You shouldn't be on this ship. You knew we could take care of everything. We'll protect the bird."

Arne leaned against the wall. Jake twisted, presenting his profile to Georgina.

"I had to come. She needs me." He rubbed his nose. "Just like you needed me in the Caribbean."

Arne grinned. "When you broke your nose. You always have to play the hero."

"I just wanted to save your sorry ass. I can still smell the fish that Dominican threw at me."

"You got the easy end of it, man. He broke three of my ribs. Why'd you never fix the nose?"

"It's a badge of honor. I saved my best friend's life. I should have a T-shirt made." Jake's voice held a hint of humor.

Well, that explained the nose.

"Tomorrow's the trade. Let's close the deal, first. All right?" Arne growled. Not an angry growl, more like an 'I owe you one' kind of grumble'.

"We'll act sooner. Get a ship here tonight to take her off. The SOB has some evil plan in mind for her." Jake held out his hand. Why? Was he waiting for a communication device?

Arne loosened his belt, removed the leather from his pants. "I'll arrange transportation with the port authorities for tomorrow, right before the trade. If you don't keep a low profile, you're on the ship with her. We'll finish the sting without you."

Jake didn't say a thing. Arne didn't flinch, nor did Jake.

"I'll take care of the arrangements. Get back on deck before you're reported missing. Don't do anything stupid." Arne smiled and shoved Jake's arm. Jake headed around to go back up the main staircase.

Arne slid the belt buckle back to review a small computer screen. Smaller and thinner than a Blackberry, the communication device had been worked into the belt. He pressed the flat face of a micro-computer. Cool technology.

"Sea King, Ariel here," Arne whispered.

She leaned in until her bucket bumped against the railing. She snapped the container back and held it close to her chest. Arne closed the clasp and walked closer. Georgina ran up the stairs and lowered down behind the bar. If found out, she'd claim she was trying to mix a drink. She peered around the edge to see who could possibly have witnessed her frantic scurry.

Tristan reclined on a lounge at the front of the ship. Jake jogged to the top deck and shot a glance in her direction. She crawled farther behind the bar, holding the bucket near the edge to get a view. Jake cleared the dishes off the table tops. As he passed by, Tristan extended his leg to stop him.

"Where have you been?" Tristan moved his sunglasses to rest on the top of his head.

"Swabbing the deck. Took care of plumbing. Is there something you need?"

"You stare at my wife," Tristan said in his pompous voice.

"Right. I'm sorry sir, it won't happen again," Jake growled.

"I know it won't. Leave." Tristan lowered his designer shades.

Georgina crept back down the stairs to her cabin. What had Tristan meant by that comment?

****

Georgina leaned against the railing of the aft deck at eleven. She rubbed the pad of her thumb over the backside of her other hand. Her internal radar sent out waves of warning signals. She bit the inside of her lip and continued to play the conversation between Jake and Arne over in her head. The sting! Was Jake a criminal planning to steal the yacht from Tristan? No, because Arne stated they'd been working on surveillance for two years. Jake must be part of the coast guard, and they planned to capture Tristan.

Her heart skipped a beat. If that was the case, why would he tell her he was a photographer? Maybe Arne was law enforcement and Jake was his friend or one of his brothers. Regardless of the spin, Jake hadn't told her the truth about himself. Then again, she hadn't told him either. She loved him, but what type of relationship would they have if they both started the affair with lies? As soon as this was over, they needed to come clean and trust each other.

"What are you doing out here, Mrs. Kaplan?"

She turned from watching the running lights create shadows on the dark ocean water. A chill ran over her body. Craig, who had threatened her with a .38 at her home in Boston, and another lackey, a short stocky man, stood behind him. A childhood saying went something like 'a chill runs over your body when someone walks over your grave'. Would her grave be sooner than later?

"I'm enjoying the night sky." She turned back to look over the railing. "Go about your business."

"I'll show you to your cabin." Craig grabbed her right arm and another man clutched her left arm from behind. She jerked her upper body, but their holds were secure. Craig pinched her skin tight in his hands, bruising the tender surface.

"I'd like to spend a few more minutes looking out to sea rather than being mauled by foul men." She twisted her body back and forth in an attempt to free herself.

"I'd rather that you were a fathom down, but the boss wants to keep you alive." Craig hauled her away from the rail. The scar on his face ran from his high forehead to beneath his granite jawbone. The white line converted the left side of his face into a twisted stripe of evil. "Steve, you go below deck."

The second man released her arm and didn't

hesitate to run down the steps.

"Now, Mrs. Kaplan, I believe it's time I taught you a lesson about respect." He moved his beefy hand around her neck. His breath smelled like fish and beer. A small upper lip blended in with the lower one as he drew his mouth into a straight line.

"Release her," Kandi said, with a forceful deep voice, from behind Craig's back. What happened to the school-girl squeak?

"It's none of your business, puta." Craig didn't glance behind him but continued to breathe heavy on Georgina's cheek and ear.

"Maybe not, but it is mine," Tristan barked as he moved Craig's hand from around her neck, and she exhaled.

Craig's face contorted into rage. His scar became white instead of its usual pink. It must have been difficult for him to hold his resentment in check. He stomped off toward the bow of the ship. Georgina rubbed her upper arms with her hands. Tristan took hold of her waist and escorted her to her room, without saying a word. For the first time, he locked her inside the cabin.

No sign of Jake. The next day, Georgina picked up Tristan's discarded newspaper and inside was a sailing diagram as developed by J.Clark's Gulf Stream. Tristan had mapped out a route which connected the Florida Current with the Gulf Stream. If they didn't get caught in the circle of the course they'd jet into the North Atlantic Drift. The nights were getting colder, so they must be on track. Her tanning session lasted thirty minutes. Free, she hastened to her room.

She suffered through the brutal agony of a shower. The sunburn stung like a thousand pin pricks as the tepid water flowed over her skin, but the shower became her sanctuary. She didn't want to leave it. When it was possible to be murdered at a moment's notice, the pain reassured her she was alive. Had Tristan murdered Jake?

The clear shower curtain flew back on the rod. She jumped back and held onto the shower handle. Blue eyes pursued her form.

Tristan.

She swallowed, forcing the bile back down, and shut off the water. Her hands instantly covered her nipples. She glared at him.

He grabbed her hair and hauled her close. He brutally kissed her, bruising her mouth and inserting his whiskey soaked tongue inside. She broke contact, shoved his hand, snatched the robe from the hook, and covered her body. A turn of her hand, and she tossed the hair already forming into coils from her forehead. She tightened the belt on the robe and stepped out of the shower. Tristan didn't move aside, so she pushed him and ran into the main cabin area. As expected, he followed.

She didn't have a choice but to play his game, his way. She didn't know if Gemma was safe. Fear kept her skin moist. Fear of the unknown and fear of the monster her ex-husband had become.

"I took you because I love you. Now I realize taking you against your will was a mistake. Come with me to talk to my friend, Aleksandr Styopas. He's on the freighter sitting twelve nautical miles to the south of us. Perhaps he could give you a lift back to Virginia." He held out his hand.

She watched his facial expression, or lack of, and ignored his hand. He hadn't said he was sorry or expressed any kind of remorse for drugging and dragging her from her Nero, Virginia home. He tucked his hands nonchalantly into his khaki pants. Why hadn't he even pretended to look regretful?

Curious about the freighter and Tristan's invitation, she walked out her cabin door. She pulled her hair back, and within a few steps leaned against the taffrail and looked out to sea. The peacefulness and tranquility of the water didn't relax her as it normally would have because of the ghostly outline of a vessel adrift in the distance.

The rapid flash of the stern light showed the end of the craft. There were very few safety lights outlining the ship. In the middle of the ocean the freighter should have been lit up like a Christmas tree. Instead, the vessel resembled a huge gray whale waiting to plunge back into the ink black sea.

Shivers cascaded over Georgina's body, reminding her it was November and she wore only a robe. She tried to find security of any sort, pulled her arms close to her waist, and turned to stare at Tristan. His relaxed state concerned her more than the thought of being transported to a freighter in the middle of the ocean. Her mind wrapped around the fact he could simply dump her overboard and leave. Fear pumped like frozen sludge through her veins leaving her shaking.

"You'll wear this," Tristan reached over to the railing and lifted a dress, a tiny bit of shiny, dark gold material. The silky fabric appeared to be of good quality and very small in size. He exhibited his once winsome dimples.

Out of the darkness Kandi whined, "Tristan, its Dior and one of my favorites."

Her soprano voice grated on Georgina's nerves. She must have been hovering nearby while Tristan showed Georgina the freighter. Kandi edged in beside him and reached out a slim hand to reclaim the scrap of a dress. Her brilliant, auburn hair gleamed in the dim light coming from the cabin.

"Georgina will wear it tonight." His cold, precise voice sliced through the ominous night.

Kandi pouted her lips, folded her arms across her azure strapless dress, and took a step back.

"If I have a choice, I'd rather be let off at the

next port. I'll find my own way home." Georgina bit her lip to keep the fury at bay and tasted the whiskey from his brutal kiss.

"Not on your life or Gemma's." The dimples disappeared, and she saw a flash of the evil lurking beneath the surface. The word danger flashed across Georgina's mind. Could Gemma really be in jeopardy?

Georgina seized the dress and walked back into her cabin, leaving Kandi and Tristan at the taffrail to argue. At least she was a similar size; well maybe Kandi had larger breasts. Georgina tried to shut the door, but Tristan had followed her and blocked it with his large topsiders.

Georgina sighed. "Look, I've been very cooperative up until now. I don't think threats are necessary, and you know my family has connections so I could make them. They'll protect Gemma too." Her voice caught.

He chuckled and rubbed the back of his neck as if he expected her to be a fluff-head and crawl into a corner. She longed to toss him overboard. Damn, he made her angry.

"You'll do what I say or she's dead, Georgina."

Goosebumps rose to the surface of her skin, bringing the chill of fear outside. She rubbed her arms. "You're not my husband now, Tristan. I want you to leave."

A tic pulsed in his clean-shaven right cheek. "I'll always be your husband."

"Legally you're not. Remember? You signed the divorce papers," Georgina calmly declared. "I've said this before, I've found someone else."

She envisioned Jake's gray-blue eyes, his crooked nose, and his gentle, sweet smile. He'd mysteriously appeared on Tristan's yacht and like Godiva chocolate with a pre-menstrual woman, disappeared. Had Tristan found out their connection and tossed Jake overboard? Where was Arne? If she could find him, she'd ask him what happened to Jake and to call in protection for Gemma.

Tristan firmly shut the door, leaving Kandi alone on the deck. "You'll never leave me again, Georgina. Regardless of the shards of paper, you're mine. I own you, and I'll make the decisions about your future." He sighed like a parent tired of explaining to a child. "We don't have much time."

That's what Jake said before he disappeared.

Georgina slid the tiny bit of material over her head, easing the robe off as the dress dropped into place. She looked at herself in the pitiful excuse for a mirror. The dress complimented her. The shiny gold-bronze silk made her ordinary brown hair sparkle with copper highlights. The halter style dress barely reached mid-thigh.

She slipped into the bathroom and wiggled into the wet thong. Kandi had already forfeited a bikini, so undies were out of the question. She'd washed the drinking glass size bathing suit. Now a wet thong was under the dress. Nearly naked and alone, she worked through the information, with her threatening ex-husband peering at her like a Peeping-Tom.

"At least the water blisters have healed over," she stated as she turned to see her side view in the mirror.

"Yes, ivory skin is out, tan is in," he stated, as if he were a fashion editor, his eyes focused on her breasts.

There had been no arguing with him and she reluctantly admitted, like the dress, the tan suited her. The color made her turquoise eyes stand out. Her eyes, with their large almond shape and unique color were her one bit of vanity. She squeezed her toes into the three-inch bronze heels she'd been wearing for the past several days. She was just a few inches shorter than Tristan's five-foot-eleven.

He stared at her, a penetrating stare with lids half-lowered.

She turned away, quickly twisted her hair to the back of her neck, and fastened the tresses with a clip. Her diamond earring studs created a prismatic light show in the porthole window, with the dark sea in the background. The water looked as cold as she felt, uncomfortable with a wet bathing suit bottom sticking to her skin and as black as her ex-husband's heart.

****

Georgina closed the journal. She was at the beginning and the end of the tale. Tomorrow she would go with Aleksandr to Norway. He told her she'd have one hour before he met with the buyer for the aluminum. She had to decide on the clothing in that period of time, and then she'd be taken to the hotel.

Radisson Hotel, he'd proudly stated. He wanted to make her first night alone with him special. Her final move to set the end of the game into play was to promise Aleksandr a sex filled night. He hadn't made advances toward her when he said good-night, so perhaps Magda waited for him with veils in place.

Georgina almost felt sorry for him at the excited, joyful look that filled his eyes when she whispered the outline of the evening into his ear. She didn't plan on being there.

God willing, she wouldn't be there.

Chapter 15

United States Department of Justice
Pennsylvania Avenue, Washington D.C.

Jake loosened the tie and unbuttoned the first button of his white oxford shirt. The pin-stripped suit fit snugly since he'd been having regular meals with Gee. He needed to get into a routine at the gym.

"Hell, Callahan, this irks me." Director Richard Long, known as the Razor, twisted the special security area badge from finger to finger. The man's dexterity was well-known throughout the bureau. In his day, Razor could slide in and out of tight places with the greatest of ease. Now, he was simply a tight-ass.

"It's only a compliance issue. You could've written the statement, and I'd have carried it." Jake bent his fingers trying to keep them limber. The gauze wrapping prevented full range of motion. The pain kept him alert. The urgency kept him seated, instead of pacing. And the paradox kept his mind sharp.

"Right-o. The directive was to escort you to the Department of Justice. I'm glad you're not wearing dungarees."

"Just say jeans," Jake said.

"What?" Long whispered.

His Bostonian accent grated on Jake's nerves. The man was an expert in his fields of security and terrorism at sea, and Jake admired him. Except today Jake's thoughts were fragmented, and the man annoyed the hell out of him.

Long's fingers twisted the badge faster as he got excited. "Not a career enhancing order, to escort a wounded agent to headquarters."

"Relax. I'm sure the meeting's simply to report that established and clear procedures were set and followed during the investigation," Jake said. An ongoing case, one in which he planned to become active again. He closed his eyes and pictured Georgina in his mind. The fear she must have felt when she went to the aft deck to meet him that night and he wasn't there. Damn.

"Jake."

Jake's eyelids flipped up as fast as a second hand on a clock. His godfather, John Jacob Maller, stood in front of him. His hair consisted of 90 percent gray and 10 percent black but his body remained physically fit, although thinner as happens to an aging person. "John. It's been awhile. How's Nina? Did she finish her doctoral yet?"

Out of the corner of his eye, Jake saw Long's mouth drop open. Interesting that Long hadn't known of Jake's relationship to the Deputy Director.

"She's well. Nina finishes in May. Her mother would have been very proud of her, God bless her. Thank you for asking. You must be Executive Assistant Long." Deputy Director of the Federal Bureau of Investigation, John Maller, held out his hand to Long.

"Yes sir." Long's back stiffened, and he pumped the Deputy Director's hand as if it was a rusty, old pump.

"Let's go into my office." John dropped Long's hand and with a nod toward his assistant, he led the way into the office, closing the door behind them.

"Have a seat. I've read your case studies, Long. Interesting techniques," John stated as he walked over to the cherry wood credenza and poured a glass of water. "Drink?"

"No, thank you." Long and Jake stated in unison.

Jake sat down in a chair across from John and regarded the office. The dark green walls should have been suffocating, but with the enormous window allowing light into the room, it resembled a peaceful retreat. Long shuffled papers as he removed the documents from his portfolio. Jake stood and walked over to the window, trying to calm his nerves. This was an incredible waste of time. He should be on a plane to Norway. Georgina would be arriving at port tomorrow.

"Sir, Mr. Maller, in this report you'll notice the case has been open for two years without the loss of any of our agents. The protocol was set, the recovery procedures in place." Long shifted the papers in frenzy, shooting some onto the floor, covering his shoe.

"Yet, an agent's life was lost and citizens of the U.S. as well."

"Yes sir. Special Agent Arne Eden and civilians Tristan Kaplan, Josh Hat, and Sergi Berga were killed when the yacht was bombed." Long dropped his 'r's' making his nasal Bostonian accent more pronounced.

"And Special Agent Callahan lost the use of his right hand. So tell me Mr. Long, what happened to the perfect, "sting" is the word I believe you used in the preliminary report?" John's deep monotone voice and his face were devoid of emotion. Long didn't realize it, but the Deputy Director was extremely angry. Jake turned from the window to see Long's expression when he answered.

"Agent Callahan shouldn't have been on that ship. I question if some of the events would have occurred if he'd not been on the yacht. Would they have drugged him? Taken him into the hold for questioning? Started to remove fingers when he didn't answer? If he'd remained on land, as he was assigned, would we even be here right now?" Long locked stares with John and then with Jake.

Jake mentally shook his head at the man's undeniable idiocy. As expected, John hesitated a moment, and with a glare caught and held Long's stare.

"Mr. Long that will be all we need today. Thank you and have a nice flight back to Boston."

Long's mouth opened like a guppy seeking air. He folded the portfolio back into its original rectangle shape. "Deputy Director Maller, if I may disclose spa—"

"I have the records. If questions should arise, I'll contact you." Maller leaned forward in his chair and placed his arms flat onto the desk surface, shifting papers in the process.

Long started to say something else. The man had balls.

Maller pierced him with a black look, which would have sent most humans into hiding.

Long rose from the chair—he was smart enough to know when to fold—and walked out.

The door shut. Jake made eye-contact with Maller and waited for the explosion. He was grateful Long didn't get a chance to go into details about the fight Jake had with Arne before he was captured. Arne believed Gee was part of the trafficking and not a victim. Jake regretted the disagreement more because Arne was killed in the explosion. His heart beat unsteady. Arne was a friend, and they'd been partners for the ten years Jake had been in the FBI.

Jake knew his field career could be over and very possible his career in the FBI would be defunct. He twisted his wrist, trying to regain mobility. First he'd get Georgina, close this case, then worry about his job.

"It's a nice day. Let's take a walk outside." John

grabbed his black overcoat, and Jake followed him to the receptionist area coat rack.

Jake slid on his coat and followed Maller out the building and into the woods he had admired from the window a few minutes earlier.

"As my namesake and protégé, I expected more from you." John lifted a finger and scratched the side of his nose.

"Yes sir." Eye contact remained solid. Jake refused to back down because too much was at stake. He'd probably have to kill a Russian trafficker by the end of the week. But time slipped away and he needed every minute.

"I'm not going to bore you with back story," Jake said. "We arranged a house next to Kaplan's ex-wife, Georgina Barrister Kaplan. We anticipated resolution within weeks, knowing she was the key. Kaplan was searching for her. When he found her, he'd make a play and she'd be the tipping point."

"And she was." John's body was tight and erect, his lips compressed. His anger wasn't necessarily directed at Jake, but at the situation. An FBI agent, a friend, was killed and someone John cared for had been injured.

Jake flinched. "She was."

The man standing before him acted as a second father. To be called on the carpet by the man he respected was difficult. Jake's stomach knotted. He had seen John's aggressive and cold persona with others, but the wrath had never been directed at him.

"Jacob, don't make me pull every bit of information out of you. Your mother, father, and I've been friends since you were an egg and sperm waiting to be put together. If I could've convinced your mother to marry me, instead of your father's ugly mug, you'd have been my son by blood instead of decreed by the priest. Tell me what happened. Not the bureaucratic bullshit either. I want to know what happened to make you a prospect for a desk job instead of a field agent." John leaned against a tree and drew in a deep breath. His hand shook slightly as he lowered his eye glasses from his head and tucked them into his shirt pocket.

For the first time Jake realized how much his job in the field affected his family. He became interested in the FBI because of John and had never regretted the decision to become a field agent. Maybe he should consider a desk job, or quit and be a photographer as he had dreamed of doing in the last few months. He pictured Gee pregnant with his child, and him shooting photos of her.

"Jake?"

Jake snapped out of the trance, leaned forward, and forcefully pressed his fingers into the palm of his hand. A tiny bit of blood seeped through the bandage. He eased off and flexed them back and forth.

"We didn't talk about Kaplan directly, but I knew she was running scared. She took every precaution not to be found. Her mother, not knowing about Kaplan's activities, let it slip she was in Virginia. The mother wanted them to reconcile. This played into our hands very well." Jake paced on the path.

"I lost him after he docked his yacht. He's clever the way he sneaks around. He went straight for Georgina. He used Special K. We found a needle under her bed, where it must have rolled after he stuck her. The lab stated the strength of the K would have brought down a gorilla. She was a rag doll after that, I'm sure. He could have killed her. That's one nasty drug."

"She didn't go willingly?" John asked.

"She wouldn't have gone with him. We retrieved her cell phone from the mail truck earlier. The last call was from Kaplan. He had to have threatened her for her to take such immediate action. I saw her after she got rid of the phone. She was ill, cold and shaking." Jake had read every document in the FBI files concerning Tristan Kaplan, aka Jack Knife, and Richard Mont. He was a sociopath. "Kaplan ran drug deals across several continents. He'd have access to any drug and that would be the only way to get Georgina on the yacht."

One field agent's note stated Tristan was a loose cannon and to expect the unexpected. And Jake wanted nothing more than to kill him after seeing Gee come back from disposing of the cell. Her paleness and faint, delicate condition created a fury in him, anger at Kaplan, and disappointment in Gee. His heart clipped a short beat. She hadn't had confidence in him at the time to tell him of her fears. Maybe he should have pursued her, gained her trust sooner. He could have lost her though and maybe jeopardized the case.

"How can you be so certain?"

"I am. No doubt in my mind." Jake muttered, "Gee bewitched me."

"Son, all women can be a bitch at some point in time. We should not let that affect the outcome of our assignment." John tugged the excess skin under his chin, further proving his godfather had aged. He wasn't the youthful man of the past.

No, not a bitch. She was his, and now she trusted him. Jake recalled the connection they had in the closet. He told her he would get her to safety, and she relied on him. Her soft small hands had bracketed his face. His nostrils flared as he recalled the scent of her skin that day: cocoa butter. Her soft, light-brown hair smelled of lemons. He reached out and closed the limited distance between them. A primal instinct to tuck her close and never let her go had overwhelmed him. The Irish in him rejected the fear of being caught and the consequences if they were found. He should have listened to his intuition.

Jake focused, having realized the amount of time that had passed. What had John said? Oh yes, bewitched, John misunderstood and thought he said bitch. Or, maybe his hearing was not as acute as it once was. Unable to resist grinning, Jake clarified, "She bewitched me. Georgina has an outgoing personality, a clever mind, a saucy mouth, and a body that makes me salivate."

"Christ, son. Don't wax poetry. Are you certain she's not part of the trafficking group?"

"Yes, John. She's innocent as a new born babe. I suspect she'd heard or even saw some action, which is why her ex-husband tried to subdue her with hopes of eliminating her. She could and would have testified against him."

"Hmm." John pushed away from the tree and walked toward the edge of the woods. Near a trio of blue spruce pine trees, he stood staring at the building. He separated his legs, like the stalwart sailor he had been at one time, and clasped his arms behind his back.

"I'm going to marry her," Jake declared, exhaled, and drew in the crisp scent of the pine.

He had overheard fellow agents equate Deputy Director John Maller to a peregrine falcon. The peregrine falcons are the fastest animal alive and can travel at two hundred miles per hour. At this point in time Jake witnessed the relationship between the falcon and John, when Maller turned around and pierced him with an intent dark stare.

"Christ, I don't know whether to tell you to reconsider or to congratulate you."

"Congratulate me. I'm in love for the first time." Jake's entire body vibrated with excitement about the self-realization. He did love Gee and wanted a future with her. The vision of married life and fatherhood flashed through his mind again, more detailed than before.

John stepped forward and drew him into a hug. "Well then, son. When's the wedding?"

"Soon as I get back from rescuing her in Norway."

John glanced at the bandage and a frown appeared on his face. He rambled down the winding sidewalk that circled around to the front of the brick building. A hawk flew overhead, its wings spread wide in a graceful glide searching for food. Jake formed his next statements while he silently followed his godfather. He noticed a cardinal fly past headed for a winter berry bush. Were these signs? Had his opportunity to find happiness with Gee flown?

John sat on a bench near the water fountain on the southwest corner of the building. Jake perched beside him and waited for the refusal. He had the authority to allow him to go or chain him to a desk, and that's what it would take for Jake to remain in the USA.

"If you value our relationship, you won't refuse me." Jake tried to shake off the memories of the attack on him, and his trepidation for Gee.

"Give me the details."

Jake crossed his arms and tilted his chin. He stuffed down his fears for Gee, his love for her, and took on a professional tone of voice. "I stayed with my assignment, Georgina Barrister, for several weeks without leads. The day she got a call from Kaplan was also the day Agent Popov called and stated they were docking in Virginia. Georgina was the target, as we anticipated. Believing I could get to the docks and capture Kaplan before she even had a sighting of him, I left Georgina safe at her house. Kaplan had already left the ship hidden away in a container of refuse. He arrived at Gee's house

201

moments after I left. Arne and Popov stayed with the yacht, and Hat trailed the assignment. We tracked Georgina through the necklace, which led us back to the ship. We didn't want to forfeit the cover, so I offered one of the crew members a few weeks vacation and a couple of grand. I boarded the vessel, claiming to take my boyfriend's place."

"Yeah, right, offered him a reduced sentence you mean." John laughed.

"He didn't think the joke was funny either." Jake rubbed his chin. "I need to work on my arrest humor. Contact was made with Arne and Popov and later to my assignment to reassure her. I made arrangements to take her off the ship. We continued to make progress tracking who Kaplan made trades with and anticipated catching him in the act. He became suspicious."

"Because you took risks with the girl?" he growled.

Jake raised his eyebrows at the angry tone in John's voice. "I never lost control, at least not until I was attacked from behind. The lab indicated I'd been injected with GHB."

Jake walked over and stood with his back in front of the camera mounted on the wall. "Next thing I knew I was tied to a chair with my right hand anchored to a table top. They started lopping off fingers. If it wasn't for Aleksandr Styopas early arrival, well, we both can imagine what would have happened. Arne wrapped my hand and dumped me on a rescue boat. He was my best friend, and I miss him. He put his identity at risk to save me, and he died." Jake rubbed his broken nose.

"So, we're guessing Arne revealed his identity and Kaplan left him on the yacht. Styopas ignited the ship, and we had the loss of lives." John rubbed his eyes.

"We'll know for certain once we get Popov's

report. She'll be able to fill in the missing spaces." Jake tucked his uninjured hand into his pants pocket.

"What about the personal side? Did you work through the possibility Mrs. Kaplan could be involved? She must be clever to have avoided capture for so long." John stood and walked toward the building to stand near Jake.

Jake rocked heel to toe. "At first I suspected she was involved with her husband's trafficking, but she's innocent. I waited for Kaplan to contact her. I knew he would because who could leave such a beautiful and intelligent woman alone for a long period of time? I wouldn't have, if she'd been my wife. I know her. I trust her, and I love her."

Yes, he was in love with her, and he wished he would have conveyed that message before the night the case went to the dogs.

John closed his eyes, and his words sounded like a murmured prayer. "The extent of your injury makes you ineligible to continue the mission."

"The physician stitched them on and assured me there shouldn't be an infection. The hand will be like new in a few days."

"Damn it, Jake, you were lucky to keep your goddamn hand." John paced down the sidewalk and back, stopping in front Jake. "She has the tracking device on her necklace? By the way, the Celtic Love Knot? A little over the top."

Jake shrugged. "I commissioned the piece myself and paid for it, so I could create whatever I wanted."

John snorted.

"And don't worry about my hand. The best governmental surgeons took care of it. May not have complete range of motion, but I have five fingers." Jake smiled, a weak smile, because of all his uncertainties. "I can't imagine her giving up the necklace, because of the knot of love."

They were meant to be together. His stomach clenched. He glanced down at his hand to see the blood had dried to a soft brown. He would not be denied.

"We'll get her out of danger, Jake. We have people in place, waiting for Styopas' arrival." John turned to walk inside the building.

Jake, at his side, withdrew his SAC badge and scanned it. They took the elevators up to the fifth floor and went into John's office.

John opened the mini-fridge and withdrew two bottles of water. He threw one to Jake.

Jake caught the plastic twelve ounce container with his left hand.

John smiled.

"Quick action, quick thought, and caught the damn thing with my left hand." Jake pressed the bottle between his arm and his side, twisting the cap with his left hand. "Remember, I'm ambidextrous."

John removed his coat, hung it on the hook behind the door, and sat behind his desk. He took a swig of the water and sat the bottle down on the brown leather blotter. He put his head on his hands and rubbed. The whiskers sounded like pieces of paper being fanned. "Jake, your parents would never forgive me, and I'm not certain I could forgive myself."

"I'm a professional. The best man in the bureau taught me everything I know."

John's involvement with Jake becoming a field agent was a touchy subject. His parents held a bit of animosity toward John as a result. Jake opened his mouth to argue and press his point. He refused to be denied, he needed to find Gee.

I'll tell him I quit the force, and I'll go solo.

He glanced at John, who was beaming with pride. Jake snapped his lips together and smiled. He'd won without a battle.

Then John's response shook him to the core, reaffirming family support was priceless.

"You know, I haven't been out in the field for a long time. Maybe it's time to make a quality control check."

"Thanks, John. I'll need to have a passport for Georgina. If I need anything in Norway I'll give you a call."

"You won't need to call. I'll be going to Norway with you." John sorted through his pockets looking for something. Not finding it, he rubbed his face as a weary man does.

"Up to this point, as an FBI special agent, I've never lost a case, and God willing I wouldn't lose this one. We'll get Georgina to safety and protect her. Styopas will be brought to justice and rot in a jail hell for the rest of his natural life. So, when do we leave?"

"Amen. Get packed, we leave now." John picked up the telephone and dialed.

Chapter 16

Madame Francine, Clothier
Oslo, Norway

Georgina's reflection in the full-length mirror didn't resemble the girl she once was, rather the woman she had become. Madame Francine led her into a changing room and there Georgina evaluated her pale face, freckled from the sunburn, with dark circles underneath her eyes. The ill-fitting, black wrinkled pants and tank top covered by a frilly shirt made her appear as a refugee, which of course she had become.

"Madame, it's rather hot in here. Must be the excitement of a grand shopping expedition. I'm sure I'll want to try on many dresses. I especially like the black mink hanging in the window." Georgina took a business card from the table and fanned, rapid minute movements, making tendrils of her untamed curls blow.

"Oui, mademoiselle. I'll turn down the heat." Madame Francine's foot was barely out of the door, when Georgina stopped her.

"Monsieur Styopas arranged a private appointment, did he not?"

Madame turned and crossed her thin, pale arms. "Oui."

"No one else is here?"

Madame shook her head.

"Would it possible to open the window and let in a breeze? A breath of fresh air would be nice. I'd like to see how warm the mink will keep me. The fur is lovely." Georgina placed the card back onto the table top.

"Oui. The fur is exquisite. I'll open this door connecting with the dressmaker's room, which has a window." Madame's accent was authentic and the clothes, beautiful. The old world style store was at Gate 38, close to the waterfront. If Georgina's luck meter read high the shop was also near the American Embassy.

Georgina fingered the silks and cottons embroidered with fresh water pearls, yellow, blue, and pink diamonds. Some dresses contained minor gems. She had spent most of her breaks from school in fashion establishments exactly like this with her mother. She focused on the past experience, perfected her rich-bitch pose, and attacked the owner's weak spot.

Greed.

"Madame Francine, if my benefactor is made comfortable with a glass of vodka, I'm confident he'll purchase the long mink in addition to the dresses I've selected." Georgina used her best Bostonian affluent voice, giving the impression she would not accept no for an answer.

She had sat along sidelines throughout the years while her mother revenge-shopped to get back at her father. Georgina witnessed the same expression on the shopping attendants' faces then, as she saw on Madame Francine's face now. Her blue eyes glittered; thousands of American dollars could be made by providing a cup of vodka and a room with a breeze.

"Oui, mademoiselle. I'll move the dresses to the dressmaker's room."

"Perfect." Georgina glanced into the lobby where Aleksandr sat in a small egg shell-shaped chair, with a magazine open on his lap. He looked bored and impatient. Behind him she could see the guards through the windows as they waited out in front of the store. She gathered some of the clothing and followed the dress-laden Madame Francine through the connecting doorway and out of sight of Aleksandr. The smell of starch, cottons, linens, and sewing machine oil greeted her as she walked into the room.

Madame Francine placed the hangers on an empty rack and flipped the hook latch to open the window as wide as the rusted hinges would allow. "Will monsieur want to move back here to see mademoiselle trying on the mink, ah, clothing?"

"Non, madame. I'll walk out when I question something. He's able to see the door we entered. It will be like I'm a model. Please make monsieur comfortable, and I promise to spend all of his funds on this beautiful clothing." Georgina caressed the soft fabric. The desire to wear the dress was strong, but the knowledge of what she must do overrode the hunger to have a pretty frock that fit.

"Your French is perfect mademoiselle," Madame Francine said.

"Merci. Please make sure monsieur is cozy. I plan a long visit in your establishment." Aleksandr hadn't had one sip of vodka in the car as the driver took them from the small sea port of Trond to Oslo. Even with the increased speed it took thirty minutes to get to the quaint boutique. He would appreciate the gesture, and she could use the time.

"Oui, take your time." With a twist of her thin hips, Madame Francine walked out of the room, heels clicking on the hardwood floor, her red silk dress flapping behind her.

The door shut, Georgina threw off the black slacks, lace ridden white blouse, and heels. She slid into a pair of cream wool pants and a quality wheat-colored cable knit sweater she'd selected from a rack. Her heart beat as fast as the click, click, click of

Madame's shoes hitting the floorboards. Would Aleksandr be happy with a glass of vodka, or would he grow suspicious and walk into the room at any minute?

Georgina shucked off the heels, withdrew the pair of thick wool socks from her bra, and pulled them onto her feet. She snatched shears from the work table and held out a strand of hair. It was risky to waste precious minutes cutting her hair, but she wanted to change her appearance, to pass as a boy. Damn, why couldn't one break come her way? Her simple stocking cap disappeared from her room, it would have been perfect. Tears pooled in her eyes with the thought of Jake and the day he arranged the haircut for her. She blinked away the salty moisture and snipped. Three huge chunks of hair flopped over her fingers, and she dropped the tresses into a rag bag. Within seconds her hair was cut into odd shapes, close to her crown and at the nape of her neck. She set the scissors on the table, closed up the sack, and tossed it behind the rack of clothes. The canvas filled with memories hit the floor with a muted thud.

She climbed onto the table top, grabbed the window ledge, and pulled herself up. Her socks made her feet slide down the wall. Falling back to the table, she heard the click, click, click of the owner as she returned. Georgina placed her fingers in the grove of the window and bounced off the table with her feet. The excitement of success made her heart beat as fast as the bells ringing in the square. At the top of the window, she lowered her right leg over the side, the other leg followed, and she slid down to the ground. She ignored the shock waves of electricity running through her legs. A quick shake and she removed the stolen sunglasses out of her pants pocket, wiped the sweat off her face, slid the shades in place, and ran.

In all of their travels, the GBs never visited Norway. Much to Georgina's regret, she didn't know which way to go. She needed to stay away from the docks. The wind carried the scent of fish, so the docks were to her left. To the right, groups of people, children, men, and women, moseyed down the sidewalk. Joyful folks sharing a day of shopping, capitalizing on the freedom they probably did not appreciate.

She paused in front of a coffee shop. A calendar in the window indicated the date was November twenty-eight. It was after Thanksgiving. Georgina hugged her arms close to her body as silent tears fell. Gemma would have already given birth to little Bobby. A catch in her throat caused her to falter. Gemma and the baby had to be safe. Georgina touched the glass, glanced at her reflection in the store window, and reaffirmed her self-worth. She was determined to regain her freedom and have a normal life.

Chills racked her body. She used the backs of her hands to wipe away the tears, and blended in with the Christmas holiday shoppers. At five-foot-five and with a bulky sweater covering her hips, she appeared to be a teen. As long as no one looked closely at her feet, she should be fine. The cold wind swirled a light dusting of snow on the sidewalk. Her socks became soaked, and too soon her feet were numb.

Run, walk, dodge, and hide in the crowds. The mantra kept looping in her head. The rhythm helped keep the panic of being caught out of her thoughts, and the pain from her frozen feet at bay.

Georgina recognized Viktor and Nikka's voices before she saw them. She inconspicuously merged into a family of three, with the boy resembling her in apparel. The family moved forward. She hovered close to them until they passed an alley. She ducked into the passageway, and with short, quick breaths of terror, she pressed against the hard, rough brick.

The alley smelled of rotten vegetables and soured milk. She held her breath and occasionally sucked a quick gasp between her teeth. Fear of a small, furry creature running over her feet and the angst of being discovered, made her shake uncontrollably. She crouched down to hide, to blend in with the pale brick of the building, and wrapped her arms around her knees.

Georgina twitched at the nearness of Nikka's voice. "I know it was her," They stood within inches of the alley. She kept her head turned toward the entrance, watching for the slightest indication of being seen. Would she be found? If so, she would fight. Capture was not an option.

"Hair too short. It was boy. A teen," Viktor said, a little too loudly. "We are wasting time."

Georgina waited until their voices faded and peeked around the wall to look both ways. Viktor and Nikka jogged toward her, one block down. Her breath caught in her lungs, as Viktor made eye contact. She could swear she saw him wink as they turned the corner. Her heart tightened. She might be able to escape. A group of migrants were crossing the street, and she maneuvered into the midst of them.

"Excuse me. You've an American voice. Do you know where the American Embassy is located?" Georgina asked running her hand through her short cropped hair. She lifted her sunglasses to the top of her head.

A petite, dark-haired girl with a yellow tongue ring and ratty backpack pointed toward the noon sun. "At Embassy Square. Fifteen blocks south."

"Thank you. Where is the rail transportation?"

"That's where we're going. Come-on." The girl bent a tattooed index finger, urging Georgina into the group. She merged with the merry band of backpackers.

"What street am I looking for?" Georgina asked the smiling youth. Although Georgina was just a couple of years older, she had aged centuries in the last few months.

"Drammensveient, number eighteen."

"What about buying a ticket, will they take American dollars?"

"Only if it's crisp American money," she said. They jogged down the stairs to the ticket machines. The backpackers took off to the right to go through the turnstile.

"If they won't take American money is there a bank nearby to exchange for Kroner?"

"Afraid not. Too late." The sweet girl waved good-bye and rejoined her friends, who had gone through the gateway.

Georgina thanked her guides and watched as they hopped on the train.

She glanced around and walked over to the ticket agent behind the plate-glass window. As she waited in line, she reached her hand inside her underpants and withdrew a twenty dollar bill. At the counter she handed the bill to the man behind the cage. "I need to go to Embassy Square."

"Only accept Kroner." He didn't lift his eyes to look at her.

Most European countries shut down business earlier than American cities. From what the backpacker stated it must be after three-thirty, so she couldn't exchange the money. Convincing him was her only hope of escaping. "It's after three-thirty, the banks are closed. Please, won't you accept American dollars? Sixty Krone or twenty American dollars. You can keep the change."

He had small, squinted eyes, which drew attention to the frown on his face. His gray military jacket emphasized the silver of his hair. A tie knotted so close to his neck she was surprised he could talk.

"199 Krone. Not refundable. Minipris ticket. Unlimited travel. All destinations."

Damn, forty dollars. She'd have to leave her hundred with him. "How much for a day ticket?"

"60 Krone."

Twelve dollars, much better. "It's a crisp twenty."

She smoothed the twenty out on the counter top. His glance met her stare, and she knew the moment his mind changed. A flicker of sympathy flew across the bright blue eyes.

He snatched the twenty from her hand.

"How many stops?"

"Three." He handed her the pass through the square cutout in the glass window and met her glance. "The train is departing." He nodded toward the track.

She pivoted. The portal to her freedom was closing. Georgina ran, twisting to get through the turnstile. Eyes focused on the slide of the electric doors, she bumped into a hard chest. Nikka grabbed her arm. Without a second's thought, she reached into her pants pocket and withdrew Madga's knife. She jabbed the blade into his hand. He jerked back and released her arm, the knife wobbling back and forth like a grotesque Halloween trick. She exhaled, sprinted to the train, turning sideways to slip through the train doors.

Her sock snagged on a bolt. The sensor opened the door. She jerked the sock free and the doors slid closed again. Nikka raced forward as the train set in motion. She craned her neck to see out the window. Nikka sucked on his hand. The knife, grasped tight in his other fist, dripped blood on the platform.

Georgina lowered onto the nearest seat and took

a deep breath. She glanced around at her fellow travelers. They stared back. An elderly woman clutched the arm of a bald, pinched-faced man, putting as much space between Georgina and her as possible. Had they witnessed the stabbing?

She crossed her arms at her waist, hugging herself. The horror of her actions and the apprehension she could be captured caused her to convulse. People around her moved to other seats.

Control, breathe, relax. The shudders reduced, and she leaned back against the seat. In a trance, she watched people leave and enter the train with each stop. An aura surrounded her, or maybe it was the socks without shoes in November, because the seats near her remained vacant. She tugged the socks higher onto her legs, nearly reaching her knees.

At the third stop she rose and held onto the silver metal bar, ready to jump off the train and seek asylum. The doors squeaked open and the stench of the dirty hot oil from the rails assaulted her nostrils. Georgina placed a finger under her nose and dashed forward. She jogged up the stairs and exited the station. The shift from dark train station to bright sunny day created a black spot in her vision. Her eyes adjusted and she noticed the white lettering on an iron sign. Drammensveien. According to the backpackers, she needed to find Drammensveien 18.

"Georgina."

She ignored the shout and took flight. What was the probability? It was logical, of course, that they would check the embassy. But, damn, why couldn't she get a break? She ran along a black iron fence that surrounded a building as she searched for a sign to indicate eighteen Drammensveien. The black iron seemingly disappeared and became a hedgerow of bushes that flowed over onto the sidewalk.

Her breath came out erratically, and her

stomach muscles braided and bunched. The heave rushed forth like a broken faucet, her breakfast of toast and tea flew into the bushes. Damn, what timing. She glanced around to see no one had spied her, and took off at a fast clip down the sidewalk. A few blocks later, there on the corner, an angular black brick building rose high in the sky.

She'd arrived at the embassy. She spit out the excess discharge, peeked around the corner, and spotted a guard. As an American, they had to help her, didn't they?

She wiped her mouth, took a quick glance back, and darted around the corner, propelling into a solid body. Strong hands held her close to a tall broad chest, the tears of frustration and defeat spun unchecked down her face.

"Georgina Kaplan?" a deep voice asked.

"Who are you?" Georgina didn't recognize the voice, but he was American. His menthol scented breath created turmoil in her stomach. She clenched her hands against the man's wool overcoat and struggled to be released from his firm grasp. She swallowed the bile and lifted her head. The first thing she noticed was his beak of a nose, then piercing dark eyes with glints of humor, topped off by graying hair.

"I'm Deputy Director John Maller with the FBI." With one hand, he reached into his overcoat and pulled out a small, leather case. He flipped it open and showed her an official-looking badge. At least the eagle nested on the leaves appeared to be authentic. Relief made her knees weak. He was an American, a government official, and a solid force.

"We need to go." He tucked his arm around her waist and led her down the street.

Wait! They were bypassing the American Embassy. She dug her cold, tender heels into the wet concrete sidewalk and glanced at place of safety. She didn't trust any one. He could be lying. The badge wasn't open long enough to determine if his credentials were real. He didn't offer her proof he was who he claimed to be. Why wouldn't they go into the consulate?

"Where are we going?" She was proud of how firm her voice sounded, considering she was shaking in her socks and her stomach threatened to erupt again.

"To the police station. I've got a car waiting at the curb." Although his quiet calm voice was convincing, she didn't trust him. Her luck meter had to be low.

"I'll just go into this building, right here." She pried his fingers from her waist and tried to wave to the guard at the gate. Maller had a chest as wide as one of the No Necks. The olive green of the guard's uniform never looked as good to her as it did at that moment. Her feet prompted her forward, until she felt a pressure on her arm. She glanced down. Maller had a firm grasp on her forearm.

"I'll take you to Jake," Maller whispered near her ear. The words were politely spoken, but had an edge. His dark, dangerous and creepy tone made her shiver.

"How do I know I can trust you?" Despite the strands of hair jutting out at odd angles from her head, she tried to bestow grace and dignity.

"You can." A scowl transformed his beak into a replica of Cyrano de Bergerac, drawing the tip almost to meet his lips. Not an attractive man. Was he a serial killer or liberator?

"Why didn't Jake meet me here?" She pulled away.

"He couldn't. Come on." He tugged at her arm. Had Jake been injured? He would have come if he was able. Or this man lied.

"Tell me something personal. Something only

Jake and I would know." She replied hotly, while looking back to see if the guard, a few steps away, took notice.

"We're wasting time." A brief flash of irritation crossed over his narrow face. She stared at him incredulously. If he knew Jake, Maller would know something personal. He would say something, and she needed to hear the words, hoped to hear them, to reaffirm Jake was alive.

"Sir?" the guard shouted as he approached.

"Bottle of water, private area, beach towel cleanup," Maller dryly replied and dropped his hand from her arm.

Georgina's mind quickly replayed the night Jake had asked too many questions and she dumped a bottle of cold water on his lap. She tapped his pants with a beach towel, which was her first exposure to his tightly muscled body. She chuckled, appreciating the memory.

The guard arrived with one hand on his shoulder communicator device and one at his belted waist. "Miss, may I help you?"

"No. Sorry. I'm pointing out the features of the building to my husband. See, hun, he's nice. Thank you for your offer." She glanced down at the ground and moved her feet to be hidden under her pant legs, and then glanced back to the guard's face. The guard didn't appear to be buying her story, but Maller must have flashed the badge at him because moments later the guard's military-clad body and government issued black boots turned and moved out of eyesight.

Maller tugged her arm. She glanced into his frowning face and skipped to keep in time with his wide stride. A solid black Audi idled at the curbside. A uniformed driver, stereotypical clothing, black suit, white starched shirt, thin tie, got out and opened the door. Maller waited, glancing both ways, until she settled onto the seat. The heated, beige leather seat wrapped around her. She wanted to remain in its decadent warmth until Jake took her back to their safe, normal life. Cripes, what did normalcy consist of? She had dreamed of living without lies, and no fear of being captured or killed. Could she live the average life?

"Where is he?" Georgina asked.

"At the police station interviewing Styopas."

"They caught him?"

"Yes, coming out of Gate 38."

"What about the bodyguards?"

"Styopas was alone. Provide a description and we'll track the bodyguards."

She nodded. Odd, she had been moments away from being safe. Instead she had shorn hair and wet feet. "Is Jake okay? Has he been injured?"

"Why do you ask?" He raised an eyebrow in question.

"Only death would have kept him away," she softly replied, while pushing her feet flat onto the floor to let the carpet absorb the moisture.

"He intended to meet you on the yacht. An incident happened, but he'll be fine." His keen, bird-like, brown eyes assessed her. "You seem confident of his loyalty."

Georgina combed her fingers through her short hair. The lump she'd had in her throat since Jake disappeared from Tristan's ship evaporated. Her heart expanded in her chest, and she rested her hands over her womb. Like a deflated balloon, she sighed and pressed her back against the seat.

"I am. He's okay then?" She turned her head, her face seeking the warmth of the smooth, soft, beige leather. She wanted to see his face when he answered.

"Yes, he's fine." Maller stared at her, like a hawk evaluating its prey. She squirmed, conscious of her feet and moved one damp foot to be on top of the other. Shivers ran over her body.

"Could you find out about my friend, Gemma Sheraton? If she's safe?"

"She's fine. So is her son. They're staying with family."

Tristan had lied. Thank God. "I need a pair of shoes. I had to lose mine when I escaped."

"Yes, sorry, I didn't think of it." He leaned forward and told the driver. "What size of boot, Georgina?" Maller asked.

"Seven," she answered.

He dialed a number on his cell. "Get me a room at the Grand Oslo Hotel." He hung up and turned toward her. "Jake claims you make him a better man."

The sound of his voice wasn't unemotional as she would have expected from an FBI agent. His tone held a bit of tenderness, surprise, and question.

Maller's hawk-like gaze unnerved her. How should she respond? What was Jake and Maller's relationship that Jake would tell him this?

She closed her eyes. No answer would be forthcoming. She didn't know this man, and until she saw Jake with her own eyes, she couldn't truly trust anyone.

****

A deep voice penetrated her sleep. "Georgina. We're at the station."

Slowly and cautiously she opened her eyes. FBI Agent Maller had been nudging her. Would she ever peel apart her eyelids to see normal surroundings again?

"Sir?" Georgina squeaked out.

"We're at the station." He picked up a shopping bag. "Here are fresh socks and boots if you'd like to change."

She removed the damp socks and slid into the

warmth and security of the leather half-boots. "Is Jake here?"

"Yes. He'll be inside."

Her hand stilled as she reached for the seat belt. She jerked her head to look at Maller, dizziness encompassed her. "Is Jake FBI?"

Why hadn't she considered this possibility straight-away? How could she have overlooked asking?

"The best in the bureau." Pride laced his voice, and his smile confirmed the truth.

Jake was FBI, which meant he had been planted next door to her. That explained why the Smiths disappeared overnight, why Amber was available on a Sunday afternoon and insisted on a release form, and how Jake arranged to be on Tristan's ship. It also explained why he spent so much time with her.

She hadn't blindly fallen in love with a pirate, but a man who was doing his job and his duty to his country. Georgina had been a means to an end. Damn lustdom and her traitorous body for trusting another man. Despite her nervous stomach and heart quickly gathering speed, she knew what she had to do.

Chapter 17

Norway Police Headquarters
Norway

"Where is she?" Jake roared.

Rivulets of sweat poured down Aleksandr Styopas' face. Reluctantly, Jake admired him his fortitude. When they picked him up outside Gate 38 he hadn't said a word, nor had he tried to escape.

"I do not know. We were to meet at our hotel room, after she completed shopping at Madame Francine's," Styopas paused, "for a long love-making session."

Jake's glance met and held Styopas stare, his snake-eyes glittering under the florescent lights.

Jake wanted to plow his fist into the villain's smiling face. A guard stepped forward with his hand on his keeper, his fingers resting on his battalion.

"Mr. Callahan, it is wise to remember you are a guest of the Norway police authorities," Karl, the Norwegian ambassador assigned to assist them, said.

"Ah, angry boy, do you forget you are not in America?" Styopas pointed to the two-way mirror, where others were watching. "I am protected by Geneva rights."

"What hotel were you staying at?" Jake kept his voice as monotone as possible. Fear that Styopas was correct made his heart stop and pound once again. He visualized Gee in his head. She'd never give in to Styopas. The man lied, but the declaration fractured his sense of self and his ability to protect the woman he loved.

Aleksandr leaned over and whispered into his attorney's ear. They spoke in Russian. A translator hadn't arrived yet. How difficult could it be to get a translator? The USSR butted up against this country. Numerous multi-language individuals were available. However, they couldn't find one who spoke his derivative of Russian.

"Radisson. I wanted my lover's stay to be as American as possible, since she, um, homesick for Boston." Styopas rubbed his face and then lowered his cuffed hands to rest on his lap.

Jake narrowed his eyes, ground his teeth together, and flexed his hand. A spot of blood leaked through the brown leather of his gloves.

Special Agent Candace Popov whispered into Jake's ear, "I'll go verify."

Jake nodded and led the way out of the room. Keep your friends close and your enemies closer. Kandi had played her role well. While on Styopas' ship, she had gained the support of several of his employees and attained written evidence to put the trafficker in jail, for life. She had obtained sufficient documentation to send Tristan Kaplan to prison, if he had survived the explosion. She dashed down the corridor and entered a room.

Jake followed and fell against the wall outside the office door. He put his head into his hands and rubbed them over his face. Georgina was out there, running scared.

"I need to find her." His voice echoed down the hallway.

A few minutes later, the door opened and closed. Agent Popov nodded her head. "Aleksandr has a room at the Radisson Royal Garden Hotel. The staff never saw a woman with him. This doesn't mean that she wasn't."

Popov's opinion of Gee radiated through harsh

tones with sharp endings, and the scorn pasted on her face.

Aleksandr? Jake sent her a glare.

She opened her little black book. "A Madame Francine from the clothing store has been located and is en route to the station."

Candace's dirty blonde hair had been pulled back in a clip and rested on the nape of her neck. She had on a black business suit, white shirt, and low heeled black shoes, which presented an opposite image of her yacht apparel.

"I see you changed your hair color. Didn't like the red, Kandi with an i?" Jake snarled as he stated it. "You didn't mind your role as Tristan's confidante. You certainly bared all."

"You're such a hypocrite. You enjoyed your assignment more than I did. At least mine couldn't get pregnant." Her voice held hints of cynicism? Censure?

Jake's head whipped around. He grabbed the lapels of her suit jacket. "What are you talking about?"

"On Tristan's ship I did a pregnancy test on your little princess. She proved positive, and she hadn't been with Tristan in over two years. He was livid. Congrats, you're going to be a father." Rage radiated from her stare, along with sadness. Jake wasn't the only one who'd fallen for his assignment. Popov loved Tristan Kaplan.

"Jake, release Agent Popov," John demanded as he marched down the hallway.

Jake gritted his teeth, released her, and stepped back.

"Agent Popov, I want to see your report at twenty-hundred hours," John said on a sigh.

"That's in one hour," she blustered.

"You better get started," John stated, in his official, straight-tie, Deputy Director Maller tone of voice.

"You don't want me to help interview Madame Francine." Bitterness flew from her mouth, as she flung her purse over her shoulder. A small book fell from the bag, landed on the floor, opening to the middle. Gee's handwriting glared at Jake from the pages.

"Stealing evidence, Agent Popov?" Fire raged throughout Jake's body heating him to fury as he bent down to pick up the manuscript. His fingertips vibrated with the urgency to flip the pages and read Gee's words.

John pried the volume from Jake's tight grasp.

"I wanted to get it fingerprinted and bagged," she mumbled.

Jake glowered at her and pivoted striding toward the interrogation room.

"We're not done with this, Jake," Popov shouted. "My assignment didn't make it out alive, should yours?"

Her flat shoes pounded on the cement floor as she stalked down the passage. A door squeaked and slammed shortly after.

Jake flipped back around to John. "I want to read it."

"Later. She's in the viewing room."

Jake silently slid into the semi-dark room. His heart rejoiced at the sight of her. She looked pale, and her hair had been haphazardly cut. He wanted to run forward and tuck her into him. Assure her he'd protect her from this day on.

"I don't know," she said in answer to a question and sighed.

"Did he meet with other people?" The interrogator should ask her the routine questions at a later time. Instead she had to view Styopas sitting a few feet away, with only a secure glass between them.

Jake glanced into the connecting room as John entered and sat down at the table across from Styopas.

"Not that I know. Except for a couple of hours each day, I stayed in my room." She shoved a short strand of hair behind her ear more from habit because it wasn't long enough to catch. She glanced at him. Her hands shook as she crossed her arms at her waist.

Their gazes met again. His heart beat as fast as the rods on his Thunderbird. Her bitter cold eyes held no affection. An arctic chill ran over his arms. She was angry. He'd talk to her and explain. But his confidence wavered the longer she maintained the freeze out.

"Could you excuse us, please?" Jake calmly commanded.

"We need to finish the interview." The agent's frown didn't affect Jake. The need to hold Gee in his arms was too strong to ignore.

"No—" she screeched.

"She's leaves tomorrow, early in the AM," the man admonished.

Jake's teeth hurt from clenching them together. "Leave us, right now."

The agent rustled papers, threw his chair back, and scampered out of the room.

Gee stood and started toward the door.

Jake walked in front of her, stopping her exit. He wrapped his arms around her and tugged her close. The sensation of holding her in his arms put his mind in a better place, and his heart filled with a sweet ache. He inhaled her scent, a merge of jasmine and vanilla. She wiggled out of his arms, extracted a man's handkerchief from her pants pocket, and blew her nose.

"Gee." Deep sadness invaded him. She had incredible strength to survive the last several months, alone, and separated from her family. She'd never given up, and she'd escaped her captor.

"Let me get you to the hotel." He sidled closer to her and placed his face to the side of hers. His breath flowed over her and blew short coils of hair out into the air. As intended, she turned her head and her beautiful turquoise glance met his. An inch. If he moved an inch his mouth would connect with hers. It had been so long since he touched her skin, kissed her, and made love to her.

The spell lost its power.

"Thank you." She lifted her arm and wiped her eyes. "I'm ready to go."

Her tart tone of voice ripped through his heart.

"Are you okay?" he whispered.

"Yesss," she blubbered. Tears cascaded down her face. Her hand shook with such ferocity, she could hardly hold onto the handkerchief. She wiped her tears with the sleeve of her sweater.

He pulled her close again, as she sucked back the sobs. "Take your time. We'll leave when you're ready."

Georgina's throat tightened, as she swallowed repeatedly trying to get control. Possibly, she only had the one shot to get her message across. An emotional outburst could not get in the way. "I don't want you to take me to the hotel, Jake. I need to sort through all of this."

"All right. Rest. I'll see you in couple of hours." His calm, controlled voice helped her to regain her composure, somewhat.

"No! I nee...ed time." She sounded as if she had a cold. Her throat hurt and tears dripped down her face. Her mind couldn't get past the fact she'd been an assignment, part of his job.

He opened the door. Outside in the hallway the agent who talked with her waited.

"Take her to the hotel. Make sure Mac drives.

You guard her with your life." Jake's glare alone should have set the man to trembling.

The agent swallowed, his Adam's apple moved up and down. He nodded.

In front of Georgina's hotel room, her legs refused to walk over the threshold. Her escort waited inside, holding the portal open. His right eyebrow rose so high it almost disappeared into his cap. She pressed forward, and he silently exited. A click, a whoosh, and the door shut, leaving her alone in a safe warm place.

Georgina removed her clothes. She washed out the undergarments in the sink and hung them on the antique heat register, resembling the folds of an accordion. She climbed into the shower, twisted the knob with a red band around it, and waited for the water to cleanse her. Her fingers wrapped around a white cloth, and she scrubbed her body until her skin was crimson and tender. Her hair, washed twice, stuck out like little shards of wood, and her heart had hardened into stone. She leaned her head against the wet cool tile and cried tears of remorse, of love lost, and of the unknown.

Georgina didn't have any pajamas or clean clothing to put on. She dried off and set the alarm for seven AM. Tomorrow, she would return to Virginia and see her godchild. She'd wrap herself into the comfort and warmth of Gemma and Bob. A plan of action firmly made, she climbed under the covers and fell into an exhausted sleep.

Too soon into slumber, Aleksandr appeared and chased her down city streets with a long blade made of aluminum. A shrunken skull swung back and forth on his black Gucci belt. She hurried as fast as her bare feet would take her through the turnstile and jumped onto the platform. The train squealed in the distance. Aleksandr was quick though. He must not have had vodka to drink as he drew closer to her.

He reached out and the head hanging from a sailor's rope at his side turned, revealing Tristan's face with his dimples fully exposed.

Aleksandr grabbed her arm and shook her. His mouth moved, but she could not hear what he was saying. The train arrived with oil and sparks flying into the dark night. The electric doors of the car opened. Gemma stood in the doorway, calling out a warning.

"Georgina." Strong arms wrapped around her shoulders and pulled her into freshly laundered cotton. She beat her fist against his chest until she heard his soft, calm voice.

"Gee," Jake said, and kissed the side of her forehead.

She inhaled his familiar woodsy, ambry scent, a far better smell than the oil and sulfur from the rail.

She glanced around. The room was unfamiliar. A vague glow came from an open doorway connecting her space with another and illuminating his face. Her journal lay open on the side chair, a broadcloth shirt and black wool jacket had been thrown on the dresser.

Jake.

"I'm sorry." Her dry throat wouldn't let words pass through with ease. She wet her lips.

"Don't be. It's understandable you'd have nightmares after all you've been through."

"I missed you so much." She dropped the blankets and pressed her breasts into his hard, muscular chest.

He kissed her, a gentle kiss on her lips. "I love you."

Her heart beat with a new urgency. She pressed her cheek against his bristled jaw. "Jake."

His fingers ran through her shorn locks. "Your hair is short."

She grasped his hand and moved it away from

her curls. The haircut reminded her of her trials. Gauze had been wrapped around his hand. She pulled the bandage closer. Why hadn't she noticed this at the police station? Maller said Jake had been injured.

She licked her dry lips again. "What happened?"

"Injury on the job. Let's talk about us." His lips felt hot on the side of her face.

"The job." She jerked and climbed back on the bed tugging the covers with her. The soft cloth touched her chin and her breasts, reminding her she was naked. "The job. I was the job. You romanced me to get to Tristan."

He scooted nearer. "No. Yes."

She couldn't back away any further. The question: did she want to run or should she stay and fight for him?

His strong fingers pried her hands away from the sheet. He wrapped his hand around hers, making a circular motion on her palm, a comfort, a loving habit from the past.

"Yes, you were my assignment, but I fell in love with you when you quizzed me about photographers. I denied my obligations the night of the rain. You became the wife of my heart."

Chapter 18

Grand Oslo Hotel
Norway

Georgina jerked her hand back and held her stomach. She clamped her teeth down to keep her lips from quivering. Her fingers shook as she smoothed down her hair. "How did you find me so fast?"

"We tracked the necklace." He frowned and moved his hand to rest on her leg.

She reached up to touch the jade pendant. The talisman that helped her keep faith throughout the trials she'd had the last few weeks. She had known as long as she wore the necklace he could find her and rejoiced in the thought the silver circles were a sign of his love.

"So, the Celtic knot was a plant and not a gift. Why?" She was surprised her tone remained calm.

"For you. The gem contained a tracking device, but the necklace was a gift from me. Please listen to my words. Listen to your heart, Gee."

"All knots, huh," she said under her breath. She fisted her hands.

His gray-blue eyes glittered with anger and possibly fear lurked underneath. "Please come back to me."

"No." Her voice was hard, like a shovel hitting a rock while digging.

"Here, take this back," she unclasped the necklace and tossed it to him. "The token doesn't have meaning for me, and there isn't a reason to track me any longer."

He caught the pendant in his left hand; the chain snaked down and slid onto the floor.

"The necklace drew us to you, and I'm thankful, because it helped me to keep you safely envisioned in my mind. As long as we had a visual on the piece, probability was that you were safe." He dropped the pendant onto the table and caressed her forearm.

"I wasn't always safe," she said, weariness in her voice.

"Tell me what happened," Jake whispered gravely like he needed to cough. "I'm not going to lose you. You're a part of me. We're meant to be together."

Tears welled in her eyes as she shook her head. His words were sweet and she wanted to believe them, but the fact he was assigned to her as a case disturbed her. She had suffered in the past few weeks, having been given away by her ex-husband and attacked by a Russian trafficker. She wasn't sure how quickly she'd trust another man, even one she loved beyond measure.

"Rest, my love. We'll talk more tomorrow." He rose from the bed and waited at the side, while she snuggled underneath the covers. She turned away from him, facing the wall, as tears of remorse, love, and fear of the unknown tumbled down her face.

Georgina had become proficient at holding her sobs inside. The sound of papers being shifted and the squeak of a chair alerted her that Jake wasn't leaving. Eventually she fell asleep. She woke only once. Jake lay sleeping beside her. Instead of leaving the bed, as the logical part of her mind told her, she spooned him.

****

Georgina snuggled into the heat radiating from Jake's body. As the sun gleamed brightly into the room, she stretched, feeling refreshed. She smiled and kissed his shoulder, until she noticed the pendant and chain on the table. All of the memories flowed back into her like a fresh wave of pain.

She slid out of the bed, drawing the top blanket with her. He leaned up, eyes wide open, and waited. The man had unbelievable patience.

Georgina ran inside the bathroom and washed her face, removing all traces of her dried tears. A knock on the hotel door made her still. She shut off the water and listened. Footsteps flapped on the floor, a squeak, followed by a shutting of the entrance.

Overnight, cosmetics and a toothbrush had appeared. With wet hands, she smoothed down her hair, brushed her teeth, and applied makeup to help cover the dark circles under her eyes. A flourish of nausea washed over her, heating her. The blanket fell to the floor as she grabbed the edges of the sink. She hoped the coolness of the stone would calm her.

"Gee?" Jake's voice came through the door.

"A moment." She forced the stomach fluid back down. Her fingers latched onto a towel on the rack. She wet it and wiped her face. She got a larger towel to tie around her. A swish of mouthwash and she felt better.

She opened the door but held onto the knob. He was gorgeous in the morning. His hair mussed, a shadow of growth splattered his jaw. She breathed deep. Ignore the chest. Do not look at the V of hair emphasizing his trunk. Manly, strong, six-pack abs. Lustdom was a thing of the past.

"I had your clothes cleaned. Do you want them?" His gaze penetrated her, looking for a weakness? Or forgiveness? His pants barely hung on his hips, although zipped, one side of the belt hung along his thigh, flapping about like a snake.

An old magazine article had claimed men normally had erections first thing in the morning.

This proved to be true. Damn, lustdom wasn't a thing of the past. Would she lust for Jake forever?

"Yes," she croaked out. Her heart struck against her ribcage, so hard the fierce pounding vibrated in her throat. The radio clicked on, alerting her it was seven o'clock, blaring "The Christmas Song" by Nat King Cole. Jake didn't move to turn the volume down.

Jake stood in front of her, holding her clothes. He had them dry cleaned. An unexpected need to sit down overwhelmed her. Her world suddenly topsy-turvy, she swayed. She tried to hold steady by gripping the door knob.

He threw the plastic covered garments onto the bed and rushed forward.

"Gee."

He grabbed her around her waist and led her to a straight-back wooden chair at the table.

She licked her dry lips. Her stomach churned and her throat convulsed, she held her mouth shut and kept swallowing.

"What is it?" he whispered.

She shut her eyes, listening to him step away, water running, and then footfalls closer to her. She peeked.

He handed her a half-filled glass.

She opened her eyes, wrapped her fingers around the glass, and took a sip.

"I'm pregnant." Her voice cracked making it sound like preg-nant. She hadn't lifted her head. Her fingers gripped onto the glass as if the liquid would be her salvation.

"Are you happy?" he asked. She couldn't decipher his voice, and she didn't dare look into his beautiful, sweet countenance. Would he judge her?

She nodded.

"I am too. I've dreamed of having a baby with you." He paused. "Why didn't you tell me when we were on Tristan's yacht?" Now, a mix of annoyance and joy laced his voice.

Hope surged, warming her and stifling the contraction of her throat. She glanced into his gray-blue eyes. "When we were on the ship, I didn't know about the baby."

His shoulders lost their tenseness, fingers unclenched, and his frown dissipated. He removed his belt and threw it on the bed.

"Actually, I wasn't certain until a few days ago." She sipped from the glass and handed the tumbler to him.

Jake lifted the glass to sip, but held it posed in front of his lips. "Now, you are?"

"Yes. I'm certain." Her voice held a hint of excitement, because she wanted their child as much as he did.

He sipped the water and placed the goblet on the floor beside the chair. "And? We'll need to get married. Come on Georgina, say it. You want to be together and so do I. Just say the words."

Need? She didn't twist her hands. She steadied her voice so it wouldn't hold a nervous ting. A wariness appeared in his eyes.

"Need to get married!" She couldn't believe he said those words. Granted they knew each other beyond the norm and had experienced things together not typical to other couples. They loved each other. Or did they?

Did he truly love her?

She shook her confused head. Had he mentioned love?

Jake crouched at the edge of her chair, close enough to reach over and touch her, but far enough away not to have his toes crunched if she jumped up. He plowed his hand through his hair and steepled his fingers in front of him. Why was he nervous?

Would he pronounce his love and ask her to

marry him instead of saying they needed to get married?

"I want to start over, no lies, no deceptions, but straight-up honesty," he declared.

She stared at him. What to say? Honesty, yes she wanted no deceptions and no lies.

"Gee, help me understand what went wrong between us?"

"Is your name Jake Callahan?"

His shoulders relaxed as if a great weight had been lifted. He sighed.

You're not back in the nook yet, Jake. She crossed her legs, willing him to continue. All the while, hoping his toes remained near enough to be crunched if he didn't say what she wanted to hear.

"Yes, Jacob Thomas Callahan. My father is Thomas Callahan, and my mother is Sara Louise McCallister Callahan. I grew up in Etincelle, Indiana. I've told you about my brothers and sisters. I've photos of them at my apartment in Boston. I've been with the FBI for ten years as a special field agent, specializing in sea trafficking. I'm thirty-four, ten years older than you." He paused. "Are you okay with marrying an older man?"

Still, no pronouncement of love. She raised an eyebrow in response.

He picked up the glass and drained the contents.

She leaned forward, placing her hands on her knees and inhaled. "And?"

"My apartment's on Candle Avenue. It's small, but cozy. My sister decorated the place, calling it a bachelor pad. It's far from a hot spot, but I couldn't change it. She was so proud." He pushed the empty tumbler under the table and sat back on the floor, placing his feet in front of him, his knees raised.

Silent, Georgina waited and met his gaze, urging him to continue.

"I studied criminal justice and political science

at Chicago University. After graduation, I joined the bureau. John Maller, who you met at the Embassy, is my godfather. My godmother passed away five years ago. As a famous photographer, she taught me everything I know. I wish you could have met her, Gee. You'd have liked her. I loved getting behind the camera in Nero. I felt closer to her, as if she were there with me." He settled comfortably onto the ragged and simple braided rug, stretching his legs out. "Ave Maria" played on the radio.

"Dance with me," he whispered.

She stared at him for at least a full minute, trying to make a decision. If she went into his arms she'd feel the connection. That instant bond they had whenever he touched her. The jolt of desire which always seemed to be present would zing through her.

"Honesty, Gee. I need to have you in my arms, to be reassured you want me as much as I want you. At the very beginning I resisted the hunger, the need to touch you, out of respect for my job with the FBI. Now I have the freedom to be with you. Please dance with me."

"Can't dance to 'Ave Maria.'" She uncrossed her arms and set forward in the chair.

He stood and held out his hand.

She rose and took his hand into hers. He led her over near the shimmer of the morning sun and eased her into an embrace. One hand on her waist, and the other holding hers, fingers entwined. He pressed his hips to hers and moved. Not a fast rough move, but a gentle sway, a rock to the left and to the right. The room, tight and small, didn't allow for much latitude. Space wasn't necessary. She wanted his embrace, to enjoy his touch.

"This song is about the immaculate heart of Mary and asking forgiveness for your sins." Jake stopped and raised her chin with his hand. Her glance connected with his. "I ask you, Georgina Grey

Barrister, to forgive me for any sins, and let me love you for the rest of our lives."

She lowered her glance. "Jake, I was an assignment to you," she retorted, her fury re-emerging. She expelled a harsh breath, jerked her hand from his, and jumped back. "I wonder if you'll fall in love with the next obligation to achieve your goal."

Her eyes felt scratchy and her throat hurt.

An expression of pain crossed over his eyes and pinpricked her heart. His shoulders slumped for a second, and then he straightened his back and stuffed his hands into his pockets.

His forlornness hammered punches into her stomach. Should she try to take the words back? No. Her bane wasn't simply his omission of his job. He romanced her for information. She wanted to set sail all of the irritation, doubts, and heartache as they rose to the surface. She'd loved before, and it hadn't worked out very well.

"Give me time to convince you that I've fallen in love with Georgina, and not my assignment."

Let the anger go, it's not healthy for you or the baby...or Jake. Georgina lowered her voice. "It's too late."

He leaned over and touched his lips to hers. She gave him a parting kiss, brief and quick, like in the old days, rendering her heart into shattered pieces, wondering if they could muddle through all of the lies and omissions. Could they have a relationship?

Georgina placed her hands flat on her stomach. Maybe he wanted to be with her because of the baby. He evolved from a loving and devoted family. His parents probably knew where he went, and what he planned to do in the future. His bachelor pad wouldn't be altered, because his sister had decorated it. Jake Callahan was a family man, and she carried his son or daughter. He would insist on being a part of his or her life.

Could she live with seeing him and not being together?

Not being a couple?

He grabbed her hand. "I love you, Gee. What else might I do to prove it to you? What can I do to demonstrate my love for you? What do you want?"

His words were blunt and a little harsh and shook her to the core. But they were what she had been waiting for. She released his hand and folded her arms at her waist.

"I love you, too," she said the words aloud. She meant them.

"I know I don't say the right things sometimes." He snatched the necklace off of the table. "This necklace is a symbol of my love for you. I commissioned the piece with your Green Lantern slippers in mind."

She lifted an eyebrow. The necklace looked like a Celtic knot.

"Your favorite superhero was one of the Green Lantern Corps. By your expression you doubt me. Don't. I read the D.C. Comic books starting with Alan Scott, but Hal Jordan was my favorite."

She smiled, which apparently gave him the desire to continue discussing her favorite hero who used a green ring to provide him with power and strength of reason. Jake provided her with a guarantee, confirmation of his love.

"The Green Lantern's power came from a power ring. A jade pendant was as close as I could come. I'm also a part of a police service, a force that uses light to fight the darkness of evil. I gave this necklace to you, with the homing device. Don't frown. The homing device was my source of power, to keep my energy supply—you, my love—close to me. With this power I could always find you and your love would always renew me. You provide me with light and power."

A large tear rolled onto her cheek. Damn, his words were sweet.

"May I?" he asked. She nodded.

He placed the sentimental talisman around her neck. "A song I heard on the radio earlier, by Shayne Ward, had a set of lyrics that say what I want, probably better than anything I could come up with."

She used the back of her hand to swipe at a tear. He rested his hands on her shoulders.

"Shayne sang: I'm not here to say I'm sorry, I'm not here to lie to you, I'm here to say I'm ready. That I've finally thought it through. I'm not here to let your love go. I'm not giving up, oh no, I'm here to win your heart and soul, That's my goal."

He held aloft the jade necklace with the silver love knot. The backside of his fingers touched her skin, and she wanted to lean into them. She'd forgive him and hope that he'd forgive her as well.

He lowered his other hand to weave her fingers with his. "My goal, Georgina Grey Barrister, is to convince you I love you. I want to spend the rest of my life with you. Will you marry me?"

He dropped the pendent, dug into his pants pocket, and pulled out a tiny, round jeweler's box. He opened the cap to reveal a blue diamond. Awkwardly he removed a ring from its velvet nest and slid the diamond on her finger. "This is a token of my love, trust, devotion, and a promise of forever. Regardless of how much time you need, I want you to know I'll wait for you. I love you, Gee."

Georgina touched the ring. She admitted she'd lusted after him from the instant she saw him clipping plants in his yard. Granted, many of the wonderfully sweet things he did may have been a part of his assignment. He didn't need to mow her yard, arrange a hair cut, provide meals, or encourage her artistic endeavors, but he had. Jake proved to be an honorable person, and regardless of how many times she tempted him to have sex with her, he hadn't. At least not until he had decided he cared about her. The ring told her that he had intended to ask her to marry him before he found out about the baby. His commitment—validated.

Jake did love her. Tristan messed with her mind, making her doubt herself and her ability to love and be loved. She now admitted she was worthy of a caring relationship. Despite Jake's dedication to his job, he was honest and loved her enough to disregard the policies of his work and her own lies.

She looked down at the ring. "Jake, I need to ask you to forgive me for my lies. I had to protect myself, so I wasn't honest with you either. About Tristan."

Jake kept coming back to her, and he fought for her. He loved her, and she wanted to be with him as much as she wanted the baby inside of her. She did love him. She'd trust him and accept his love. Together they'd made a life growing inside of her, and for as long as God granted them time, she'd remain by his side. If he'd forgive her.

"Why didn't you trust me?" His voice held a smidgen of anger.

She whispered, "I wanted to tell you."

"I thought you would the night you returned from the post office, but you didn't."

She jerked her head in surprise. Of course he knew about the phone. "Jake, you can't imagine how much I wanted to lean on you. To confide in you. I was afraid. I witnessed, photographed, Tristan killing a man. I didn't want you to get involved and possibly be murdered."

He hugged her close. "It's in the past. Although, I'd like to have the photo for the case file."

She nodded.

He pushed a short stand of hair behind her ear, placed two fingers under her chin, and lifted her head. "I forgive you. So, will you marry me?"

She met his gaze.

He lowered his hand to rest at her waist.

His love was so profound he took her breath away. She licked her lips. His stare followed the movement and her heart beat as fast as the drums of the little drummer boy, vibrating from the radio.

"Yes, I'll marry you. We'll create a family together." She wrapped her arms around his neck.

He kissed her with a passion she'd never experienced before, not even the first night they'd consummated their relationship. She pressed her lips closer to his. He lifted her, carried her a few feet, and lowered her gently in front of the bed. He slowly trickled his fingers down the sides of her breasts. The towel fell to the floor.

She stood naked, without barriers, without lies, and her heart open to receive his love. Her breasts had expanded over the past month and her nipples puckered as he slid his fingers around them.

She whispered his name and placed her hands under the waistband of his pants. He helped her to push them down, and they landed with a soft thud.

He'd lost weight in the few weeks they'd been separated, but his chest remained solid and broad. She caressed his tight abs. The glint of the engagement ring reminded her of the binding vows, stated by him in person, and soon by her on paper. The oath made from his heart, more binding than if a man of cloth were present, reaffirming the love they shared.

"Please I need you to make love to me," she whispered.

"I love you and want you so much." He kissed her hand and lowered her to the bed, then placed a knee beside her. "Are you okay with my weight on top of you?"

"Only if you merge with me. I need you to be

inside of me." She ran her hands through his hair, along the sides of his neck, over his chest, stopping to massage his nipples, onto his stomach, and around to his back.

"The first time I saw you without a shirt I thought I was in my own personal hell. I called it lustdom. I couldn't take my eyes off of you. My body begged to have your hands touch me everywhere."

"Your body is begging now. You keep putting your hips against mine. I smell the musk of your excitement. Your lips are moving, but I know they want to be a part of mine." He bent down and kissed her, his staff reaching out. Her sex throbbed in expectancy.

One thrust and he was inside. She kissed his lips. He leaned his cheek against hers, letting her body adjust as her vagina sucked in his firm length. She savored the connection. He moved, pulled out, and plunged. Moans and whimpers came from the back of her throat.

She lifted her hips, her body trembled against his. His silky hard strokes brought her closer to a climax. She caught the rhythm. Her orgasm washed over her. Clutching him close, she held onto him as he exploded, imbedding his love inside her.

"I love you," she whispered.

"I love you," he replied.

The bell tower struck eight times as her love flowed through the husband of her heart, and she came onto him with the hope and love of a new beginning. Love everlasting.

A word about the author...

jj Keller is an author of suspense, paranormal, and urban fantasy novels. She enjoys reading and crafting. Traveling and meandering in her herb garden are her favorite pastimes. She lives with her husband, sons, and dog, on a small oasis in the Indiana countryside.

Visit jj Keller at www.jj-keller.com

Thank you for purchasing
this Wild Rose Press publication.
For other wonderful stories of romance,
please visit our on-line bookstore at
www.thewildrosepress.com.

For questions or more information,
contact us at info@thewildrosepress.com.

The Wild Rose Press
www.TheWildRosePress.com